THE FRONTIER DANCE

THE FRONTIER DANCE

DEE WHITMAN

Contents

Prologue ... 1
1. A New Start In Golden Valley ... 5
2. A Saloon Star Is Born ... 11
3. The Founders ... 23
4. Building Friendships ... 31
5. Jimmy's Leadership ... 37
6. The Growing Town ... 49
7. Haunted By The Past ... 57
8. Breaking Down Walls ... 65
9. Thornfield's Arrival ... 77
10. Confronting The Past ... 83
11. The Connection Deepens ... 89
12. Town Relationships ... 103
13. Shoshone Friendships ... 109
14. Steps Toward Something New ... 119
15. A Community Forms ... 129
16. A Gift Of Gratitude ... 139

17	Fayteen's Letter	155
18	Golden Valley's Role	165
19	Unexpected Reunion	171
20	The Truth Unveiled	181
21	The Saloon Festival	191
22	Langston's Threat	197
23	The Rescue Mission	209
24	A New Foundation	219
25	Preparing For Forever	229
26	Flames Of Foe And Friendship	239
27	Golden Valley Unites	245
28	The Final Confrontation	253
29	Dreams In The Making	259
30	Realities Of Frontier Life	269
31	Dreams Beyond Golden Valley	277
32	A Ghost From The Past	283
33	Past Made Whole	299
34	Uncharted Paths	305
35	The Golden Plate	315
36	New Beginnings, Old Secrets	323

Copyright © 2024 by Dee Whitman

Cover Design by DEW Media as part of SKW Publishing.
All rights reserved. No part of this book may be reproduced in any manner whatsoever without written permission except in the case of brief quotations embodied in critical articles and reviews.
First Printing, 2024

Prologue

Plopping herself down into the worn velvet chair, Fayteen let out a long, tired sigh. She had just finished the final performance of her tour—a whirlwind of singing, dancing, and endless travel that had consumed the better part of her life for the past year. The applause from the crowd still echoed in her mind, but the excitement that had once fueled her seemed to have fizzled out, replaced with a weariness that sank deep into her bones. She needed a break.

The late 1850s had brought a lot of change to the country, and the world of show business was no exception. Fayteen had seen the insides of enough theaters and dance halls to last a lifetime. From the bustling streets of Philadelphia to the rugged towns of the West, she had toured across the country, living out of trunks and performing for every kind of audience imaginable. And though she had built her reputation and saved enough money to live comfortably for a while, something was missing—a sense of home, a sense of peace.

She glanced around her small dressing room, cluttered with costumes and trinkets from every stop along her journey. The scent of roses from a bouquet of flowers left by an admirer filled the room, but it did little to lift her spirits. Her heart longed for something quieter, something more meaningful than the endless cycle of performances.

Rubbing her tired eyes, Fayteen picked up the newspaper that had been left for her earlier that day. Thumbing through the pages lazily, she was about to set it aside when something small but intriguing caught her attention—a tiny advertisement buried among the job listings.

"Small town on the edge of expansion looking for a dance troupe leader. All applicants to Jimmy Hawthorne, Golden Valley, Idaho."

The words stood out like a beacon, sparking a flicker of curiosity in her exhausted mind. Golden Valley. She had never heard of the place. But something about the way it was described—"on the edge of expansion"—tugged at her. It wasn't a flashy city or a booming metropolis. It was a small town, one that seemed to be on the verge of becoming something more. There was a simplicity to it, an opportunity, perhaps, to step away from the chaos of show business and find something quieter. Something... real.

She leaned back in her chair, considering the idea, but exhaustion quickly clouded her thoughts. She was too tired to make any decisions tonight. The weariness of the road had taken its toll, and her body ached for rest. Maybe it was best not to act on impulse. She had learned from her years in the entertainment world that not every opportunity was as good as it seemed.

Still, she couldn't shake the pull of that small ad. Jimmy Hawthorne. She had no idea who he was, but something about the name seemed solid, dependable. This could be her chance to finally slow down, to find a place where she could belong—where she didn't have to be constantly on display, where her voice and her dancing weren't the only things that defined her.

But could she leave the spotlight behind so easily? Could she trade the thrill of the stage for the quiet life of a small town in the Idaho Territory? As tempting as it sounded, there was always a risk in starting over. She had built a name for herself, and walking away from that wouldn't be easy.

The soft knock on her dressing room door startled her from her thoughts. One of the stagehands peeked in, his face creased with concern.

"Miss Fayteen, there's someone here askin' for you," he said, his voice hesitant. "Looks like trouble."

Fayteen sat up, her pulse quickening. Trouble had a way of following her, especially after a show. Fans could be demanding, and sometimes, they were more than just admirers. She had dealt with her share of persistent men who thought they were entitled to more than just a song.

She stood, straightening her skirts, her exhaustion replaced by a sudden sense of alertness. "I'll be right there," she said, her voice steady.

As she moved toward the door, she caught a glimpse of herself in the mirror—long blonde hair cascading over her shoulders, her sky-blue eyes still holding a hint of the performance's fire. She was tired, yes, but she wasn't weak. She had survived worse than this. Whatever was waiting for her outside that door, she could handle it.

But as she left the dressing room and walked down the narrow corridor, her thoughts returned to the ad. Maybe this was her chance to step away from the drama, the constant danger that came with being in the public eye. Maybe Golden Valley could offer her the peace she craved, a place to rest her weary soul.

She reached the end of the hallway, where a burly man stood waiting—trouble, just as the stagehand had said. His eyes were cold, a reminder of the darker side of her life on the road.

But as she faced him, her mind wasn't on this man or whatever problem he thought he was bringing her way. Her mind was on that small town, that small ad.

Golden Valley. Jimmy Hawthorne. A new beginning.

Maybe after tonight, once this storm had passed, it would be time to seriously consider that next step.

1

A New Start In Golden Valley

Fayteen Everhart stepped off the wagon, her lithe frame silhouetted against the dusty haze that swirled around her boots. She swept a hand through her long, golden hair, letting it cascade down her back as she took in the sight of Golden Valley. Small and slender, with sky-blue eyes that gleamed with curiosity, she had the look of a woman who'd seen much of the world but was ready to start anew. For a town so young, Golden Valley already bustled with life—buildings lined the main stretch, some still in the process of being hammered together. Yet her gaze was immediately drawn to one structure in particular, standing tall and proud at the heart of the town, its rugged charm tempered with a hint of ambition. She felt a smile tug at the corner of her lips. This town might be a far cry from the cities she'd danced in, but there was a spark here, something that hinted at possibilities waiting to unfold.

The Golden Nugget Saloon rose up three stories high, a building unlike any other in the frontier town. Its wood gleamed in the afternoon sun, polished cedar and mahogany crafted with care and precision. Broad windows were framed with thick, red velvet curtains, and finely etched glass panels reflected the sun's rays, casting a warm glow across the street. It looked almost like it belonged in a larger city, where people with money and manners would gather.

As she approached, a tall man with broad shoulders and long, sun-streaked hair came out to greet her. His piercing blue eyes held her gaze for a moment, and she could see something intense and thoughtful in his expression.

"Miss Everhart?" he called, his voice carrying easily over the noise of the street.

"That's me," she replied, stepping toward him and holding out her hand. "You must be Mr. Hawthorne."

"Just Jimmy," he said, giving her a warm, steady handshake. "Welcome to Golden Valley. Hope the journey wasn't too rough?"

She shrugged, glancing back at the wagon. "Seen worse. Rode next to a busted wagon half the way, but it held up. Made it here in one piece, so I reckon it was a good trip."

He chuckled and nodded for her to follow him. "Glad to hear it. C'mon inside, I'll show ya 'round. Figured ya might wanna get a look at where you'll be workin'."

As they stepped inside The Golden Nugget, Fayteen felt a sense of awe at the sight before her. This was no rough-and-tumble saloon. The bar stretched along one side of the room, a rich, polished mahogany that gleamed in the light of the chandelier above. Rows of plush chairs and tables with intricately carved legs were arranged across the floor, each covered with crisp, dark green tablecloths. To the right, a grand staircase led up to the second and third floors.

Jimmy caught her look and gave a slight nod. "Spared no expense on this place. That wood's mahogany, with some cedar mixed in. Strong and beautiful, holds up nice. Got it shipped special."

She ran her fingers along the back of one of the chairs, feeling the quality of the craftsmanship. "I've been in plenty of saloons, but this... this is somethin' else. You've got taste, Mr. Hawthorne."

He smiled. "Thank ya, Miss Everhart. Just Jimmy, remember?"

"Just Fayteen, then," she replied, a hint of a smile on her lips.

He motioned to the far end of the room, where a stage rose up, framed by lush red curtains that matched those at the windows. A gilded arch adorned the top of the stage, and small oil lamps had been placed around the perimeter, casting a warm glow. The stage was large enough to hold several dancers at once, with room to spare.

"This here's where you'll be workin'," he said, nodding toward the stage. "I put a lot into gettin' this set up right. Curtains came from back east. Had 'em stitched with extra detail so they'd catch the light. Figured the troupe might appreciate havin' a proper stage."

"It's beautiful," she murmured, imagining herself there, under the lights. "Can't say I've seen a saloon with a stage this fine."

"We like to keep things a bit more... upscale," he replied. "Now, I'll be straight with ya. You'll be leadin' the dance troupe, and you'll meet the other girls soon enough. They dance, sure, but some of 'em entertain in other ways, too. All of 'em made the choice themselves, and I make sure they're looked after. Anyone messes with 'em, they find themselves outside on the dirt real quick."

She turned to him, surprised at his honesty. It wasn't often she heard men talk about saloon girls with such respect, and it made her appreciate his character all the more. "Long as they're treated right, I got no quarrel with it."

He gave a small nod, his expression thoughtful. "Glad to hear it. Now, they work on contract with me. They got fair pay, good rooms, and I make sure they got what they need. Anyone causes trouble, they'll be out on their ear."

Fayteen nodded, glancing around at the elegant surroundings again. "Reckon you run a tight ship, Jimmy. Not what I expected, but I like it."

He smiled, his gaze steady. "I don't do things halfway, Miss Everhart. I'll let ya meet the girls now."

He led her down a hallway and into a spacious room with a large mirror on one wall and plush, upholstered chairs arranged around it. Eight women were gathered there, fixing their hair, chatting, and laughing softly. As they looked up, their expressions turned from curiosity to friendly smiles.

"Ladies," Jimmy said, his voice commanding but warm, "this here's Miss Fayteen Everhart. She'll be leadin' the troupe. So, give her a warm welcome, and mind her direction."

One of the women, a tall redhead with a lively grin, stood up first. "Name's Ruby. Nice to meet ya, Miss Everhart." She gestured to the others. "This here's Lily Mae, Josie, Anna, Maggie, Pearl, Sadie, and Belle."

Fayteen smiled, nodding at each of them in turn. "Pleasure's mine. Just Fayteen's fine, though."

Lily Mae, a petite girl with blonde curls, stepped forward, grinning. "Heard you got a voice on ya. We could use some fresh talent on that stage."

Fayteen chuckled, feeling a bit more at ease. "I've done my share of singin' and dancin'. Lookin' forward to sharin' the stage with y'all."

Maggie, a woman with kind eyes and a warm smile, gave her a nod. "Well, we're glad to have ya. Jimmy don't let just anyone work here, so we trust ya got somethin' special."

Ruby winked. "We'll keep the fellas comin' back, that's for sure."

Jimmy cleared his throat, bringing their attention back to him. "Remember, Fayteen's here to raise the bar. I expect y'all to show her the respect she deserves. You'll find she knows what she's doin'."

He turned back to Fayteen. "I'll let ya settle in. Rehearsals start tomorrow. Make yourself at home. If ya need anythin', just give a holler."

As Jimmy walked back down the hall, Fayteen looked around at the women, all of them now watching her with open curiosity and warm smiles. This wasn't the rough, ramshackle saloon she'd been in before. These women had pride in their work, and Jimmy treated them like family.

Sadie spoke up, crossing her arms with a grin. "Welcome to Golden Valley, Fayteen. Reckon you'll like it here. Ain't no place like The Golden Nugget."

Fayteen nodded, feeling a sense of calm settle over her. "Looks like I'm in good company."

The women laughed, and Ruby clapped her on the shoulder. "Darn right. We're glad you're here."

She took a deep breath, looking back down the hall where Jimmy had gone. This place was different—finer, more polished—and it felt like a fresh start. She had a feeling she could make a life here, one worth sticking around for.

2

A Saloon Star Is Born

The next evening, the air inside The Golden Nugget buzzed with a sort of electric anticipation. Word had spread fast that a new performer was debuting, and folks from all around had filled the tables, waiting to see what all the fuss was about. Fayteen took a deep breath as she stood backstage, listening to the hum of voices and the clinking of glasses beyond the curtains.

She adjusted the deep blue gown she'd chosen for the performance, smoothing out the skirt and ensuring every bit of lace and ribbon was in place. The dress was simple but elegant, the color chosen to match her eyes—a suggestion from one of the girls. She'd tied her hair back, letting loose tendrils fall around her face, a careful balance of refinement and allure.

A few feet away, Ruby, Lily Mae, and the other dancers watched her, sharing encouraging smiles and small nods. Ruby gave her a nudge, a twinkle in her eye. "Don't be worryin' now.

Those fellas out there are in for a treat, and they don't even know it yet."

Fayteen laughed softly. "Oh, I don't know about that. They've seen their share of dancers, I'm sure."

"Not like you, they haven't," Josie chimed in, her tone reassuring. "Ya got somethin' different, Fayteen. The way ya sing—well, it's like a whole story wrapped up in a tune. They're gonna love it."

Fayteen smiled, grateful for their words. She looked at the stage, hearing the low murmur of the crowd and feeling the rush of anticipation building within her. This was her moment to set herself apart, to do what she did best.

She turned to the girls. "All right, then. We're gonna make sure tonight's somethin' they won't forget. Lily Mae, Josie, you'll take the left side of the stage, and Ruby, you and the others take the right. I'll be center, and we'll bring it together like we practiced."

They nodded, expressions turning serious as they moved into position. Over the past day, they'd rehearsed endlessly, working on every step, every flick of the wrist and sway of the hip. Fayteen had introduced them to new moves, emphasizing grace and precision. She wanted the dance to tell a story, to evoke emotion and give the audience something to remember. Each movement had to have purpose, every glance a part of the tale she wanted to weave.

As she took her position, she felt a sense of calm wash over her. She closed her eyes, focusing on the melody she'd practiced and the lyrics she knew by heart. When the piano struck its first note, she opened her eyes, ready.

The curtains drew back, revealing a packed house. The stage lights warmed her skin, and the crowd went silent, a ripple of curiosity and admiration flowing through them as they took her in. Fayteen felt the familiar stir of excitement rise in her chest, a feeling she'd known since she first took to the stage as a young girl.

She began to sing, her voice soft at first, weaving through the melody with a tender grace. As her voice grew stronger, she let the emotions pour out, her hands and arms moving fluidly, guiding the audience through the tale of lost love and bittersweet memories.

The girls moved with her, their steps precise and deliberate, each one adding to the flow of the performance. Fayteen could sense their dedication, their focus on every step and gesture, and she felt a surge of pride. She'd spent hours working with them, emphasizing timing, the importance of synchronization, and how to use every movement to pull the audience in. She'd encouraged them to feel the music, to let it resonate in their bones and move them.

The crowd was spellbound, their eyes following her every move, drawn into the story she was telling. Fayteen glanced over at Jimmy, standing at the back of the room, his arms crossed and his gaze fixed on her. Their eyes met, and a sudden, intense connection surged between them, something deeper than mere attraction. For a moment, the rest of the room fell away, and it was just the two of them, locked in a silent understanding.

Fayteen turned her attention back to the song, letting the melody carry her, but the memory of Jimmy's gaze lingered, warm and unsettling in equal measure.

As the final note faded, a hush fell over the room, the audience holding their breath as if under a spell. Then, as though released all at once, applause erupted, cheers and whistles filling the air. Fayteen smiled, her heart racing with the thrill of it, feeling a satisfaction she hadn't known in years.

She stepped back as the curtains closed, and the girls surrounded her, their faces glowing with excitement.

"Fayteen, that was amazin'!" Lily Mae exclaimed, her eyes wide with admiration. "I could feel it, every note. You got somethin' real special."

Ruby nodded, clapping a hand on Fayteen's shoulder. "I don't think I've ever seen this place that quiet before. You had 'em hangin' on every word."

Fayteen smiled, her cheeks flushed with pride and gratitude. "Thank you, all of ya. Couldn't have done it without your help."

As the girls started talking excitedly about the performance, Fayteen took a step back, letting their voices wash over her. She glanced toward the doorway, catching a glimpse of Jimmy as he slipped into the room. His expression was thoughtful, his eyes meeting hers with a warmth that made her heart skip.

He approached, nodding toward her with a slight smile. "Well, Miss Everhart, reckon ya just gave this town somethin' to talk about. They're gonna be comin' back night after night, hopin' for more of that."

She gave a small laugh, brushing a loose curl from her face. "Glad to hear it. I've been waitin' a long time for a place like this, somewhere to really... make a mark."

Jimmy nodded, his gaze steady. "I can see that. And ya did more than that tonight. You brought somethin' special to the stage, somethin' folks'll remember. And the girls—you got 'em workin' together better'n I've ever seen."

Fayteen glanced over at the troupe, who were still beaming, caught up in the excitement of the night. "They got talent. Just needed a bit of direction, that's all."

"Well," he said, stepping a little closer, his voice lowering, "ya did a fine job with 'em. And I think you've found yourself a home here, Fayteen. I don't reckon there's anywhere else quite like Golden Valley."

Her heart thudded at his words, and she felt a warmth spreading through her. For a moment, she thought about reaching out, letting her hand brush his arm, but she held back, aware of the eyes around them, the unspoken understanding that lingered in the space between them.

He cleared his throat, stepping back. "Tomorrow, I'd like you to go over the routine with the girls again. I got a feelin' they're gonna want another show soon, and I'd like to keep 'em talkin'."

"Will do," she replied, nodding, grateful for the distraction from the pull she felt toward him. "We'll work on it, maybe add a few new steps, keep things fresh."

"Sounds good," he said, his expression softening. "Well, reckon I'll leave ya to it. Good work tonight, Fayteen."

"Thank you, Jimmy," she said, watching him as he turned to leave. As he disappeared down the hall, she felt the familiar stir of excitement mingling with something new, a feeling that lingered long after the curtain had fallen.

The following day, Fayteen arrived early, eager to work with the troupe. She knew the performance had gone well, but she wanted to build on it, to create something even more captivating. She glanced around the empty stage, imagining the routines she had in mind, each step, each movement connecting the girls to the story in a way that would pull the audience in and hold them there.

One by one, the dancers trickled in, some with their hair pinned up and others still a bit bleary-eyed from the late night. Ruby gave her a nod, a little smirk on her face.

"Ya sure got the boys talkin' last night, Fayteen. Can't even tell ya how many fellas came up after, askin' about ya."

Fayteen grinned, shaking her head. "Long as they keep talkin', that's all that matters. Now, ladies, we've got work to do. I want to start by running through some new steps, seein' what works."

Lily Mae raised an eyebrow. "New steps already?"

Fayteen chuckled, clapping her hands to gather their attention. "Ain't much use in waitin' around. We've got their attention now, and we're gonna keep it. We'll start with some basics to get warmed up, then move on to a sequence I've been thinkin' on."

She led them through a series of steps, demonstrating each movement with a graceful ease. The girls followed her lead, moving in time with her, but Fayteen could see where they could use more coordination. She stopped and adjusted their positions, emphasizing the importance of precision in each movement.

"Now listen," she said, catching their eyes. "When we dance, we ain't just movin' our feet. We're tellin' a story. Every step, every flick of the wrist, it's gotta mean somethin'. We want the crowd to feel it. They should be able to tell what we're thinkin' just by watchin' us."

Maggie nodded, catching on quickly. "So we're bringin' emotion into it?"

"That's right," Fayteen replied, pleased with the quick understanding. "When ya look out at that crowd, don't just see faces. See people who've had their own troubles, who came here lookin' to forget for a while. We're here to give 'em that, to make 'em feel somethin' beyond the everyday."

She began a sequence, moving slowly, and they followed along, mirroring her steps. Fayteen demonstrated a sweeping motion with her arm, then a quick pivot, a sway of the hips that added a subtle allure.

"Lily Mae, when ya turn here, keep your gaze low and steady," she instructed. "It's about drawin' them in, makin' 'em wonder what you're thinkin'. And Ruby, add a bit more swing to the hip there—make 'em lean forward in their seats."

They worked through the routine, repeating each section until it felt natural. The more they practiced, the more Fayteen saw them loosening up, letting go of any reservations. She encouraged them, smiling and nodding as they picked up on her guidance, adding their own flair to each move.

After an hour of steady practice, Fayteen called for a break, and the girls settled around the edge of the stage, catching their breath and sharing quiet laughter.

Sadie leaned back, stretching her arms above her head. "Ya know, Fayteen, I don't think we've ever worked this hard before, but I like it. Feels like we're actually doin' somethin' worth seein'."

Ruby nodded. "Yeah, we've been dancin' for a while, but nothin' like this. You got a way of makin' it mean somethin'. Never thought I'd be puttin' this much thought into a step."

Fayteen smiled, feeling a warmth spread through her. "Well, I'm glad to hear it. You're all talented, more than you realize. If we keep buildin' on that, there's no limit to what we can do here."

She stood, motioning for them to join her again. "Now, let's go through it once more, then we'll move on to the next part. This time, I want ya to really get into it. Think of someone or somethin' that matters to ya, somethin' that makes ya feel alive. Put that into your steps."

The girls rose, positioning themselves around her. Fayteen took a breath and began the sequence again, watching as the girls followed with renewed focus. Each step became more deliberate, more meaningful, as they poured themselves into the dance, transforming it into something powerful, something that reached beyond the stage.

The door creaked open, and Fayteen caught a glimpse of Jimmy standing in the shadows, watching. His arms were crossed, and there was a look of deep concentration on his face.

She felt a thrill run through her, a renewed determination to make this performance unforgettable.

She stepped back, letting the girls take the lead for a moment, guiding them through the motions with subtle gestures and whispered encouragements. As the music rose, she joined them again, leading them through the finale with a flourish, their movements fluid and in perfect harmony.

When they finished, Fayteen turned to see Jimmy clapping quietly, a hint of a smile on his lips. He stepped forward, nodding in approval.

"Reckon ya got yourself a real fine act here, Fayteen," he said, his voice low and warm. "Didn't think I'd ever see the girls movin' like that. Ya got a talent for leadin', no doubt about it."

The girls beamed, sharing proud glances with each other, and Fayteen felt a rush of satisfaction. She stepped down from the stage, wiping a bead of sweat from her brow.

"Thank you, Jimmy. They're hard workers, and they've got the passion. Just needed a little direction, is all."

He nodded, his gaze steady on her. "Ya got a knack for bringin' out the best in folks. They can see it, and so can the crowd. Word's spreadin' fast, and I think tonight, we'll have ourselves an even bigger crowd than last night."

Fayteen met his gaze, feeling a quiet intensity pass between them. She was still getting used to the way his eyes held hers, like he could see something deeper, something she wasn't even sure she was ready to acknowledge. But there was something there, something real and unmistakable, and it made her heart race just a little faster.

She broke the gaze, turning back to the girls. "All right, ladies. You heard the man. We got a show to put on, so let's keep rehearsin'. Tonight, we're gonna show 'em somethin' they ain't never seen before."

With renewed energy, they returned to their positions, and Fayteen led them through the routine once more. This time, she added minor adjustments, little details to make each movement more striking, more memorable. She guided Lily Mae's arms into a graceful arc, helped Sadie with a spin, and showed Ruby how to hold her chin just right, adding a sense of mystery.

The afternoon passed in a blur of movement and music, each repetition bringing them closer to perfection. By the time the sun was setting, casting warm golden light through the windows, Fayteen knew they were ready.

She dismissed the girls for a break before the performance, watching them head to their rooms to prepare. As she turned to leave the stage, she felt Jimmy's hand on her arm, gentle but firm.

"Reckon you're gonna be the talk of Golden Valley before the week's out," he said, his eyes softening.

She smiled, meeting his gaze once more. "That's the plan. Thank you, Jimmy. I wouldn't be here without your support."

He gave a slight nod, and for a moment, it felt like he was about to say something more. But then he let go, stepping back with a quiet smile. "Well, I'll let ya get ready. Lookin' forward to seein' what you got planned for tonight."

With one last glance, Fayteen turned and headed for her room, feeling a warmth spread through her. The excitement of the performance, the connection with the girls, and the lingering sensation of Jimmy's touch—it all swirled together, creating a sense of purpose she hadn't felt in a long time.

As she prepared for the evening's performance, she knew that Golden Valley was going to be more than just a stop along the way. She'd found something here, something worth holding on to. And tonight, she was going to pour every bit of herself into that stage, ready to leave her mark on this town and the man who'd made it all possible.

3

The Founders

The morning sun had barely crested over the hills when Jimmy found himself leaning against the bar in The Golden Nugget, watching the quiet stillness of the empty room. The saloon was always an impressive sight, but it held a different kind of beauty in the early light, when everything was hushed and waiting. He ran a hand over the polished mahogany, taking in the faint scent of cedar and whiskey that lingered in the air.

It hadn't been an easy road to get here. Jimmy had grown up in Cedar Ridge, Montana, a place that held far too many memories of hardship. His father had left when he was just a boy, chasing gold in far-off places, leaving Jimmy with his grandparents. He could still remember his grandfather's hands, rough and calloused from years of work, guiding him as he learned to whittle, shaping pieces of cedar into little animals he'd line up along the windowsill.

Jimmy had been restless, even as a boy, dreaming of something bigger. By the time he hit his twenties, he was ready to leave, setting out for the Boise Basin in Idaho Territory, where gold fever had struck hard and fast. He'd made his fortune there, panning alongside rough men who'd come from all over, hoping to change their luck. Jimmy had been one of the lucky ones, striking a claim that paid off big. He could've gone anywhere after that, but he chose to build Golden Valley, something that would last, a place where people could put down roots and build new lives.

As he walked outside, Jimmy took a deep breath, letting the cool morning air fill his lungs. He glanced down the main street, taking in the sight of the town he'd helped create. His gaze fell on the general store, its shutters already open, and a faint smile played at the corners of his mouth. He headed that way, his boots crunching on the gravel as he went.

The Mercantile, owned by Henry and Ada Wickham, was one of the first businesses to go up after The Golden Nugget. Henry had been an old friend from the Basin, a reliable man with a keen business sense and a knack for finding what folks needed before they even knew they needed it. He and his wife, Ada, and their two boys, Elijah and Peter, had settled in Golden Valley with the same dream Jimmy had—a place to call home.

As Jimmy entered the store, the familiar jingle of the bell overhead announced his arrival, and Henry looked up from the counter, grinning.

"Mornin', Jimmy," Henry said, his voice carrying a friendly warmth. "You're out and about early."

Jimmy tipped his hat, glancing around the store, which was stocked with everything from sacks of flour and bolts of fabric to mining tools and canned goods. "Mornin', Henry. Figured I'd come by, see how things are goin'. Heard tell ya got a shipment in yesterday?"

Henry nodded, gesturing to a stack of crates by the wall. "Just came in from Boise. Got some new tools, couple of finer fabrics for the ladies. Ada's excited—says folks'll be flockin' in for 'em."

As if on cue, Ada appeared from a back room, a warm smile lighting up her face when she saw Jimmy. "Well, if it isn't the man himself! I was just sayin' to Henry, we oughta stock a bit more for the ladies. With all these new folks comin' in, seems we're goin' through supplies faster than we thought."

Jimmy chuckled. "You're right, Ada. Town's growin' faster than any of us expected. I'm glad you two are here to keep up with it. Wouldn't be the same without ya."

Ada gave him a friendly pat on the arm. "We're glad to be here, Jimmy. This town's startin' to feel like home. And thanks to you, we've got a good start. Folks respect you, knowin' you're buildin' somethin' real."

They chatted for a few more minutes, with Henry mentioning that he'd ordered some special tools for Gideon Grady over at the blacksmith's. Jimmy nodded, making a mental note to stop by and check on the Grady family next.

As he walked down the street, he reflected on how each person who'd come to Golden Valley had brought something unique. They weren't just building a town; they were building a community, a place where folks looked out for one another.

Jimmy made his way to the blacksmith's shop, where the steady rhythm of hammer on anvil could be heard even from a distance. The scent of iron and smoke drifted through the air, and he spotted Gideon Grady, a tall, muscular man with thick forearms, working on a horseshoe.

"Mornin', Gideon," Jimmy called out, watching as the man turned, a welcoming grin breaking through his usually gruff expression.

"Mornin' to ya, Jimmy," Gideon replied, setting down his hammer. "Just workin' on this shoe here. Martha's out back tendin' to the horses, if ya want to say hello."

Jimmy nodded, stepping into the shop, glancing around at the array of tools and projects Gideon had scattered about. The man was a master of his trade, and it showed. Every piece was crafted with care, and folks knew they could count on Gideon for quality work.

"You're keepin' busy, I see," Jimmy said, leaning against a nearby post.

Gideon laughed, a deep, booming sound. "Busier than ever, thanks to you. Martha and I were talkin' just last night about how this town's growin' like a weed after the rain. Don't reckon we'd have settled down here if it weren't for you, Jimmy."

Just then, Martha appeared from the back, leading a sturdy bay horse. She smiled when she saw Jimmy, giving him a nod. "Good to see ya, Jimmy. This town's startin' to feel like family. Every day, seems like new folks are comin' in, needin' horses shod and wagons fixed."

Jimmy returned her smile. "That's the idea. Golden Valley's got a future, and I'm countin' on folks like you two to help make it happen."

They talked a bit longer, with Gideon mentioning the tools Henry had ordered for him, and Jimmy promised to bring them by later. As he left the blacksmith's, he glanced down the road toward the café, his stomach reminding him that he hadn't eaten yet. Hattie and Lou McBride ran the café, and he could already smell the warm, comforting aroma of fresh coffee and baked bread wafting through the air. Hattie was widowed and had brought her daughter Lizzie with her for a new beginning after her husband's death.

He entered the café, the little bell above the door ringing as he stepped inside. The café was cozy, with tables covered in checkered cloths and vases of wildflowers set in the center of each one. It was a place where folks could come and rest a spell, share a meal, and trade stories.

Lou, the younger sister, spotted him first and waved him over. She had a bright, infectious smile and a way of making everyone feel welcome. "Mornin', Jimmy! Come on in, have a seat. We got fresh coffee and biscuits just out of the oven."

Jimmy tipped his hat, taking a seat by the window. "Well, ya know I can't pass up your cookin', Lou."

Hattie, the elder sister, appeared from the back, a plate of biscuits in one hand and a pot of coffee in the other. She set them on the table with a warm smile. "Thought you'd be comin' by sooner or later. Ain't nobody makes biscuits like us, and don't you forget it."

Jimmy laughed, taking a biscuit and savoring the buttery, flaky goodness. "You got that right, Hattie. Ain't nobody in the territory could do it better."

They chatted over breakfast, with Lou talking excitedly about all the new faces they'd seen lately. "Seems like every day, we're meetin' folks from all over. They're hearin' about the town, hearin' about what you're buildin', and they're comin' to see for themselves."

Jimmy nodded, his gaze thoughtful. "That's what I was hopin' for. Golden Valley's got a chance to be somethin' special. It ain't just about the gold—it's about buildin' a place where folks can live and work, raise families, and make somethin' of themselves."

Hattie poured him another cup of coffee, nodding in agreement. "Well, you're doin' a fine job, Jimmy. And Lou and I are glad to be a part of it."

He finished his coffee, leaving a few coins on the table before he stood. "Much obliged, ladies. Don't know what this town would do without ya."

He made his way to the one-room schoolhouse at the edge of town, where a petite, auburn-haired woman was arranging books and small chairs. Miss Cora Abernathy, the schoolteacher, was new to Golden Valley, but she'd already made an impression on the townsfolk with her progressive ideas and kind demeanor.

She looked up as he approached, a warm smile lighting up her face. "Mornin', Mr. Hawthorne."

"Just Jimmy," he replied, smiling. "Looks like you're settlin' in fine."

Cora glanced around the small room, her eyes filled with pride. "It's comin' along. I've got some books on the way, and I've been gatherin' supplies. Figured if the town's growin', we'll have children comin' in soon, and they'll need learnin'."

Jimmy nodded, leaning against the doorframe. "I'm glad to have you here, Miss Abernathy. Education's important, and these kids'll be better for it."

She nodded, her eyes reflecting a fierce dedication. "They deserve it, Jimmy. Every child deserves a chance to learn, to grow up knowin' more than their folks did. I intend to make sure they get that chance here."

As he left the schoolhouse, Jimmy felt a sense of satisfaction settle over him. He walked back down the main street, the sounds of construction, laughter, and life filling the air. Golden Valley was growing, and it wasn't just the buildings. It was the people, each one bringing a piece of themselves, their dreams, and their hard work. Together, they were building something that could last.

And Jimmy knew that as long as they kept movin' forward, as long as they held onto that sense of purpose, Golden Valley would thrive. It would be a place where people could belong, a place where he could build his future.

4

Building Friendships

Fayteen hadn't been in Golden Valley long, but it was already starting to feel like home. There was a warmth here she hadn't expected—a sense of community that went beyond the walls of The Golden Nugget and seeped into her bones. She'd come to the frontier looking for a fresh start, a place where she could leave her past behind, and it seemed she'd found it.

The day after her first performance, she gathered the girls for rehearsal in the empty saloon. The sunlight streamed through the windows, casting warm patches on the polished wood floor. Ruby, Josie, Anna, Maggie, Pearl, Sadie, and Belle were already there, chatting and laughing as they waited for her to begin.

Lily Mae Dawson sidled up to her, her blue eyes sparkling with mischief. She was younger than the rest, barely twenty, with a knack for making anyone smile. Her blonde curls bounced as she spoke, her voice light and teasing. "Ya sure made an impression last night, Fayteen. Folks couldn't stop talkin' 'bout ya."

Fayteen chuckled, giving her a playful nudge. "It was a team effort, Lily Mae. Couldn't have done it without y'all."

The other girls nodded, a mix of admiration and camaraderie in their faces. Fayteen had quickly found a rhythm with the troupe, her years of performing giving her the confidence to lead. And yet, it wasn't just about the dancing. It was about forming bonds, building something real with these women who had their own dreams and struggles.

As they began the rehearsal, Fayteen took a moment to appreciate the way the girls moved, their steps growing more fluid, more confident with each repetition. She called out gentle corrections, guiding them into a seamless routine that told a story, each movement reflecting a deeper emotion.

"Remember," she said, catching their eyes, "we're not just here to entertain. We're here to make folks feel somethin'. When ya dance, let yourself go. Think about what matters to ya and let that show."

Lily Mae nodded, her expression thoughtful. "It's more than just dancin', ain't it? It's like... we're sharin' a part of ourselves."

"That's right," Fayteen replied, her voice softening. "Dance is more than steps. It's a way to speak, a way to let out what we carry inside."

The girls seemed to take her words to heart, their movements growing more deliberate, more expressive. By the time they finished the routine, they were laughing and clapping, the air filled with a sense of shared accomplishment.

As they took a break, Fayteen found herself drawn to Lily Mae, who was seated on the edge of the stage, swinging her legs and humming a tune. Fayteen sat beside her, leaning back on her hands and taking in the familiar comfort of the empty saloon.

"Ya know," Lily Mae said, her voice quieter now, "I never thought I'd find a place like this. Never thought I'd meet folks who care."

Fayteen glanced at her, surprised by the vulnerability in her tone. "Golden Valley's somethin' special. A place where people can come together, build somethin' real. And ya got a place here, Lily Mae. We all do."

Lily Mae smiled, a hint of gratitude in her eyes. "Thanks, Fayteen. Ya got a way of makin' folks feel like they matter. I reckon I'm lucky to know ya."

Fayteen felt a warmth spread through her, a sense of connection she hadn't felt in a long time. She reached out, giving Lily Mae's hand a gentle squeeze. "We're all lucky. And we're just gettin' started."

Later that afternoon, Fayteen decided to pay a visit to Miss Cora Abernathy. She'd heard a lot about the schoolteacher—how she was different from most, with a mind full of new ideas and a passion for helping children learn. Cora was still settling into her one-room schoolhouse, arranging desks and setting up books for the children who would soon be filling the space.

When Fayteen arrived, she found Cora sitting at a small desk, reading over a stack of papers. She looked up, her eyes brightening as she saw Fayteen.

"Well, if it isn't Golden Valley's newest star!" Cora said, setting down the papers and standing to greet her. "Come on in, Fayteen. It's a pleasure to finally meet ya."

Fayteen smiled, stepping inside and taking in the simple but inviting space. The walls were lined with chalkboards, and rows of small desks filled the room, each one a little worn but full of character. "I've heard a lot about ya, Miss Abernathy. Folks say you're a breath of fresh air."

Cora laughed, waving a hand. "Please, just Cora. I don't think anyone's ever called me a breath of fresh air before, but I'll take it. Heard you put on quite a show last night."

Fayteen nodded, leaning against the edge of a desk. "It went well, I think. Folks seemed to enjoy it. But it's more than just dancin'. I want it to mean somethin'."

Cora nodded thoughtfully, her gaze warm. "Sounds like you've got a good heart, Fayteen. That's rare, and it's somethin' folks are gonna remember. I can tell you're not just here to entertain—you're here to make a difference."

They talked for a while, their conversation drifting from the challenges of teaching to the joys of working with children. Cora shared her vision for the school, her desire to teach the children not just to read and write, but to think for themselves, to grow into people who could shape the world around them.

"It ain't easy," Cora said, glancing out the window. "But it's worth it. I want these kids to have a future, one that's brighter than what most folks expect for 'em."

Fayteen felt a surge of admiration for the woman beside her, a kindred spirit who understood the importance of building something that lasted. She reached out, placing a hand on

Cora's arm. "You're doin' somethin' real, Cora. And if ya ever need help, I'm here. We're all in this together."

Cora smiled, her eyes softening. "Thank ya, Fayteen. Means a lot, knowin' there are folks who understand."

As Fayteen left the schoolhouse, she felt a renewed sense of purpose. The friendships she was building here, the people she was meeting—they were more than just acquaintances. They were becoming family, each one adding to the tapestry of her new life in Golden Valley.

Her next stop was the café, where she found Lou McBride bustling about, carrying trays of steaming coffee and fresh biscuits. The café was lively, with patrons chatting and laughing over their meals, and Fayteen was struck by the warmth of the place, the way it felt like a gathering spot for the whole town.

Lou spotted her and waved her over, a bright smile lighting up her face. "Well, if it isn't our star performer! Come on over, Fayteen. Sit yourself down and let me get ya somethin' warm."

Fayteen took a seat by the window, watching as Lou bustled about, her energy infectious. Lou set a plate of biscuits and a mug of coffee in front of her, giving her a friendly wink. "House special. Can't let ya leave without tryin' 'em."

Fayteen laughed, taking a bite and savoring the buttery, flaky goodness. "These are incredible, Lou. Ya got a real talent for this."

Lou grinned, taking a seat across from her. "Well, thank ya kindly. Hattie and I, we've been bakin' since we were kids. Never thought we'd end up out here, but I gotta say, I'm startin' to love it."

Fayteen nodded, taking a sip of the coffee. "I feel the same way. Thought I was just passin' through, but now... it feels like I've found somethin' worth holdin' onto."

Lou leaned forward, her expression softening. "Ya know, Fayteen, I think you've got a rare gift. I saw ya up there on that stage last night, and it wasn't just dancin'. Ya got a way of speakin' to folks, makin' 'em feel somethin'. People need that."

Fayteen felt a flush of gratitude, the weight of Lou's words settling into her heart. "Thank you, Lou. Means a lot comin' from you."

They talked for a while, sharing stories and laughing over their shared experiences. Lou's lively personality complemented Fayteen's quieter strength, and by the time they finished, Fayteen felt like she'd known Lou for years.

As she left the café, Fayteen felt a growing sense of belonging. The connections she was forming, the friendships she was building—they were creating a foundation for something lasting, something real. Golden Valley was becoming more than just a stop on her journey; it was becoming home.

That night, as she lay in bed, Fayteen reflected on the day's events, the people she'd met, and the bonds that were starting to form. Lily Mae, Cora, Lou—each one brought something unique to her life, filling the empty spaces with laughter, warmth, and a shared sense of purpose. She knew that, with these women by her side, there was no limit to what they could build together.

And as she drifted off to sleep, Fayteen felt a quiet peace settle over her, a feeling that she was exactly where she was meant to be.

5

Jimmy's Leadership

The Golden Nugget was in full swing, the saloon alive with the sounds of laughter, clinking glasses, and the lively notes of a piano tune. Jimmy moved through the room with an easy stride, his eyes sweeping over the crowd. He wasn't just watching the patrons; he was watching his girls, too, ensuring that everyone was safe and that the rules he'd set were being respected.

He'd always run The Golden Nugget with a clear set of guidelines, and he expected everyone to follow them. The dancers—Fayteen, Lily Mae, Ruby, and the rest—were more than just entertainment. They were part of his family here, and he treated them with the same respect he expected from his patrons. Anyone who crossed the line found themselves face-to-face with the business end of his Colt, or worse, tossed into the dirt outside the saloon.

He caught sight of a couple of rough-looking men at the bar, their gazes lingering a little too long on Anna, who was serving drinks with a bright, practiced smile. Jimmy made his way over, giving the men a hard look as he approached.

"Evenin', gents," he said, his voice low and calm but carrying an unmistakable authority. "Just a reminder that my girls are here to work, not to be bothered. You keep your hands to yourselves, understand?"

The men glanced at each other, and then at Jimmy. One of them, a wiry man with a scar along his jawline, gave a sneering smile. "We're just havin' a little fun, that's all."

Jimmy held his gaze, his expression hardening. "Fun's one thing. Crossin' the line's another. My girls are here by choice, and they got my protection. Respect 'em, or find yourself out on the street."

The man's smile faded, and he gave a grudging nod. Jimmy watched as the two of them returned to their drinks, keeping their eyes away from the dancers. Satisfied, he nodded to Anna, who gave him a small smile of thanks before returning to her work.

As he turned to continue his rounds, Jimmy noticed a familiar figure standing near the entrance. Ahanu Laughing River, a man from the nearby Shoshone tribe, had a quiet strength about him that drew attention without any need for words. He was tall, with dark eyes that held a spark of wisdom and humor, and he wore his long black hair tied back, dressed simply but with a quiet dignity that spoke of his heritage.

Jimmy walked over, smiling as he extended a hand. "Ahanu, it's good to see ya. Didn't expect ya to be in town tonight."

Ahanu shook his hand, nodding with a smile. "Thought I would come to see how my friend Jimmy handles his world. Seems you have your hands full tonight."

Jimmy chuckled, glancing back at the crowd. "Always do, but that's the way I like it. Why don't we step outside? It's quieter there, and we can catch up."

They made their way to the saloon's porch, where the night air was cool and fresh. Jimmy leaned against the railing, taking in the quiet around them, a stark contrast to the raucous sounds inside. Ahanu stood beside him, his gaze on the distant hills, his expression calm.

"Your saloon is a lively place," Ahanu said, a trace of amusement in his voice. "But it seems you keep things in order."

Jimmy nodded. "Reckon I have to. Those girls work for me, and I won't let anybody disrespect 'em. They deserve better, and it's my job to see they get it."

Ahanu looked at him, a thoughtful expression in his eyes. "You take care of your own. That is good. In my people's ways, we call that *wa'kun*, a sacred duty to protect. It's something we live by."

Jimmy nodded, intrigued by the word. "*Wa'kun*, huh? Sounds like we got some things in common. I figure respect is respect, no matter where you're from."

Ahanu gave a slight nod, his gaze distant. "That is true, my friend. Respect is at the heart of our ways. When we take from the earth, we offer back. We honor the land, the animals, our ancestors. All things are connected, and to live without respect for that connection is to invite trouble."

They fell into a comfortable silence, the quiet of the night wrapping around them. Jimmy had always admired Ahanu's calm, his steady presence. There was a wisdom in his friend that he respected, a knowledge that came from a place deeper than books or experience.

"Tell me somethin', Ahanu," Jimmy said, breaking the silence. "What's it like, growin' up with your people, learnin' your ways? I only got a piece of that growin' up—my granddad taught me some things, but it ain't the same."

Ahanu glanced at him, a glimmer of something close to pride in his eyes. "It is like growing up with the earth as your teacher. We learn from the mountains, the rivers, the animals. Every season brings its own lessons. We have ceremonies to honor those lessons, to remind us of our place in the world."

Jimmy listened intently, soaking up the words. He'd spent much of his life moving from place to place, chasing after dreams and fortunes, never settling long enough to truly connect with the land around him. Hearing Ahanu speak of these customs made him realize how much he'd missed.

Ahanu continued, his tone quiet. "We have a ceremony each spring, called the *Sun Dance*. It is a time when we gather, fasting and praying for strength. The dance is a gift, an offering to the Creator, to show that we honor the life we have been given. It is a way of renewing ourselves, of finding balance."

Jimmy's eyes widened slightly. He'd heard stories of the Sun Dance, but hearing it from Ahanu made it feel more tangible, more real. "Sounds like there's a lot of meaning in it. I can see why it matters so much."

Ahanu nodded, a faint smile crossing his face. "There is meaning in everything, Jimmy. Even the small things. When I hunt, I thank the animal, and I use every part. When I walk the land, I speak to the trees, the stones. They remember us, just as we remember them."

Jimmy considered this, his mind turning over the words. He'd grown up with a respect for the land, but he'd never thought to see it as something alive, something that remembered. He felt a new appreciation for Ahanu's way of life, a way of living with purpose and intention.

"Tell me more," Jimmy said, his voice softening. "I want to understand."

Ahanu seemed pleased, as though he'd been waiting for this moment. He spoke of the Shoshone way of life, of the seasons and their meanings, of the ceremonies that marked each turning of the year. He told Jimmy about the coming-of-age rituals for young men, about the vision quests that took them deep into the mountains to seek guidance from the spirits.

"We believe that each person has a spirit guide," Ahanu explained. "Someone who watches over us, who helps us find our path. When a boy becomes a man, he goes into the wilderness alone, fasting and praying, until his spirit guide reveals itself. It could be a wolf, an eagle, a bear. Each one has its own wisdom, its own gifts to share."

Jimmy felt a sense of wonder as he listened, picturing a young man alone in the wilderness, seeking something beyond himself. It was a test of strength, of courage, but it was also a journey inward, a search for something deeper.

"That's a powerful thing, Ahanu," he said, his voice tinged with awe. "I can see why ya carry yourself the way ya do. It's like... ya got a peace about ya."

Ahanu smiled, his gaze steady. "Peace comes from balance, my friend. When you know who you are, when you walk with respect, you find balance. And with balance comes peace."

They sat in silence for a while, watching the stars begin to emerge, each one a tiny point of light in the vast sky. Jimmy felt a deep gratitude for Ahanu's friendship, for the way he'd shared a part of himself, a part of his culture, with him.

"Ahanu," Jimmy said, breaking the silence, "I don't reckon I'll ever be able to understand it all, but I want ya to know... I respect what ya do. The way ya live, the way ya honor the land—it's somethin' special."

Ahanu placed a hand on Jimmy's shoulder, a gesture of quiet solidarity. "Respect goes both ways, Jimmy. You have a good heart. I see it in the way you look out for your people, the way you care for this town. You are walking a good path."

Jimmy nodded, a sense of pride settling over him. In that moment, he felt connected to something larger, something that went beyond himself or his saloon. He knew that, in his own way, he was honoring the people around him, building a community that could stand the test of time.

As they sat there under the stars, Jimmy realized that Golden Valley wasn't just a place he'd built; it was a place he was learning to belong to. With friends like Ahanu, he was finding his own sense of balance, his own path.

"I want to understand more, Ahanu. I've spent my life on the move, always chasin' somethin'. Maybe it's time I learned how to be still, how to know this land I'm tryin' to build on."

Ahanu's face softened, a glimmer of approval in his eyes. "That is the first step, my friend. The willingness to learn. If you truly want to understand, meet me here at first light. I will show you things you will not find in any saloon."

Jimmy nodded, feeling a surge of anticipation. "I'll be here. I want to learn all you can teach me."

The next morning, Jimmy rose before the sun, the early morning air crisp as he made his way to the edge of town, where Ahanu was waiting. They set off together, heading toward the hills, the landscape around them gradually brightening as dawn broke over Golden Valley.

Their first stop was near a small, trickling creek, where Ahanu crouched down, examining the tracks in the soft earth. He gestured for Jimmy to join him, pointing to a series of faint prints in the mud.

"Tell me what you see here," Ahanu said, his tone gentle but probing.

Jimmy knelt beside him, studying the tracks. "Looks like... deer, maybe? Four-toed, small print."

Ahanu nodded, a faint smile on his face. "You are right. Young deer, likely passed here at dawn, maybe an hour before we came along. In my people's ways, we call the deer *bah'chi*. They are quick, light, and they teach us to be gentle, to tread softly on the land."

They followed the tracks for a while, Ahanu pointing out subtle changes in the landscape—broken twigs, bent grass, faint impressions left by animals that had crossed the path before them. Jimmy watched in awe, his respect for Ahanu growing as he realized how much he didn't know, how much he'd overlooked in the world around him.

"You see," Ahanu explained, "it is about reading the signs, understanding what they tell us. The land speaks to us, if we know how to listen."

They continued through a meadow where wildflowers swayed in the breeze, their colors vibrant against the green backdrop. Ahanu paused, crouching down to pluck a small, delicate flower with purple petals. He handed it to Jimmy, his gaze thoughtful.

"This is *yampah*," Ahanu said. "It is a healing plant, one we use in our medicines. It soothes the stomach, and we dry it to use in teas. We believe that every plant has a purpose, a way of helping us. Nature provides what we need, if we know how to honor it."

Jimmy turned the flower over in his hand, marveling at its simplicity and the knowledge it held. "Didn't think there'd be so much to it. I've been around plants my whole life, but I never thought of 'em as anything more than... well, just plants."

Ahanu smiled, his expression warm. "It is about seeing the world as a whole, each part connected. In our ways, we call it *biya'min*, the balance. We take only what we need, and we give thanks. It's a way of honoring the gifts we have been given."

They continued deeper into the forest, Ahanu pointing out various plants, each one with a purpose—some for healing, others for sustenance. He taught Jimmy how to recognize edible roots, to distinguish between medicinal herbs and those that were best left alone.

As they walked, Ahanu began to share stories, tales of his people and the lessons passed down through generations. He spoke of how the Shoshone viewed the world, of how they lived in harmony with the land and honored the spirits of their ancestors.

"We believe that when a man dies, his spirit returns to the earth, joining the land, the trees, the rivers. He lives on, part of all that surrounds us," Ahanu explained, his voice quiet but filled with conviction. "It is why we respect all life, why we take only what we need. It is all connected."

They reached a small clearing where a group of Shoshone men had gathered, preparing for a hunt. Ahanu introduced Jimmy, explaining that he was a friend who wanted to learn, to understand their ways. The men welcomed him with quiet nods, their expressions open and respectful.

One of the men, named Mahpee, handed Jimmy a bow and arrow, showing him how to hold it, how to draw the string back with a steady hand. Jimmy took a deep breath, focusing on the target—a small bundle of sticks tied with rope—and released the arrow. It struck close to the center, and the men nodded approvingly.

"You have a good hand, Jimmy," Mahpee said with a smile. "With time, you could learn to hunt as we do, to move with the land, not against it."

Jimmy felt a surge of pride, grateful for the chance to learn, to be part of something beyond himself. He spent the next hour practicing, listening to the men's stories, their laughter filling the air as they shared tales of past hunts, of the challenges they'd faced, the lessons they'd learned.

Afterward, Ahanu led him to a nearby stream, where they rested, the sound of the water a soothing backdrop to their conversation. Ahanu spoke of the Shoshone's connection to nature, of how they believed the spirits of their ancestors watched over them, guiding them through life's trials.

"In my tribe," Ahanu said, "we have a ceremony, the *Ghost Dance*. It is a prayer for peace, for protection. We dance to call upon our ancestors, to ask for their guidance. It reminds us of who we are, where we come from."

Jimmy listened, captivated by the beauty and depth of the customs Ahanu described. He realized that the Shoshone's way of life was about more than survival—it was about connection, a respect for the past and a hope for the future.

"I can see why it matters so much," Jimmy said, his voice filled with awe. "I feel like I'm finally startin' to see the world the way you do, Ahanu. There's a peace in it, a purpose."

Ahanu nodded, placing a hand on Jimmy's shoulder. "You have the heart for it, Jimmy. You care for your people, you honor your commitments. That is what matters. Our ways may be different, but in the end, we seek the same things—balance, respect, a sense of belonging."

They sat together in companionable silence, watching the stream flow by, its waters clear and cool. Jimmy felt a sense of calm settle over him, a feeling he hadn't known in years. He realized that this friendship, this connection to Ahanu and his people, was helping him find his own path, his own sense of purpose.

As they made their way back to Golden Valley, Ahanu continued to share his knowledge, teaching Jimmy about tracking animals, about reading the signs of the land. He showed him how to recognize the calls of birds, how to find his way by the position of the sun and stars.

By the time they returned to the edge of town, Jimmy felt a sense of fulfillment, a gratitude for the day's lessons and the friendship that had grown between them.

"Thank ya, Ahanu," he said, his voice filled with sincerity. "I've learned more today than I ever thought possible. I see things differently now."

Ahanu smiled, nodding. "We walk different paths, my friend, but we share the same earth. Remember what you learned today. Honor it, and you will find your way."

They parted ways with a quiet understanding, a sense of mutual respect that went beyond words. As Jimmy walked back to The Golden Nugget, he felt a new resolve, a determination to live with purpose, to honor the land and the people around him.

He realized that he wasn't just building a town—he was building a life, one that could stand the test of time, one that would leave a legacy. And with friends like Ahanu, he knew he had found the guidance he needed, the strength to walk his own path with honor.

6

The Growing Town

Golden Valley was flourishing, and the transformation was evident everywhere Jimmy looked. Each day brought new faces and fresh energy to the town, and with it, a sense of purpose that made him proud. What had begun as a small outpost was growing into a thriving community, with new buildings rising alongside The Golden Nugget, each one marking another step toward the town's future.

The doctor's clinic was among the newest structures, its walls freshly painted in a soft white, with a green door that gave it a welcoming touch. Dr. Emmett Harper had arrived not long ago, and his reputation as a skilled and compassionate physician had already spread through town. He'd come with a nurse, Eliza Wakefield, a young woman with a gentle manner and a quiet resilience that was evident in the way she approached her work.

Jimmy approached the clinic just as Dr. Harper was organizing supplies on the porch, with Eliza by his side, carrying a basket filled with small bottles and bandages. She looked up and smiled when she saw Jimmy.

"Mornin', Dr. Harper, Miss Wakefield," Jimmy greeted them, tipping his hat.

"Good morning, Jimmy," Dr. Harper replied, shaking his hand with a firm, steady grip. His hair was flecked with gray, and his face held the calm assurance of someone who'd seen enough to know how to handle whatever might come his way.

Eliza nodded in greeting, her eyes bright with a warmth that seemed to put everyone at ease. "Mornin', Jimmy. It's good to see you."

"Just wanted to make sure you were both settlin' in fine," Jimmy said, glancing at the clinic. "Folks'll rest a bit easier knowin' there's a doctor in town. And from what I hear, you're the best around."

Dr. Harper smiled, a humble expression on his face. "Thank you, Jimmy. This town's shown us nothin' but kindness. We're glad to be here, and we'll do what we can to keep everyone healthy."

Eliza chimed in, glancing over her supplies. "We've been gettin' the place in order, and we're thinkin' of startin' a small herb garden out back for natural remedies. The folks here are used to takin' care of themselves, but it'll be good to have a place they can come to when they need help."

Jimmy nodded, impressed. "That's a fine idea. If ya need anythin' to get it goin', let me know. Golden Valley's gonna need a clinic as we grow, and we're glad you two are here."

As they talked, Jimmy felt a surge of satisfaction.

He continued down the street to the newly constructed church, where Reverend Amos Thornton was inspecting the final touches on the wooden structure. The simple building had a small steeple and a cross above the door, and it was surrounded by a neat, modest churchyard. Reverend Thornton, a man in his early thirties with a gentle but determined manner, looked up when he saw Jimmy approaching.

"Mornin', Reverend," Jimmy called, tipping his hat as he drew closer.

"Good mornin', Jimmy," Reverend Thornton replied, extending his hand. "Thank you for comin' by. We're nearly finished, and I have to say, the folks here have been a blessing, helpin' me get everything set up."

Jimmy shook his hand, feeling a pang of remembrance as he took in the sight of the church. It brought him back to the days of his youth, when he'd attended services with his grandparents. His grandfather's strong, steady voice as they sang hymns, his grandmother's gentle hand on his shoulder as they listened to the preacher—it was a time he hadn't thought of in years, but standing here with Reverend Thornton brought it all rushing back.

Reverend Thornton seemed to notice his momentary silence and gave a small smile. "Church has a way of bringin' back memories, don't it? It's a place for families, for reflection."

Jimmy nodded, his gaze distant. "It does. My grandparents took me to church every Sunday. Never thought I'd be back in one, but reckon it's good to have a place like this. The town needs it."

The reverend nodded, looking around with a sense of quiet pride. "A town is more than just its buildings, Jimmy. It's the people, the spirit they bring. I'm glad to be here, to help foster a sense of community, of connection. We're all walkin' this path together, after all."

They talked a while longer, Jimmy offering his help if the reverend needed anything as he settled in. As Jimmy made his way back to The Golden Nugget, he felt the weight of those memories, the feeling of home that he hadn't known he'd missed.

Back at The Golden Nugget, he found Fayteen sitting at the bar with Antonio, the mysterious pianist who'd taken up residence in the saloon. Antonio was playing a quiet tune, his fingers moving over the keys with effortless grace, his gaze distant and focused. The man was a mystery—he rarely spoke, but his music had a way of capturing the room, of reaching deep into the soul of anyone who listened.

Fayteen looked up when Jimmy entered, a bright smile on her face. "Jimmy, I've been thinkin'. This town's growin' faster than we ever expected, and I reckon folks could use a place to gather, to relax and enjoy some music."

Jimmy leaned against the bar, nodding for her to continue. "What've you got in mind?"

She straightened, her enthusiasm infectious. "Well, we've already got a stage and Antonio here. What if we started hostin' regular events? Not just dancin', but music, singin', maybe a chance for folks to come together, to feel like they're part of somethin' bigger?"

Antonio's fingers paused on the keys, and he glanced over, a slight smile on his face. "I can play anything ya need," he said softly, his voice carrying a hint of an accent. "Music has a way of bringin' people together. I'd be glad to lend a hand."

Jimmy nodded, picturing the gatherings Fayteen described. "We've got those rooms out the back, too. Once they're finished, folks'll have a place to stay if they're passin' through. I like the idea, Fayteen. Let's make this place more than just a saloon."

Fayteen's eyes sparkled with excitement. "We could host weekly music nights, where Antonio plays and I sing. Maybe even bring in other musicians from time to time, make it a real event. Folks'll come from all around, and it'll put Golden Valley on the map."

Jimmy smiled, the vision taking hold in his mind. "All right. Let's do it. This place was always meant to be more than just a drinkin' hole. It'll be a place folks remember, a place they'll want to come back to."

The plan took shape over the following days. Jimmy hired Eli Thorne, the local sawmill owner and skilled carpenter, and a few more men to finish the back rooms, ensuring each one was comfortable and inviting, with rich wooden furnishings and warm quilts. Fayteen worked with Antonio to plan the music for the first gathering, her enthusiasm spreading through the saloon, drawing in everyone who heard about it.

She also spent time with Dr. Harper and Eliza, getting to know the new faces in town, forging bonds that strengthened her connection to Golden Valley. Fayteen found a kindred spirit in Eliza, whose quick smile and gentle nature made her easy to talk to. One afternoon, after Fayteen had helped tidy up the clinic, Eliza invited her over to the small café across the street. They settled at a table near the window, sipping tea and watching the comings and goings of the town.

Eliza glanced out, her eyes drifting thoughtfully over the bustling scene. "You know, it's funny—I grew up back East, in a small town outside of Philadelphia," she said, a soft smile spreading across her face. "I never thought I'd end up way out here. But after studying nursing, I knew I wanted to be somewhere I could really make a difference. And Golden Valley... well, it just felt right."

Fayteen nodded, intrigued. "Philadelphia, you say? I've been there! I've performed in cities all over, from Boston down to Charleston. Philadelphia has such a spirit to it, don't you think? I remember walking along its old streets, the buildings standing tall, the history just humming all around you. But I always ended up moving on to the next place, always looking for somethin' more." She took a sip of her tea, her gaze softening. "Turns out, my heart had plans I didn't even know about."

Eliza laughed, leaning forward with a glint of excitement. "Isn't it strange how life can change like that?" Eliza said, laughing. "I had dreams of going to New York, working in a big hospital there. But the more I learned, the more I realized I wanted to be where I could help people in a real, meaningful way. Not just another face in a crowd. Here, I feel like I'm part of somethin' that matters."

Fayteen's eyes sparkled. "It's the same for me. There's a sense of freedom here, of bein' able to create somethin' all our own. I reckon that's why I agreed to take on this dance troupe. These girls have their stories, their own hopes and hurts, and we're all finding our way together. Sometimes I look out at this town, at the saloon Jimmy's built, and I realize—this is more than just another stop along the road. It's home."

Eliza reached across the table, placing a comforting hand on Fayteen's. "And you're good for this place, Fayteen. I can see it. I think we're all lookin' for a bit of that peace, that purpose. I know Dr. Harper feels the same way. He came out here with a strong heart, wanting to bring medicine to folks who've never had a real doctor before. He says it's the work that keeps him grounded, makes him feel alive."

Fayteen nodded, touched by the insight. "I think that's what makes folks like you and Dr. Harper so special. You see the good in people, and you're willin' to put in the hard work to help them, even when it isn't easy. I'll be sendin' my girls to you often enough—this work we do, it takes a toll, both on the stage and in other ways. I want to be sure they're healthy, that they've got someone to turn to if they need help."

Eliza smiled, her eyes warm with understanding. "You know you can count on us. This town has a long road ahead, but with people like you, Jimmy, and Dr. Harper, I think we can make it somethin' beautiful. We're all here to help each other, and that's what makes it worthwhile."

***

The excitement in the town was palpable as word spread about the upcoming event. People stopped by the saloon to ask about the music, to see the new rooms, and to share in the growing sense of community that was taking hold. The Golden Nugget was transforming, not just into a saloon but into the heart of Golden Valley, a place where dreams were shared and where new friendships were forged.

On the night of the first event, Fayteen stood on the stage, her heart swelling with pride as she looked out over the gathered crowd. Antonio sat at the piano, his fingers poised over the keys, ready to bring the room to life with his music.

As the first notes filled the air, Fayteen began to sing, her voice carrying through the saloon, reaching every corner of the room. Jimmy watched from the back, a sense of contentment washing over him. This was more than he'd ever dreamed, more than he'd ever hoped for when he'd first arrived in Golden Valley. He'd built a town, a place where people could find what they needed, a place where they could belong.

And as he watched Fayteen sing, he knew that this was only the beginning. Together, they were building a legacy, one that would last long after the music had faded and the lights had dimmed.

7

Haunted By The Past

The first music night at The Golden Nugget had been a resounding success. The townsfolk filled the saloon, clapping and cheering, swept away by Fayteen's voice and the skilled notes of Antonio's piano. The sense of community that had taken root was flourishing, each event adding another layer to the bond shared by Golden Valley's residents.

As Fayteen watched the crowd filter out into the night, laughter and murmurs lingering in the air, she felt a quiet contentment. She'd found something here, something worth holding onto. The Golden Nugget was no longer just a stage for her performances; it was a place where she was building a new life, where she could finally feel at peace.

But peace, she'd come to understand, was fragile.

The memory crept in that night as she sat alone in her room, the flickering candle casting shadows on the walls. Her success in Golden Valley, the warmth of the people she'd met—it all seemed too good to be true. She'd worked so hard to bury the past, to leave behind the darkness that had once threatened to consume her. But no matter how hard she tried, the memories had a way of clawing their way back.

She closed her eyes, gripping the edge of her vanity, as a familiar unease settled over her. Images of Silas Thornfield slipped into her mind, unbidden and relentless. She'd been young, barely more than a girl, when he'd first taken an interest in her. Silas, her father's boss—a man of means, a man with a charming smile and a vicious streak hidden beneath his polished exterior.

He'd always found reasons to linger near her, his hands too familiar, his words too suggestive. At first, she'd thought it was just her imagination. But soon enough, his interest turned to something darker, something that left her with a hollow ache in her chest and a creeping shame she couldn't shake.

He'd cornered her one afternoon, his fingers digging into her arm as he whispered things no man should ever say to a young girl. She remembered the way his breath had smelled, the way his voice had dripped with menace, promising pain if she ever dared to speak of it. Little did he know the pain she was in, caused by him. Nor did he see the trickle of red coursing down her legs that day.

She shook herself from the memory, breathing deeply to push it away, to bring herself back to the present. Fayteen had fought her way out of that life, escaping the hold Silas had over her. But no matter how far she'd run, the scars he'd left behind lingered, a constant reminder of the darkness she'd fought to overcome.

The next day, she buried those memories beneath her usual bright smile, throwing herself into rehearsals with the girls, letting the rhythm of the dance and the camaraderie of the troupe carry her forward. But a sense of unease hung over her, a shadow she couldn't quite shake.

That evening, as the saloon filled with patrons, Fayteen felt a familiar tension settling over her. She took the stage, her gaze sweeping the room, her voice carrying over the crowd as she sang, her heart pounding with a mixture of nerves and excitement. The songs helped her forget, if only for a little while, giving her something to hold onto as the memories continued to linger.

It was then that she noticed him—a man seated at the back of the saloon, his eyes fixed on her with a cold, unsettling intensity. He was tall, with greasy hair slicked back and a scar that ran along his left cheek. His gaze held a familiarity that made her stomach twist, a reminder of Silas Thornfield that she'd rather not have faced.

Jimmy noticed him too. He'd been watching Fayteen throughout her performance, a sense of pride swelling within him as he saw the way the crowd responded to her, how they were captivated by her voice, by the quiet grace she brought to the stage. But when he saw the man in the corner, saw the way his eyes lingered on Fayteen, his jaw tightened.

Jimmy made his way across the room, positioning himself near the bar, keeping the man in his line of sight. He didn't like the way the stranger was watching her, the way his gaze seemed to follow her every movement. Jimmy's protective instincts flared, a familiar sense of vigilance taking hold as he assessed the newcomer.

When the performance ended, Fayteen stepped down from the stage, her heart still racing from the intensity of the song, from the thrill of being onstage. She moved to the bar, reaching for a glass of water, when she felt Jimmy's presence beside her, his expression guarded.

"Who's that fella in the corner?" Jimmy asked, his voice low.

Fayteen glanced over her shoulder, her heart skipping a beat when she saw the man's cold eyes still fixed on her. She turned back to Jimmy, her expression uneasy. "I don't know. Haven't seen him around before. But he gives me the creeps."

Jimmy frowned, his gaze hardening. "I'll keep an eye on him. If he tries anything, he'll answer to me."

The stranger moved toward them then, his gait slow and deliberate as he approached the bar. He stopped a few feet away, his gaze shifting from Jimmy to Fayteen, a smirk curling his lips.

"Evenin', miss," he said, his voice oily and too familiar. "Heard ya singin'. Quite a voice ya got there."

Fayteen forced a polite smile, her fingers tightening around the glass in her hand. "Thank you."

The man leaned against the bar, his eyes never leaving her. "Name's Curtis Blackwood. Just passin' through, but reckon I could stay a while if there's more entertainment like that."

Jimmy's posture stiffened, his eyes narrowing as he sized up Curtis. "Enjoy the show, did ya?"

Curtis shrugged, his gaze drifting back to Fayteen. "Mighty fine show. Maybe I'll stick around, see what else this town's got to offer."

Fayteen felt a chill creep down her spine. There was something about Curtis, something in the way he spoke, the way he looked at her, that brought back that old fear, that reminded her of the darkness she'd tried so hard to leave behind.

Jimmy's voice cut through the tension, firm and unyielding. "If you're stayin', you'll mind the rules. This ain't the kind of place where ya can do as ya please. Understand?"

Curtis gave him a mocking smile, but there was a hardness in his eyes, a challenge. "Reckon I understand just fine. I'll be seein' ya around, miss," he said, giving Fayteen one last lingering look before sauntering back to his table.

Jimmy watched him go, a sense of unease settling in his chest. He turned back to Fayteen, concern etched into his features. "You all right?"

She nodded, forcing a smile that didn't quite reach her eyes. "I'm fine, Jimmy. Just... he reminds me of someone I used to know."

Jimmy's gaze softened, his hand resting gently on her shoulder. "If he bothers ya, I'll deal with him. You don't have to face this alone."

Fayteen felt a surge of gratitude, the warmth of Jimmy's presence a balm against the memories that still lingered. She knew that he'd protect her, that he'd stand by her no matter what. But she also knew that some battles had to be fought within, that the shadows of the past didn't disappear so easily.

Over the next few days, Curtis Blackwood became a regular presence at The Golden Nugget, always seated at the back, his gaze never straying far from Fayteen. She did her best to ignore him, to push away the memories his presence stirred, but it wasn't easy. The fear she'd felt around Silas, the sense of being trapped, of having nowhere to run—it all came rushing back, a reminder of the life she'd left behind.

Jimmy stayed vigilant, his watchful eyes never leaving Curtis. He made it clear to everyone that Fayteen was under his protection, that any disrespect would be dealt with swiftly. But he could see the toll it was taking on her, the way her shoulders tensed when Curtis entered the room, the way her laughter faded when she caught his eye.

One evening, as they prepared for another performance, Jimmy pulled her aside, his expression serious. "Fayteen, if ya need to talk, I'm here. I don't need to know everything, but if there's somethin' I can do, just say the word."

She met his gaze, a flicker of vulnerability passing over her face. "Thank you, Jimmy. It's just... he reminds me of someone I knew back in Kansas. Someone who... hurt me."

Jimmy's jaw tightened, a surge of protectiveness rising within him. "Ain't nobody gonna hurt ya here, Fayteen. Not while I'm around."

She smiled, a genuine warmth breaking through the tension. "I know. And I'm grateful for that. I just... sometimes it's hard to shake the memories."

Jimmy nodded, his hand resting gently on her shoulder. "Take it one day at a time. You got people here who care about ya. You're part of this town now, and we take care of our own."

With Jimmy's words, Fayteen felt a sense of peace, a reminder that she wasn't alone. She'd found something here, something worth fighting for. Golden Valley wasn't just a place to hide—it was a place to rebuild, a place to reclaim the parts of herself she thought she'd lost. And as she stood beside Jimmy, she knew that whatever shadows her past might cast, she had the courage to face them. She wasn't running anymore; she was ready to stand her ground.

8

Breaking Down Walls

The last note of Fayteen's song hung in the air, a delicate thread connecting her to the quiet, expectant faces in the crowd. As she stepped off the stage, the patrons burst into applause, their cheers filling The Golden Nugget. She felt a warmth spread through her, a sense of belonging that was still new to her, but one she was beginning to trust.

The evening settled into a comfortable hum as patrons lingered over drinks, laughter and conversation flowing around the room. Fayteen slipped through the crowd, a faint smile on her lips, making her way back to her room. She needed a moment to catch her breath, to let the memories of the performance sink in.

As she closed the door, leaning against it with a soft sigh, she was startled by a gentle knock. Her heart leaped, and she knew, even before she opened the door, who it would be.

"Jimmy," she said, smiling as she stepped back to let him in. "Come on in."

He removed his hat, running a hand through his long, wavy hair as he crossed the threshold, his expression a mix of relief and something deeper, something unspoken. They exchanged a quiet glance, and then he took a seat in the chair beside her bed, gesturing for her to join him.

"I just wanted to see how you were doin'," he began, his voice low. "It's been a long night, and I could tell you had a lot on your mind."

She nodded, feeling the weight of her past settle around her. "Thank you, Jimmy. I guess I've been thinkin' about some things I thought I'd put behind me."

They sat together in silence for a moment, the flickering light from the oil lamp casting soft shadows across the room. Then Jimmy cleared his throat, his voice barely above a whisper.

"Mind if I tell you somethin'?" he asked, his gaze steady.

She looked at him, nodding, feeling a strange, quiet anticipation. "Of course. I'd like that."

Jimmy took a deep breath, his gaze turning distant, as if he were looking back over the years. "When I was just a little boy, my ma ran off. I never really knew why. I was six, maybe seven. She just disappeared one night, and my pa—he didn't stick around long after that. Left me with my grandparents, went off chasin' gold, and never came back."

He looked down, his hand resting on his knee, his fingers tracing an invisible pattern on his trousers. "My grandpa, he was a firm man, real fun though and lovin', and he taught me a lot. He taught me how to work hard, how to build things with my own hands. And my grandma, well... she was somethin' special. Sweet as honey, but with a wicked sense of humor. She had a way of makin' everything feel right, even when it wasn't. I guess she was the one who taught me how to keep goin', no matter what."

Fayteen reached out, placing her hand over his. "She sounds like a wonderful woman."

He smiled, a faint, bittersweet expression. "She was. And I owe her a lot. But even with them, I always felt like somethin' was missin'. When I hit my teenage years, I got it in my head that I'd go find my pa. Figured he was out there somewhere, maybe just waitin' for me to show up. But after a few years, I realized he wasn't waitin' for anybody."

He looked at her, his eyes filled with a quiet sadness. "I never found him, Fayteen. I reckon I've been tryin' to make somethin' of myself ever since, tryin' to build a place where I can belong, where folks can find what they're lookin' for."

She squeezed his hand, feeling the weight of his story settle over them. "Jimmy, you've done more than just make somethin' of yourself. You've built a town, a place where people like me can feel safe. That's somethin' to be proud of."

He gave her a small, grateful smile, and for a moment, they simply sat together, the silence between them filled with understanding. Then he turned to her, his expression serious.

"What about you, Fayteen?" he asked, his voice gentle. "What brought you here? I know there's more than just a desire for the stage."

She took a deep breath, steeling herself. "I don't usually talk about it. I've tried so hard to put it behind me, but... maybe it's time."

He nodded, his gaze unwavering, giving her the space to speak.

"When I was young, there was a man—Silas Thornfield. He was my father's boss. My parents, they were good folks, kind and loving. But they didn't see him for what he was. Silas... he took things from me, things I can never get back. I tried to tell my parents, but they didn't believe me, not really. They loved me, but they couldn't believe someone like him, someone they respected, could do such a thing."

She paused, the words catching in her throat. Jimmy's hand tightened around hers, his eyes filled with a quiet, unspoken anger.

"They refused to talk about it, refused to acknowledge it. So, the moment I could, I left. I ran as far as I could, went to every city I could find, tryin' to escape. I wanted to be someone, someone no one would ignore or silence ever again. I figured if I could find the spotlight, if I could stand on a stage and make people see me, then maybe I could take back what he took from me."

Jimmy's expression softened, a look of understanding crossing his face. "You wanted to reclaim your voice, to make somethin' of yourself on your own terms."

She nodded, a tear slipping down her cheek. "Yes. I didn't want to be a victim anymore. I wanted to prove that I was more than what he did to me. And for a while, it worked. I traveled all over this country, I sang, I danced. But I always felt like I was runnin' from somethin', like I'd never really be free of him."

He reached up, gently brushing the tear from her cheek, his touch soft and comforting. "Fayteen, you've built a life for yourself. You've made somethin' out of nothin'. And that takes strength, a strength most folks don't have."

She smiled, a flicker of hope igniting in her chest. "Thank you, Jimmy. I've never really told anyone all this before. I thought if I could just keep runnin', maybe I could leave it all behind. But bein' here, talkin' to you... I feel like maybe I don't have to keep runnin'."

He took her hands in his, his gaze steady. "You don't have to run anymore. Not here. You've got people who care about you, people who'll stand by you. I'm here for you, Fayteen. Whatever you need, you can count on me."

They sat in silence, their hands intertwined, a quiet understanding passing between them. The walls they'd both built, the defenses they'd held onto for so long, were beginning to crumble, giving way to a new sense of trust, of shared purpose.

"Jimmy," she whispered, her voice trembling, "I've never felt this way before. I've spent so long tryin' to protect myself, tryin' to keep everyone at arm's length. But with you... I feel like I can finally breathe."

He leaned closer, his gaze filled with a gentle intensity. "You're not alone, Fayteen. You never have to be alone again."

They talked through the night, sharing memories of their childhoods, the struggles they'd faced, the dreams they'd both been chasing. Jimmy told her more about his grandparents, the way his grandmother would sing to him as they worked, her voice rich and warm, weaving old folk songs into the rhythm of their days. She'd sing while she kneaded dough or churned butter, her laughter mingling with the notes as she encouraged him to join in. He still remembered how, as a boy, he'd belt out the tunes with her, making up silly verses that sent her into peals of laughter. Those songs made even the hardest days feel lighter, and they were a reminder that he was loved, deeply and without reserve.

He spoke of his grandfather, too, a man with a voice as big as the Montana sky and a laugh that could fill any room. His grandpa had a way of turning every chore into an adventure. When he taught Jimmy to ride horses, he'd tell him, "This land is as much yours as it is anyone's, so you might as well know it." Jimmy remembered his first time up on that old bay mare, holding the reins with both hands, his knuckles white and his heart pounding. His grandpa had walked beside him, offering quiet encouragement until Jimmy's nerves gave way to joy, and he was soon galloping through the fields, feeling the wind rush past his face.

There were other lessons too, ones that came in quiet moments, like when they plowed the fields together, the steady rhythm of the horses pulling the plow, his grandfather's voice carrying over the open land as he explained the importance of good, honest work. There was a gentleness to his teaching, a patience that made even the hardest tasks feel worthwhile. And then there were the days they spent chasing off snakes from the fields, his grandpa wielding a long stick with a deftness that amazed him, laughing as they watched the serpents slither away.

Jimmy shared how, on Sundays, his grandma would pack a lunch for after church—thick ham sandwiches, fresh berries they'd picked the day before, and cookies she'd baked that morning. They'd spread a blanket on the grass beneath the big cottonwood tree near the church, enjoying the cool shade as they ate and talked. Sometimes, his friends would join them, and after lunch, they'd race to the creek nearby, setting up contests to see whose frog could jump the farthest. They'd cheer and holler, laughter filling the air as they watched the frogs leap, splashing into the cool water.

And there were evenings, long after the sun had dipped below the mountains, when they'd gather around the fire, his grandpa telling stories that seemed as old as the land itself. Stories of brave pioneers, of wild animals and narrow escapes, tales that made the shadows dance along the walls and filled the night with a sense of magic. His grandmother would listen, smiling, occasionally interjecting with her own memories, and Jimmy would sit there, wrapped in a blanket, feeling as though he was part of something timeless and unbreakable.

He told Fayteen how those memories had shaped him, how they had given him a foundation to stand on even when the world felt uncertain. His grandparents had taught him the value of hard work, of laughter, and of the strength that came from knowing you had a place in the world. And though he'd left Cedar Creek behind, those days remained a part of him, a reminder of the love and wisdom they had given him, and the dreams they had encouraged him to chase.

Fayteen shared tales of her childhood too, of the moments before Silas darkened her life, of the simple joys her parents had given her, the love that had carried her through the darkest days. She spoke of Kansas in the summertime, of warm breezes that rustled the tall prairie grasses and made the sunflowers sway like dancers. As a young girl, she would run barefoot through those fields, her laughter mingling with the chirping of crickets and the calls of meadowlarks. There were days when she would twirl and spin, arms outstretched to the sky, feeling as though she could lift off the ground and fly, as light as the cottony clouds drifting above.

She remembered Sundays at the little wooden church on the edge of town, where the air was filled with the voices of the congregation singing hymns that seemed to reach heaven itself. She loved those mornings, when her mother would dress her in a clean white dress and ribbon her hair, and her father would hold her hand as they walked to church, his steady grip making her feel safe. She would sing along with the hymns, her voice rising clear and strong, unburdened by the weight of worry or sorrow. Back then, she had no idea that singing could be anything but pure joy, a way to share her heart with God and the people around her.

Her days were filled with simple pleasures: the thrill of climbing the big oak tree near her house, its sturdy branches cradling her as she looked out over the fields; the sweet taste of wild blackberries she'd pick with her friends, their laughter echoing as they stained their fingers and lips. Sometimes, her parents would take her to the lake, where they'd spread a blanket on the grass and lay out a picnic of ham sandwiches, apple slices, and her mother's famous lemon pie. Her father would show her how to cast a fishing line, his hand over hers as he taught her the gentle rhythm of reeling in, his laughter rumbling as she squealed with excitement over her first catch—a little sunfish that glistened in the sunlight.

Evenings were filled with stories shared by the fire, her father's voice weaving tales of adventure and courage, her mother smiling as she embroidered, nodding along with the familiar lines. There were nights when they'd sit outside under the stars, her father pointing out the constellations, his arm around her shoulders as he told her about the myths of Orion and the Seven Sisters. She would lean against him, content and sleepy, watching the stars twinkle and feeling as though the world was as big as the sky itself, full of wonder and beauty just waiting to be discovered.

In those early years, life had felt endless and bright, like a meadow stretching out to meet the horizon. There was no room for fear, no shadows to dim her days. She had been free then—truly free—her heart light and open, untouched by darkness. Those memories, wrapped in sunlight and laughter, had carried her through the years, a reminder of the love she had known and the joy she could still find.

As dawn's first light began to filter through the window, Jimmy stood to leave, squeezing Fayteen's hand one last time. She looked up at him, feeling a renewed strength she hadn't known was there, fueled by the honesty they'd shared through the night.

Just as he reached the door, a loud crash from the saloon below shattered the quiet morning air, followed by the sounds of raised voices and hurried footsteps. Jimmy froze, his eyes meeting hers, his expression instantly shifting to one of alert readiness.

"What in tarnation...?" he muttered, reaching for the Colt at his side. He turned back to Fayteen, his expression tense. "Stay here. I'll handle this."

But Fayteen stood as well, a fire igniting in her eyes. "No, Jimmy. This is my home too. I'm comin' with you."

He gave her a brief, fierce nod, their bond solidifying in that shared moment. As they moved toward the door, the sounds from below intensified, and a cold feeling swept through her. She had no idea what awaited them downstairs, but for the first time, she wasn't afraid.

As Jimmy and Fayteen stepped into the hallway, the muffled sound of voices drifted up from the saloon floor below. It was quiet, the kind of quiet that hinted at something brewing, something they couldn't yet see. They moved cautiously down the stairs, their footsteps barely a whisper against the wood, both of them tense with anticipation.

Just as they reached the bottom step, another loud crash shattered the silence, followed by the unmistakable sound of breaking glass. Fayteen gripped Jimmy's arm, her heart pounding as they looked at each other, wide-eyed.

"What in the world?" she whispered, fear flashing in her eyes.

Jimmy raised a hand, motioning for her to stay back. "Wait here," he murmured, moving toward the noise, his eyes scanning the dark corners of the empty saloon. He spotted the source—a shattered window, glass strewn across the floor, the frame splintered as if someone had thrown something heavy against it. Some glasses behind the bar had been smashed, too.

Just then, he noticed a shadow darting past the broken window, disappearing into the early morning mist. He cursed under his breath, his hand instinctively moving to his revolver. Whoever had done this was long gone, but the message was clear. Someone was watching, lurking, ready to stir up trouble.

Fayteen moved to his side, her face pale but determined. "What do you think it was?" she asked, her voice steady despite the tremor in her hands.

Jimmy shook his head, his gaze hardening. "Don't know. But whoever it was, they wanted to make a point. Reckon we'll find out soon enough."

They stood there for a moment, the weight of the unknown settling over them, the sense that something dark was lurking just beyond their sight. But as the morning light crept in, they knew one thing for certain: whatever came next, they would face it together.

9

Thornfield's Arrival

The first signs of evening drifted into The Golden Nugget, filling the saloon with warm light as the patrons began to settle in, the anticipation of music and dancing thick in the air. Jimmy had spent part of the afternoon repairing the broken window from that morning's incident, boarding it up until the glazier could arrive from Boise. He didn't know who had caused the damage, but he'd kept a wary eye on the saloon's door, sensing that more trouble was on the way.

As Fayteen readied herself backstage, smoothing her dress and adjusting her hair, she couldn't shake the sense of unease that lingered after the long night she and Jimmy had shared. She'd taken comfort in his presence, but as evening approached, she steeled herself to face whatever the night might bring.

Antonio began to play a lively tune on the piano, the familiar sound filling the saloon as the dance troupe girls took the stage, their laughter and bright costumes catching the crowd's attention. Lily Mae, the boldest of the troupe, winked at a group of miners as she led the other girls in a playful, flirtatious dance. The men cheered, raising their glasses as the dancers swirled and spun, filling the room with a sense of joy and celebration.

Fayteen stepped onto the stage, her gaze sweeping over the crowd, but then her eyes landed on a figure near the bar, and the world seemed to narrow. Silas Thornfield was watching her, his lips curling into a smug, satisfied smile. He looked older, rougher than she remembered, but his presence sent a chill down her spine, stirring memories she'd fought to bury.

Jimmy, who'd been leaning against the back wall, noticed her sudden change in demeanor and followed her gaze, wondering if this was the man Fayteen had been running from for so long.

As Fayteen's voice faltered, Lily Mae quickly stepped forward, leading the girls in a bolder, faster dance, one designed to pull the crowd's attention away from the tension simmering near the bar. The other dancers joined in with knowing smiles, raising the energy in the room as they spun, flirted, and filled the saloon with laughter. Antonio caught on as well, launching into a rousing melody that had the patrons clapping along, their focus entirely on the performance.

Jimmy made his way to the bar, positioning himself between Fayteen and Silas. From behind, he heard Fayteen mutter that this was Silas Thornfield. He didn't need to draw his revolver; the look in his eyes spoke volumes. "You've got no business here, Thornfield," he said, his voice steady, but unmistakably firm. "You're not welcome in Golden Valley."

Silas's gaze flicked back to Fayteen, his eyes cold and calculating. "I came a long way to see her," he sneered. "Didn't think she'd end up here, of all places. But I reckon she still remembers who she really belongs to."

Fayteen felt a wave of anger replace her fear, her voice steady as she stepped forward, refusing to shrink beneath his stare. "You don't own me, Silas. You never did. Whatever hold you thought you had, it's gone. I'm done lettin' you haunt me."

Silas's smirk faded, his expression darkening as he realized she wasn't intimidated. "You got a smart mouth, girl," he growled. "Maybe it's time someone taught you a lesson in respect."

Jimmy's hand shot out, gripping Silas by the shoulder, his face a mask of cold fury. "You take one more step toward her, and you'll answer to me."

Silas looked at him, his sneer returning. "You think I'm afraid of you, boy? I've seen worse than you in my time."

But Jimmy didn't flinch. "You'll see a lot worse if you don't walk out of here now. Fayteen's made herself clear. She doesn't owe you a thing."

The crowd, captivated by the dancers, had begun to settle into a rhythm of cheers and laughter, oblivious to the tense exchange taking place at the bar. Lily Mae shot Fayteen a quick, reassuring smile, twirling with an exaggerated flourish as she led the girls through a particularly flirtatious routine, her eyes twinkling as she winked at the patrons. She knew exactly what she was doing—keeping the attention away from the man at the bar, buying Fayteen and Jimmy the time they needed.

Silas pulled away from Jimmy's grip, adjusting his coat with a sneer. "You think you can hide from me, Fayteen? Think you're some kind of high-and-mighty star now, do ya? Don't forget where you came from. Don't forget who put you in your place."

Fayteen met his glare, the last shreds of fear replaced by a fierce resolve. "I've got nothin' to prove to you, Silas. You can try to tear me down, but you'll fail. I've built a life here, a real life, and you don't get to take that from me."

For a moment, he stood there, his face twisted with anger, his fists clenched at his sides. But then he turned, a low growl escaping his lips as he backed away, throwing a final look over his shoulder. "This ain't over, Fayteen. I'll be back. You can count on that."

Jimmy watched him go, his jaw clenched as he fought the urge to follow him, to make sure he wouldn't come back. But he knew that Fayteen didn't need violence to protect her; she needed someone who believed in her, who would stand by her no matter what.

As the door swung shut behind Silas, Lily Mae led the girls in a final flourish, their laughter rising above the music as they took a collective bow, their performance a bright distraction from the dark cloud that had just left the saloon.

The crowd erupted in applause, oblivious to the undercurrent of tension that had just passed through the room. Fayteen took a shaky breath, her eyes meeting Jimmy's as the dancers returned backstage, the noise and energy of the crowd filling the space around them.

Jimmy reached out, resting a hand on her shoulder, his voice gentle. "You did good, Fayteen. He's got no power over you anymore."

She nodded, a faint smile breaking through her resolve. "Thank you, Jimmy. For standin' by me. I needed to face him, to say those things out loud. I've spent so long tryin' to bury it, but now... now I feel free."

He gave her a small, reassuring smile. "You're stronger than you know. And whatever comes next, I'm here for it. This is your life, and you get to decide who's part of it."

She took a deep breath, the relief of her words settling over her. The weight of her past had lingered for so long, but she could feel it lifting, replaced by a sense of strength she hadn't known she possessed. Silas might have been a dark chapter in her life, but she was ready to move forward, to reclaim the story for herself.

As the crowd began to thin, Jimmy and Fayteen made their way back to the bar, the tension easing as the familiar warmth of The Golden Nugget settled around them. She knew that Silas wasn't gone for good, but she felt a renewed sense of purpose, a determination to stand tall, no matter what shadows lingered on the horizon.

10

Confronting The Past

The following afternoon, Fayteen wandered through the quiet streets of Golden Valley, her thoughts tangled with memories of the night before. She'd stood up to Silas in the saloon, but she knew it wasn't over. A storm was brewing within her, a storm of anger and pain that she'd kept buried for too long. She wasn't sure if she could truly feel free until she let it all out, every last piece of it.

As she walked, she spotted him. Silas Thornfield stood at the edge of town, leaning against a post, watching her with a smug, knowing look. He made no move to approach, simply waiting for her to come to him, his eyes daring her to face him.

And for the first time, Fayteen felt ready.

She strode up to him, her posture straight and her jaw set, a fire burning in her eyes. She was done with fear, done with the silent shame that had haunted her since she was a girl. It was time to end this, once and for all.

"Silas," she called out, her voice sharp and clear. "I'm done hidin' from you. I'm done lettin' you control my life."

He smirked, crossing his arms as he looked her up and down. "Didn't know you had it in ya, Fayteen. But you can shout all you want. We both know you'll never be free of me."

She took a step closer, her fists clenched at her sides. "You think you've won, don't you? Think you've got some kind of hold over me. But you're wrong. You're just a coward—a miserable, pathetic man who uses fear to keep people in line. And I'm done bein' afraid of you."

Silas's expression faltered, but he quickly recovered, his smile widening as he took a step toward her. "You've got quite a mouth on you. Reckon you've forgotten who made you, who you really are."

Fayteen laughed, a bitter sound that echoed through the empty street. "You didn't make me. I made myself. I survived you, and I'll keep survivin' you, no matter what you try to throw at me. I won't let you drag me back into the darkness. Not now, not ever."

He scowled, his eyes narrowing. "You think you're somethin' special, don't you? Think you've found some kind of safe haven here? These folks don't know the real you, Fayteen. You can put on a show, but deep down, you're still just the scared little girl you've always been."

Her voice rose, filled with a force she hadn't known she possessed. "I am somethin' special, and I don't need your permission to believe that. I've fought my way here, carved out a life for myself. And you—you're just a reminder of where I came from, a reminder of what I'll never let myself fall back into."

Silas took a step back, a flicker of uncertainty in his eyes, but he tried to mask it with a sneer. "You can say whatever you like, girl. I'll be back, and you'll remember who's in charge."

She advanced on him, the anger that had simmered for years finally breaking free, her voice trembling with the weight of her fury. "You don't scare me. I see you for what you are—a weak, pathetic man who takes his misery out on others because he can't face himself. You've got nothin' on me, Silas. You never did. I'll tell anyone who'll listen about what you did to me. I'll yell it from the rooftops if I have to, but I'll make sure the world knows exactly who you are."

His face twisted in anger, but she saw the flicker of fear behind his eyes, the realization that she wasn't the scared girl he remembered. She was stronger now, stronger than he could ever understand.

"You can't hide from this, Silas," she spat, her voice laced with fury and a raw, unyielding strength. "I'm finished letting your twisted sins weigh me down. I'm done letting your darkness shadow my life. The shame? The guilt? That's yours to carry, not mine. You'll have to live with what you did—the filth, the disgusting acts, the way you shattered an innocent girl's life without a second thought. You think you can escape it? Think again. Every step you take, every corner you turn, you'll be dragged down by the horror you've carved into this world. That's on you, Silas. I'm free of it, free of you. And now, you're the one who'll bear the weight, all by yourself."

Silas opened his mouth to retort, but she cut him off, her voice ringing through the street with a force that startled even herself. "Go on. Run. You're good at that, aren't you? You'll never break me again. I'm free of you, and there's nothin' you can do to change that."

He took a step back, his mouth opening and closing as he struggled for words, but nothing came. She saw the truth in his eyes—the fear, the shame, the recognition that he'd lost his power over her. She turned her back on him, walking away without another word, leaving him standing alone in the fading light.

As she made her way back to The Golden Nugget, a wave of emotion washed over her, a mix of relief, anger, and a newfound sense of peace. She'd faced him, voiced the truth she'd kept locked away for so long, and she knew now that she could finally move forward, free of the chains he'd tried to bind her with.

By the time she arrived back at the saloon, the evening crowd had gathered, filling the room with laughter and chatter, the familiar sounds of life in Golden Valley. She stepped onto the stage, feeling the weight of the past lifting from her shoulders, replaced by a sense of purpose that filled her with strength.

Antonio began to play a slow, haunting melody on the piano, his fingers moving across the keys with a sensitivity that matched her own emotions. She took a deep breath, closing her eyes as the first notes filled the room, and then she began to sing, her voice carrying the weight of everything she'd just experienced, every painful memory, every moment of fear and anger, all wrapped up in a song that was as much a declaration of freedom as it was a release.

The lyrics flowed from her like a confession, a promise to herself and to everyone listening that she was done with the shadows, done with the darkness that had haunted her for so long. She sang of strength, of resilience, of finding the courage to face whatever came her way. She sang of the scars she carried, not as a mark of shame, but as a testament to her survival, to the fire that burned within her.

Jimmy watched from the back of the room, his eyes fixed on her, a sense of awe filling him as he took in the raw emotion in her voice, the way she seemed to pour her soul into every note. He'd known she was strong, but seeing her like this, seeing the fire in her eyes, the way she stood tall and unbroken—it struck him to the core.

He felt his chest tighten, a realization settling over him as he watched her. He was falling for her, falling for the fierce, courageous woman who'd faced her darkest fear and come out stronger. She was more than he'd ever dreamed, more than he'd ever dared hope to find.

As the last note faded, the room fell into a stunned silence, every face turned toward Fayteen, caught in the spell of her voice. And then, as if released all at once, the crowd erupted into thunderous applause, cheers echoing through the saloon, filling the air with the sound of admiration and support.

Fayteen stepped down from the stage, her heart still racing, her face flushed with the emotion of her performance. She barely had time to catch her breath before she felt strong arms wrap around her, lifting her off the ground. She let out a startled laugh, looking down to see Jimmy grinning up at her, his blue eyes bright with pride and something deeper.

He spun her around, laughter bubbling up between them, his smile wide and infectious as the crowd cheered even louder, clapping and whistling in celebration. When he finally set her down, he kept one arm around her shoulders, turning to face the crowd.

"Drinks are on the house!" he bellowed, his voice booming over the noise, met with an enthusiastic roar of approval. The patrons surged toward the bar, still cheering, their spirits lifted by the unexpected celebration.

Fayteen turned to him, her eyes shining with laughter, her heart full. "You didn't have to do that," she said, though she couldn't stop smiling.

He shrugged, his gaze warm, his hand lingering on her shoulder. "Reckon I did. What you just did up there... I've never seen anything like it. You're amazin', Fayteen, and it's about time you knew it."

She felt a flush rise to her cheeks, a quiet happiness settling over her. "Thank you, Jimmy. I've never felt this way before... I don't have the words to describe it!"

He gave her a soft smile, his voice gentle as he replied, "Well, I'm just so dang proud of you, Fayteen!" He wasn't ready to finish the rest of that sentence yet.

They stood together, watching the crowd as they celebrated, the laughter and joy filling the air. And as Jimmy's arm tightened around her shoulders, she knew, with a quiet certainty, that this was just the beginning of something beautiful, something she'd never let go.

11

The Connection Deepens

The morning after the celebration, the saloon was quiet, the soft light of dawn filtering through the windows as Jimmy and Fayteen sat together at one of the tables. The echoes of laughter and music still seemed to hang in the air, and Jimmy could feel a quiet happiness settle over him, a sense of peace that he hadn't known he was missing.

Fayteen sipped her coffee, watching him with a curious smile. "You don't talk much about your mining past," she said softly. "I'd like to know more, if you're willin' to share."

Jimmy leaned back in his chair, a thoughtful expression crossing his face. "Reckon I've never been one to dwell on it, but maybe it's time. I've been chasin' gold for as long as I can remember, goin' from one place to the next. I've had my share of wild times along the way."

He grinned, a mischievous glint in his eye. "Back in the early days, I was workin' a claim with a couple fellas up near the Salmon River. Now, one of 'em—Clive—had a real knack for findin' trouble. One day, he got it into his head that we oughta try diggin' in a spot the locals said was haunted. Apparently, they'd seen lights dancin' around there at night, and they reckoned it was spirits guardin' somethin' valuable."

Fayteen raised an eyebrow, leaning in. "Did you believe him?"

Jimmy chuckled, shaking his head. "Not a lick, but Clive was so worked up about it, I figured I'd go along for the ride. So we set up camp, and sure enough, that night, we saw the lights he'd been talkin' about. Turns out, it wasn't ghosts—it was a bunch of glowin' mushrooms. But Clive swore up and down that they were the eyes of lost souls. Ran halfway down the mountain before he'd listen to reason."

Fayteen laughed, her eyes sparkling with amusement. "Sounds like you've had some colorful characters in your life."

"Oh, plenty," Jimmy agreed, grinning. "And that wasn't even the worst of it. One time, we hit a vein of gold so rich, you'd think we struck the gates of heaven. We were hollerin' and carryin' on, celebratin' like fools. Next thing I know, one of the fellas, Ralph, strips down to his drawers and starts dancin' a jig right there in the mine shaft, swingin' his pickaxe like he's leadin' a parade."

Fayteen's laughter rang out, filling the empty saloon with a warmth that made Jimmy's heart swell. "What happened then?"

"Well," Jimmy said, smirking, "he got so caught up in his celebratin' that he missed his step and tumbled right into a muck pit. Came out lookin' like a ghost, covered head to toe in mud. We laughed about that one for weeks. He tried to act like it didn't bother him, but he wouldn't go near the muck pit again, that's for sure."

They shared a quiet moment, their laughter fading into a comfortable silence. Fayteen looked at him with a soft smile. "I like hearin' your stories, Jimmy. You've got a way of makin' life sound like one big adventure."

He shrugged, a faint smile playing at the corners of his mouth. "I suppose it has been. But lately, I've found somethin' better than gold. I've been learnin' things I never thought I'd take an interest in, things that make this place feel more like home than anywhere I've ever been."

He glanced out the window, his expression turning thoughtful. "You remember Ahanu, the Shoshone fellow I introduced ya to?"

Fayteen nodded. "I do. You seem real fond of him."

Jimmy's face softened, a look of admiration crossing his features. "He's taught me things I never even thought about. Out here, folks like us, we're always thinkin' about what we can take from the land—gold, timber, whatever else we think'll make us rich. But Ahanu... he sees the land as somethin' sacred, somethin' worth protectin'. He's shown me ways to understand it, to listen, almost like it's speakin' to ya."

Fayteen tilted her head, intrigued. "What kind of things has he taught you?"

Jimmy leaned forward, his eyes bright with excitement. "Did you know you can tell the time of year just by lookin' at the plants? Ahanu showed me how to spot the signs of the seasons changin', just by watchin' the way certain flowers bloom or the way the leaves change. He said it's all part of the land's rhythm, like the beat of a drum."

He paused, a smile crossing his face. "And he's got a sense of humor, too. One time, he took me out into the woods, and he starts tellin' me about the 'spirit of the bear'—how you've gotta be quiet and respectful, or the bear'll come for you in the night. I was listenin' real serious, thinkin' he's tellin' me somethin' sacred. Turns out, he'd rigged up a little trick with some branches and leaves to make it sound like a bear was comin' through the brush. Scared me half to death."

Fayteen laughed, covering her mouth as she imagined Jimmy's reaction. "Ahanu sounds like quite the character."

"Oh, he is," Jimmy replied, nodding. "He's got a way of lookin' at things that makes ya stop and think. The Shoshone don't just see the world, they feel it. Ahanu says everythin'—the rocks, the trees, the water—it all has a spirit. And I reckon he's right. Spend enough time out there, and you start to feel like you're part of somethin' bigger than yourself."

Fayteen's expression grew serious as she listened, her gaze searching his face. "Sounds like you've found more than just gold out here, Jimmy. Sounds like you've found a piece of yourself."

He met her eyes, a quiet intensity in his gaze. "Maybe I have. It's funny, I used to think I needed to keep movin', keep chasin' somethin' I couldn't even name. But now... now I feel like I'm right where I'm supposed to be. And that's thanks to Ahanu, and thanks to you."

They shared a lingering look, a moment of unspoken understanding passing between them. Jimmy broke the silence, leaning back with a sigh. "Ahanu's got his ways, all right. Last week, he took me out to teach me about trackin'. Now, I thought I was a pretty good tracker—figured I'd show him a thing or two. But he led me around in circles for hours, trackin' my own footprints without me even realizin' it. Said it was a lesson in humility."

Fayteen burst into laughter, her eyes shining with amusement. "Sounds like he's got you all figured out."

Jimmy chuckled, shaking his head. "Reckon he does. He keeps tellin' me I've got too much fire in my heart, that I need to learn to listen more. I think he might be right."

Fayteen reached across the table, her hand resting on his. "I think you're doin' just fine. You've got a way of bringin' people together, makin' folks feel like they belong. That's a rare thing, Jimmy."

He looked down at her hand, a warmth spreading through him. "Funny thing is, I never felt like I belonged anywhere. But now... now I think maybe I've found a place where I do."

They fell into a comfortable silence, each lost in their thoughts. Jimmy took a deep breath, feeling a sense of contentment settle over him. He wasn't used to sharing his life, but with Fayteen, it felt easy, natural. She had a way of bringing out the best in him, of making him feel like he was finally where he was meant to be.

He glanced over at her, a smile playing on his lips. "I got one more story for ya. It's about the time I thought I struck it rich, only to find out I'd dug up a pile of fool's gold."

Fayteen raised an eyebrow, intrigued. "Oh, do tell."

"Well, I was workin' a claim down near Orofino, diggin' like my life depended on it. I started findin' these shiny rocks, and I thought I'd finally hit pay dirt. I was dancin' around, hollerin' like a madman, thinkin' I'd found enough gold to last a lifetime. Took it all the way back to town, only for the assayer to tell me it was nothin' but iron pyrite. I reckon I coulda died of embarrassment right then and there."

Fayteen laughed, shaking her head. "You must've been so disappointed."

Jimmy chuckled, rubbing the back of his neck. "Oh, I was. But I learned somethin' that day—that not everythin' that glitters is gold. Sometimes the real treasure's the folks you meet along the way, the ones who stick by you even when things don't turn out the way you planned."

They sat together, sunlight streaming through the windows as the saloon filled with warm light. Jimmy leaned back in his chair, a smirk playing on his lips.

"You know," he said, glancing at Fayteen, "next time Ahanu takes me out to teach me somethin', I reckon I'll try to act like I know what I'm doin'—at least for a few minutes. Don't want him thinkin' I'm completely hopeless."

Fayteen chuckled, shaking her head. "Oh, I'm sure he's seen right through that already."

Jimmy laughed, scratching his chin thoughtfully. "Well, reckon you're right. But maybe I'll get him back one of these days. I'll have to get a little creative, though. I bet he wouldn't expect me to rig up some branches to sound like a bear sneakin' up on him."

She grinned, a mischievous glint in her eye. "You mean after he taught you that same trick? I'd pay good money to see that."

Jimmy raised an eyebrow, a playful smile spreading across his face. "Is that so? Well, maybe one of these days we'll both head out there, give Ahanu a little surprise. Reckon he could use a taste of his own medicine."

He leaned in, lowering his voice conspiratorially. "And who knows? Maybe we'll dig up some fool's gold just for old times' sake. If nothin' else, we'll get a good laugh out of it."

Fayteen burst into laughter, the sound filling the saloon as Jimmy joined in, their laughter echoing through the empty room. And as they shared a grin, the promise of future mischief hanging between them, they knew they'd found something special in each other—a friendship, a shared sense of adventure, and maybe even something more.

TOWN RELATIONSHIPS

It was one of those warm summer evenings in Golden Valley, the kind where the sun lingered on the horizon, casting a golden glow over the town as folks milled about, enjoying the coolness of the approaching night. In the middle of it all, Ethan McGraw, a young miner with a quick smile and a reputation for his work ethic, was making his way toward The Golden Nugget. He'd spent the day digging in the hills, his arms sore and his clothes dusted with dirt, but he hadn't been able to shake the anticipation that filled him with each step closer to the saloon. He knew he'd better get cleaned up, though, because you're not getting into the saloon dressed like a miner!

Ethan wasn't one to visit The Golden Nugget often, but lately, there was a particular reason for his evening trips: Lily Mae Dawson, the lively dancer with a smile that could light up the darkest corners of the saloon. The first time he'd laid eyes on her, he'd been captivated, and since then, he'd made a habit of dropping by whenever he had a little extra coin in his pocket.

They'd met one night a few weeks back, during one of the busier evenings at the saloon. Ethan had been nursing a drink at the bar, trying to shake off the weariness of a long day's work, when Lily Mae had taken the stage with the other dancers. As the music picked up and the dancers twirled and laughed, his eyes had been drawn to her, mesmerized by the way she moved, the grace and energy she brought to each step. He'd felt his heart quicken, his tiredness forgotten as he watched her command the room.

Later that evening, while the girls mingled with the patrons, Lily Mae had wandered over to his side of the bar, her cheeks flushed from the performance, her smile wide and inviting.

"Well, don't you look like someone who's worked a long day," she'd teased, leaning against the bar with a sparkle in her eyes. "Tell me, what's a hardworkin' miner like you doin' in a place like this?"

Ethan had managed a sheepish smile, rubbing the back of his neck. "Just needed a little break, I reckon. Figured I'd come see what all the fuss is about. Gotta say, I see why folks keep comin' back."

She'd laughed, a musical sound that made him feel lighter. They'd talked for a while, their conversation flowing easily as if they'd known each other far longer. She told him about her life with the troupe, the friends she'd made, the nights she'd spent on stages across the West. He'd shared stories from the mines, tales of the camaraderie among the men, the occasional excitement of unearthing a gold vein, and the dreams he held for the future.

From that night on, he'd made a point of seeking her out whenever he had the chance. Their conversations grew longer, their laughter louder, and before long, he found himself falling for her, captivated by her spirit, her warmth, and the kindness that lay beneath her playful exterior.

Tonight, as he approached the saloon, he spotted her sitting on the steps, watching the sunset. She looked up as he drew near, a smile spreading across her face.

"Ethan," she greeted, moving over to make room for him. "Didn't expect to see you tonight. Thought you'd be busy diggin' in those hills."

He took a seat beside her, resting his elbows on his knees. "Had to come see you, didn't I? Can't let you have all the fun without me."

She laughed, bumping his shoulder with hers. "You sure know how to make a girl feel special. But you know… Jimmy's got rules. He's not big on us girls courtin' the patrons."

Ethan's expression grew serious, a flicker of worry passing through his eyes. "I've heard about those rules. Figured I'd have to talk to him sooner or later. Don't reckon he'll be too happy about it, though."

Lily Mae's gaze softened, her hand resting on his arm. "Jimmy's protective, that's all. He looks out for us girls, makes sure no one's takin' advantage. I suppose it's a good thing, but sometimes... sometimes it makes things complicated."

Ethan placed his hand over hers, giving it a gentle squeeze. "Well, I'm willin' to fight for you, Lily Mae. If it means havin' to talk to Jimmy, then I'll do it. I'm not plannin' on goin' anywhere, you know."

She looked at him, her eyes bright with gratitude and something deeper, a glimmer of hope that he'd be the one to change things, to give her a glimpse of the life she'd dreamed of beyond the saloon walls.

The following evening, Ethan made his way back to The Golden Nugget, steeling himself for the conversation he knew he'd need to have. Fayteen, who'd been watching the budding romance with a keen eye, spotted him as he entered, a determined look on his face. She approached him with a warm smile, sensing the reason for his visit.

"Ethan," she greeted, gesturing for him to sit with her. "I've noticed you've been spending time with Lily Mae. I reckon you've got somethin' on your mind."

He nodded, taking a seat across from her. "You're right. I want to talk to Jimmy. I know he's got rules about the girls and all, but I care about Lily Mae. I'm not lookin' to cause trouble, but I want to do things proper."

Fayteen nodded thoughtfully, her expression encouraging. "Jimmy's protective of the girls, but he's fair. If you're willin' to talk it over with him, I'll back you up. Sometimes rules need a little bendin', especially for the right reasons."

Just then, Jimmy approached, catching the tail end of their conversation. He crossed his arms, his brow furrowing as he looked between the two of them. "What's this about bendin' rules?"

Ethan straightened, meeting Jimmy's gaze with a steady resolve. "I know you've got rules, Mr. Hawthorne. I know you look out for Lily Mae and the other girls, and I respect that. But I care about her, and I want to court her proper. I'm askin' for your permission to do that."

Jimmy studied him for a moment, his expression unreadable. "It's more than just my permission, son. There's a reason I've got rules about these things. These girls have had their fair share of men lookin' to take advantage, and I'm not gonna let that happen here. So if you're thinkin' of gettin' involved, you'd better be prepared to treat her with the respect she deserves."

Fayteen interjected, her voice calm but firm. "Jimmy, I've watched Ethan and Lily Mae together. He's not like the others, and I think he's proven he's got honorable intentions. Besides, if anyone understands the importance of second chances and startin' fresh, it's you."

Jimmy sighed, rubbing a hand over his chin as he considered their words. Finally, he looked at Ethan, his gaze stern but not unkind. "All right, Ethan. I'll allow it, but there'll be conditions. You're welcome to court Lily Mae, but you'll do it respectfully. No sneakin' around, no skippin' out on work. And if I hear you've done anything to hurt her, you'll answer to me."

Ethan nodded, relief flooding his face. "Thank you, sir. I promise I'll treat her right."

Jimmy nodded, the ghost of a smile tugging at the corners of his mouth. "See that you do."

As Ethan turned to leave, Fayteen reached out, touching Jimmy's arm. "Thank you for this, Jimmy. Lily Mae deserves happiness, just like the rest of us."

Jimmy met her gaze, a glimmer of admiration in his eyes. "You're a good influence, Fayteen. Reckon I'd have been a bit more hard-headed if it weren't for you. I trust your judgment."

Later that night, Lily Mae found Ethan waiting for her outside the saloon, a bouquet of wildflowers in his hand, freshly picked from the fields beyond the town. Her face lit up with a mixture of surprise and joy as she accepted them, her heart swelling at the simple, thoughtful gesture.

"Jimmy said yes," Ethan told her, his voice filled with excitement. "He's lettin' us court, under a few conditions. But I reckon I'd follow any rule he laid down if it meant spendin' time with you."

She smiled, her cheeks flushing as she took his hand, leading him down the quiet street. "Well then, I guess we're gonna have to make the most of it, aren't we?"

They wandered through the town, talking quietly as the stars began to dot the sky, their laughter mingling with the soft rustling of the trees. Ethan shared stories of his childhood, tales of growing up on a small farm before heading west to seek his fortune. Lily Mae listened, sharing her own dreams, her hopes for a future that extended beyond the saloon walls, a future filled with love, family, and a place to call home.

As they walked, they felt a sense of possibility opening up before them, a sense that they'd found something rare and beautiful in each other, something worth fighting for. They knew there would be challenges, but they also knew, with a quiet certainty, that they were ready to face them together.

As they strolled through the moonlit streets of Golden Valley, hand in hand, they knew they were building a foundation, brick by brick, for a future that shone just as bright as the stars above.

12

Town Relationships

It was one of those warm summer evenings in Golden Valley, the kind where the sun lingered on the horizon, casting a golden glow over the town as folks milled about, enjoying the coolness of the approaching night. In the middle of it all, Ethan McGraw, a young miner with a quick smile and a reputation for his work ethic, was making his way toward The Golden Nugget. He'd spent the day digging in the hills, his arms sore and his clothes dusted with dirt, but he hadn't been able to shake the anticipation that filled him with each step closer to the saloon. He knew he'd better get cleaned up, though, because you're not getting into the saloon dressed like a miner!

Ethan wasn't one to visit The Golden Nugget often, but lately, there was a particular reason for his evening trips: Lily Mae Dawson, the lively dancer with a smile that could light up the darkest corners of the saloon. The first time he'd laid eyes on her, he'd been captivated, and since then, he'd made a habit of dropping by whenever he had a little extra coin in his pocket.

They'd met one night a few weeks back, during one of the busier evenings at the saloon. Ethan had been nursing a drink at the bar, trying to shake off the weariness of a long day's work, when Lily Mae had taken the stage with the other dancers. As the music picked up and the dancers twirled and laughed, his eyes had been drawn to her, mesmerized by the way she moved, the grace and energy she brought to each step. He'd felt his heart quicken, his tiredness forgotten as he watched her command the room.

Later that evening, while the girls mingled with the patrons, Lily Mae had wandered over to his side of the bar, her cheeks flushed from the performance, her smile wide and inviting.

"Well, don't you look like someone who's worked a long day," she'd teased, leaning against the bar with a sparkle in her eyes. "Tell me, what's a hardworkin' miner like you doin' in a place like this?"

Ethan had managed a sheepish smile, rubbing the back of his neck. "Just needed a little break, I reckon. Figured I'd come see what all the fuss is about. Gotta say, I see why folks keep comin' back."

She'd laughed, a musical sound that made him feel lighter. They'd talked for a while, their conversation flowing easily as if they'd known each other far longer. She told him about her life with the troupe, the friends she'd made, the nights she'd spent on stages across the West. He'd shared stories from the mines, tales of the camaraderie among the men, the occasional excitement of unearthing a gold vein, and the dreams he held for the future.

From that night on, he'd made a point of seeking her out whenever he had the chance. Their conversations grew longer, their laughter louder, and before long, he found himself falling for her, captivated by her spirit, her warmth, and the kindness that lay beneath her playful exterior.

Tonight, as he approached the saloon, he spotted her sitting on the steps, watching the sunset. She looked up as he drew near, a smile spreading across her face.

"Ethan," she greeted, moving over to make room for him. "Didn't expect to see you tonight. Thought you'd be busy diggin' in those hills."

He took a seat beside her, resting his elbows on his knees. "Had to come see you, didn't I? Can't let you have all the fun without me."

She laughed, bumping his shoulder with hers. "You sure know how to make a girl feel special. But you know... Jimmy's got rules. He's not big on us girls courtin' the patrons."

Ethan's expression grew serious, a flicker of worry passing through his eyes. "I've heard about those rules. Figured I'd have to talk to him sooner or later. Don't reckon he'll be too happy about it, though."

Lily Mae's gaze softened, her hand resting on his arm. "Jimmy's protective, that's all. He looks out for us girls, makes sure no one's takin' advantage. I suppose it's a good thing, but sometimes... sometimes it makes things complicated."

Ethan placed his hand over hers, giving it a gentle squeeze. "Well, I'm willin' to fight for you, Lily Mae. If it means havin' to talk to Jimmy, then I'll do it. I'm not plannin' on goin' anywhere, you know."

She looked at him, her eyes bright with gratitude and something deeper, a glimmer of hope that he'd be the one to change things, to give her a glimpse of the life she'd dreamed of beyond the saloon walls.

The following evening, Ethan made his way back to The Golden Nugget, steeling himself for the conversation he knew he'd need to have. Fayteen, who'd been watching the budding romance with a keen eye, spotted him as he entered, a determined look on his face. She approached him with a warm smile, sensing the reason for his visit.

"Ethan," she greeted, gesturing for him to sit with her. "I've noticed you've been spending time with Lily Mae. I reckon you've got somethin' on your mind."

He nodded, taking a seat across from her. "You're right. I want to talk to Jimmy. I know he's got rules about the girls and all, but I care about Lily Mae. I'm not lookin' to cause trouble, but I want to do things proper."

Fayteen nodded thoughtfully, her expression encouraging. "Jimmy's protective of the girls, but he's fair. If you're willin' to talk it over with him, I'll back you up. Sometimes rules need a little bendin', especially for the right reasons."

Just then, Jimmy approached, catching the tail end of their conversation. He crossed his arms, his brow furrowing as he looked between the two of them. "What's this about bendin' rules?"

Ethan straightened, meeting Jimmy's gaze with a steady resolve. "I know you've got rules, Mr. Hawthorne. I know you look out for Lily Mae and the other girls, and I respect that. But

I care about her, and I want to court her proper. I'm askin' for your permission to do that."

Jimmy studied him for a moment, his expression unreadable. "It's more than just my permission, son. There's a reason I've got rules about these things. These girls have had their fair share of men lookin' to take advantage, and I'm not gonna let that happen here. So if you're thinkin' of gettin' involved, you'd better be prepared to treat her with the respect she deserves."

Fayteen interjected, her voice calm but firm. "Jimmy, I've watched Ethan and Lily Mae together. He's not like the others, and I think he's proven he's got honorable intentions. Besides, if anyone understands the importance of second chances and startin' fresh, it's you."

Jimmy sighed, rubbing a hand over his chin as he considered their words. Finally, he looked at Ethan, his gaze stern but not unkind. "All right, Ethan. I'll allow it, but there'll be conditions. You're welcome to court Lily Mae, but you'll do it respectfully. No sneakin' around, no skippin' out on work. And if I hear you've done anything to hurt her, you'll answer to me."

Ethan nodded, relief flooding his face. "Thank you, sir. I promise I'll treat her right."

Jimmy nodded, the ghost of a smile tugging at the corners of his mouth. "See that you do."

As Ethan turned to leave, Fayteen reached out, touching Jimmy's arm. "Thank you for this, Jimmy. Lily Mae deserves happiness, just like the rest of us."

Jimmy met her gaze, a glimmer of admiration in his eyes. "You're a good influence, Fayteen. Reckon I'd have been a bit more hard-headed if it weren't for you. I trust your judgment."

Later that night, Lily Mae found Ethan waiting for her outside the saloon, a bouquet of wildflowers in his hand, freshly picked from the fields beyond the town. Her face lit up with a mixture of surprise and joy as she accepted them, her heart swelling at the simple, thoughtful gesture.

"Jimmy said yes," Ethan told her, his voice filled with excitement. "He's lettin' us court, under a few conditions. But I reckon I'd follow any rule he laid down if it meant spendin' time with you."

She smiled, her cheeks flushing as she took his hand, leading him down the quiet street. "Well then, I guess we're gonna have to make the most of it, aren't we?"

They wandered through the town, talking quietly as the stars began to dot the sky, their laughter mingling with the soft rustling of the trees. Ethan shared stories of his childhood, tales of growing up on a small farm before heading west to seek his fortune. Lily Mae listened, sharing her own dreams, her hopes for a future that extended beyond the saloon walls, a future filled with love, family, and a place to call home.

As they walked, they felt a sense of possibility opening up before them, a sense that they'd found something rare and beautiful in each other, something worth fighting for. They knew there would be challenges, but they also knew, with a quiet certainty, that they were ready to face them together.

As they strolled through the moonlit streets of Golden Valley, hand in hand, they knew they were building a foundation, brick by brick, for a future that shone just as bright as the stars above.

13

Shoshone Friendships

The morning sun cast a gentle glow over Golden Valley as Jimmy hitched the horses to the buggy, his movements easy and familiar as he prepared for the day's trip. Fayteen joined him, her eyes bright with anticipation. She had heard so much about the Shoshone people from Jimmy, particularly his friend Ahanu, and she was eager to see the reservation for herself, to learn more about the land and the people who had called it home long before Golden Valley had taken root.

"Reckon we'll have quite a day ahead of us," Jimmy said, offering her a hand as she climbed into the buggy. "Ahanu said they'd be happy to show us around, and I figured it's high time you met Sahale. She's got a way with herbs and medicines that I reckon you'd find interestin'."

As they set off, the landscape around them shifted from the bustling town to the open fields and rolling hills beyond. The smell of sage and wildflowers filled the air, and Fayteen breathed it in, savoring the sense of freedom that came with the wide-open spaces. She glanced over at Jimmy, grateful for the chance to experience this part of his life, to see the land through his eyes.

"Ahanu's told me about the healing methods his people use," she said, her voice filled with curiosity. "I've always been fascinated by medicine, the way different plants can bring comfort and health. I'm eager to meet Sahale."

Jimmy smiled, the warmth in his eyes evident. "Sahale's got a gentle spirit, but she's got a fierce knowledge of the land. She and Eliza have already met a couple times, and they get along like a house on fire. Reckon you and she will too. She's got a way of seein' right through people, though, so don't be surprised if she catches onto somethin' you're feelin' before you've even thought about it."

As they neared the reservation, the landscape changed, the trees growing taller and the river running clear and fast alongside them. They reached the edge of the reservation, where a small group of Shoshone men and women waited to greet them. Ahanu was among them, his expression warm as he waved them over.

"Welcome, Jimmy, Fayteen," Ahanu said, his voice as calm and steady as always. "We are honored to have you here. Sahale is waiting near her garden. She's been looking forward to meeting you, Fayteen."

They exchanged greetings, the formality quickly giving way to friendly smiles as Ahanu led them to a shaded area where a large, well-tended garden stretched out, filled with herbs and plants Fayteen didn't recognize. Beside the garden stood a woman with long, dark hair streaked with silver, her eyes kind and wise. She wore a simple dress made from soft buckskin, and as she turned to greet them, Fayteen felt an immediate sense of calm radiating from her.

"Sahale," Ahanu said, gesturing to Fayteen, "this is Fayteen, Jimmy's friend. She has come to learn from you, to see what you can teach her about the healing ways."

Sahale nodded, a gentle smile crossing her face as she extended her hand. "It is good to meet you, Fayteen. Ahanu has spoken of you. He says you have a spirit like the wind, strong and untamed."

Fayteen took her hand, smiling. "I'm honored to meet you, Sahale. I've heard much about your skills, and I'd be grateful to learn from you."

Sahale inclined her head, motioning for Fayteen to follow her through the garden. Jimmy and Ahanu remained nearby, talking quietly as Sahale introduced Fayteen to the plants, explaining the purpose of each one, her voice soft but filled with conviction.

"This plant here," Sahale said, pointing to a tall herb with slender leaves, "is yarrow. We use it for wounds, to stop bleeding and aid in healing. The earth provides for us, gives us all we need to stay healthy and strong. But one must listen to the plants, understand their language, their purpose."

Fayteen leaned closer, studying the plant with interest. "I've heard of yarrow, but I never knew how to use it. You seem to know every leaf, every flower."

Sahale nodded, a faint smile touching her lips. "It is not difficult when you respect the land, when you treat each plant as a friend. The earth is our mother, and she cares for us, if only we listen."

As they moved through the garden, Sahale shared stories of her ancestors, of the ways they had lived in harmony with the land, passing down their knowledge from one generation to the next. Fayteen listened intently, feeling a sense of wonder at the depth of Sahale's connection to the earth, the reverence in her voice as she spoke of the plants she tended.

They were soon joined by Eliza Wakefield, the town's nurse, who greeted Sahale with a warm smile and an eager hug. Eliza was a young woman with a sharp mind and a passion for learning, and she had already formed a fast friendship with Sahale, captivated by the Shoshone healer's knowledge.

"Eliza!" Fayteen called, embracing her. "I didn't know you'd be here!"

Eliza grinned, her eyes bright. "Jimmy told me you'd be comin' out today. I've been learnin' from Sahale whenever I can. She's been teachin' me about plants I never even thought to use, things we don't learn about in our own medicine."

Sahale placed a hand on Eliza's shoulder, her gaze warm. "Eliza has been a good student, eager and willing to listen. She has a gift for healing, and she understands that medicine is not only found in bottles and powders, but in the very soil beneath our feet."

Eliza beamed, turning to Fayteen. "Today, Sahale was showin' me how to make a poultice from willow bark. It's got properties similar to the aspirin we use, but it's much gentler on the stomach. I swear, the plants out here hold more remedies than I ever learned back East."

Sahale nodded, moving to a nearby patch of willow saplings. "The willow tree is a friend to those in pain, soothing both body and spirit. I am glad you appreciate this knowledge, Eliza. Many do not see the value in what is freely given."

Fayteen watched as Sahale explained the process, her hands deftly stripping the bark, her voice filled with a quiet authority. She found herself feeling grateful to witness the exchange, to see the bond forming between Eliza and Sahale, each of them bringing their own knowledge, their own perspectives, and blending them into something powerful.

After spending some time in the garden, Sahale invited them to join her near the river, where she had laid out various herbs and roots for them to explore. Jimmy and Ahanu joined them, the group gathering around as Sahale explained the uses of each plant, the ways they could bring relief to those in need.

Ahanu shared stories as well, tales of his own experiences with the healing arts, of how the tribe had relied on Sahale's skills during times of sickness, her remedies bringing comfort to those who had lost hope. Fayteen listened, feeling a deep sense of respect for the Shoshone people, for their wisdom and their resilience.

Jimmy watched Fayteen with a quiet smile, seeing the way her eyes lit up with each new discovery, her curiosity a perfect match for Sahale's quiet guidance. He felt a sense of pride, knowing she was embracing this part of his life, the part that had taught him to see the world with fresh eyes.

As the afternoon wore on, Sahale offered them a tea made from wild mint and sage, the warm, earthy aroma filling the air as they sipped from small clay cups. Fayteen closed her eyes, savoring the taste, feeling the warmth spread through her, a sense of peace settling over her.

"This tea will cleanse your spirit," Sahale explained. "It is good for the soul, for clearing away the troubles of the mind. In times of worry, we come here, to the river, and we drink this tea, letting go of what we cannot change."

Eliza sighed, a smile on her lips. "I could get used to this. There's a simplicity in it, a beauty I never found back in the city."

Sahale nodded, her gaze gentle. "We are all part of the earth, connected by the same breath, the same heartbeat. When we honor that connection, we find balance, both within ourselves and with each other."

Fayteen felt the truth of Sahale's words resonate within her, a sense of belonging that went beyond the town, beyond the life she had known. She reached for Jimmy's hand, her eyes meeting his as they shared a quiet moment of understanding.

"This place... it has a way of changin' you," she murmured. "I never thought I'd feel so at home in a place so far from where I came from."

As the afternoon sun dipped lower, casting a warm, golden glow over the reservation, Sahale looked thoughtfully at Fayteen. There was a quiet intensity in her gaze, an understanding that went deeper than words.

"Fayteen," she said softly, gesturing for her to step closer, "I see the song within you, a song you have carried since long before you came to this place. It is a gift, a voice that speaks to the heart. You honor the spirit with each note, each movement."

Fayteen felt a warmth rise in her chest, a mixture of surprise and gratitude. "You really think so?"

Sahale nodded, her smile gentle but certain. "Yes, but it is a song you have not yet fully embraced. There is more to it, more waiting to be found. Come with me. I would like to show you something."

Sahale led Fayteen to a small clearing near the riverbank, where a circle of smooth stones lay nestled beneath a stand of tall cottonwoods. The ground was soft underfoot, the air alive with the sounds of the river and the gentle rustling of leaves. Sahale raised her arms, her movements slow and graceful, inviting Fayteen to mirror her.

"This is a dance we women perform," Sahale explained, her voice a quiet hum in the stillness. "It is a dance of gratitude, of respect for the life that flows through all things. It is a dance that reminds us of our place in the world, of the connection we share with the earth and with each other."

She began to move, her steps light and fluid, a gentle rhythm that seemed to echo the pulse of the land itself. Fayteen watched, captivated by the way Sahale seemed to flow like water, her movements a graceful expression of unity with the earth. Tentatively, she joined in, matching Sahale's steps, feeling the rhythm guide her.

As they danced together, Fayteen felt a sense of release, a letting go of the fears and uncertainties that had weighed on her. She closed her eyes, allowing the movement to carry her, to free her from the thoughts that had tethered her to the past. She was no longer dancing for an audience, no longer performing for applause or approval; she was dancing for herself, for the pure joy of expression.

Sahale began to sing softly, her voice rising and falling like a prayer, the words foreign but the melody as familiar as an old friend. Fayteen listened, feeling the notes seep into her, filling her with a warmth that felt like home.

"Now," Sahale said, her voice a soft command, "sing with me. But do not sing my song. Sing your own."

Fayteen hesitated, a flicker of uncertainty crossing her face. She'd always sung other people's songs, songs written by strangers, melodies that spoke of other lives, other stories. But as she stood there, surrounded by the ancient trees and the river's song, she felt a new melody rising within her, a song that had been waiting, unspoken, for far too long.

She opened her mouth, letting the notes spill out, a quiet, trembling sound that grew stronger as she found her voice. She sang of the journey that had brought her here, of the dreams she'd carried, the struggles she'd endured. She sang of hope, of resilience, of the strength she'd found in herself and the love she was learning to embrace. The melody was simple, raw, but it was hers, a song that spoke of her heart, of the woman she was becoming.

Sahale joined in, harmonizing with her, the two voices blending into a single, soaring note that filled the clearing, rising above the trees and dancing with the wind. They sang together, their voices intertwined, a celebration of life, of healing, of the power that lay within each of them.

When the song ended, Fayteen felt a quiet peace settle over her, a sense of belonging that went beyond words. She looked at Sahale, her eyes filled with gratitude.

"Thank you," she whispered, her voice thick with emotion. "I didn't know... I didn't know I had that within me."

Sahale smiled, her gaze warm and knowing. "We all have a song, Fayteen. It is the breath of our spirit, the voice of our soul. Sing it often, and you will find your path, no matter where it may lead."

Jimmy, who had been watching from a respectful distance, stepped forward, a soft smile on his lips. He'd heard her song, felt the raw power of it resonate deep within him. He took her hand, his gaze filled with a quiet admiration.

"Reckon that was the most beautiful thing I've ever heard," he said, his voice barely a whisper.

Fayteen met his gaze, her heart swelling with a newfound confidence. She felt like she'd been stripped bare, her soul laid open, but she was stronger for it, ready to face whatever lay ahead.

As they made their way back to the buggy, Sahale touched Fayteen's arm, her expression serious. "Remember this day, Fayteen. Remember your song, for it will guide you when the path grows dark. Trust in it, and trust in yourself."

Fayteen nodded, a sense of purpose settling over her as she climbed into the buggy beside Jimmy. They waved their goodbyes, the warm smiles of Sahale and Ahanu following them as they set off, the quiet strength of the Shoshone's teachings lingering with her.

The journey back to Golden Valley was filled with a comfortable silence, each of them lost in their thoughts. Fayteen felt the weight of the day's experiences settle over her, a mixture of joy, gratitude, and a quiet certainty that she was exactly where she was meant to be.

And as the sun dipped below the horizon, casting a golden glow over the land, Fayteen knew she would carry the memory of this day with her always, a reminder of the strength that lay within her, a strength she was only just beginning to discover.

14

Steps Toward Something New

The Golden Valley Mercantile was alive with activity that morning, townsfolk bustling in and out, exchanging greetings and lively conversation as they went about their errands. Fayteen stepped inside, the bell above the door chiming, and took a moment to breathe in the familiar scent of pine, flour, and freshly polished wood. It was a small but well-stocked place, with shelves stacked high with everything from kitchen goods to tools, and it held a warm, welcoming feel.

Behind the counter, Henry Wickham greeted her with a smile, his eyes bright with curiosity. "Mornin', Miss Fayteen! What can I do for ya today?"

Fayteen returned his smile, moving toward the counter. "Just pickin' up a few things. I've been so busy lately, reckon I haven't had the chance to stop in and visit with folks."

Henry nodded, ringing up her items as he glanced over at Ada, who was dusting a display nearby. "Well, folks have sure noticed you around, especially since that little display out in the street the other day."

Fayteen's cheeks flushed, but she kept her smile. "Reckon I was a bit more fiery than usual. Sometimes a girl has to stand up for herself, though, no matter what people think."

Ada joined them, offering her a kind smile. "Well, we're glad you did. It takes courage to face someone like that, and you handled it well. Folks have been talkin' about it, but mostly outta respect."

Fayteen felt a wave of relief at Ada's words. She'd been worried about how the townsfolk would perceive her, especially since most had only seen her performing on stage at The Golden Nugget. She hadn't exactly planned to air her personal business so publicly, but Silas's presence had pushed her beyond her usual restraint.

They chatted for a few more moments, and then Fayteen took her items, thanking Henry and Ada before stepping back out into the sunlight. As she started down the street, she spotted Reverend Thornton, who was finishing up a conversation with one of the townsfolk near the church steps. He caught sight of her, a thoughtful expression crossing his face.

"Miss Fayteen," he called, waving her over. "Would you mind stoppin' by the church for a moment? I'd like to have a word, if you're able."

Fayteen hesitated, a flicker of uncertainty in her heart, but she nodded, curious to hear what he had to say. She followed him up the steps and through the church doors, the cool, quiet interior a welcome change from the bustling street outside.

They took a seat in one of the pews, and Reverend Thornton turned to her, his expression gentle. "I wanted to talk with you about what happened the other day. I wasn't there, but I heard some things, and I thought you might be in need of a friendly ear, maybe a bit of spiritual counsel."

Fayteen nodded slowly, grateful for his kindness. "Thank you, Reverend. It's been a lot to take in, and I reckon I wasn't expectin' things to come to a head like that."

He smiled, his gaze warm and understanding. "Sometimes we're faced with situations we didn't choose, but they reveal our strength all the same. I can see you've got a strong spirit, Fayteen, and I respect that. But I also know that carrying anger and pain can weigh heavy on a person's heart."

She looked down, her fingers tracing the wood of the pew. "I reckon I've been carryin' a lot of that. I thought leavin' my old life behind would help, but it seems the past has a way of catchin' up with ya."

The reverend placed a gentle hand on her shoulder. "It does, but we have the power to face it and let it go, with the right support. If there's one thing I've learned, it's that forgiveness isn't always about the other person. Sometimes, it's about findin' peace within yourself."

Fayteen felt a tear slip down her cheek, but she quickly brushed it away, nodding. "I want to let it go. I want to start fresh, but sometimes it's hard to see the way forward."

Reverend Thornton smiled, offering her a handkerchief. "You're already on the right path, Fayteen. Just remember, you don't have to carry these burdens alone. If you ever need a friend, someone to pray with, or just to talk to, my door is always open."

She took the handkerchief, feeling a warmth spread through her heart. "Thank you, Reverend. That means a lot to me."

He gave her a reassuring nod, and after a moment, she rose to leave, feeling a renewed sense of hope. As she stepped out of the church and onto the sunlit street, she took a deep breath, savoring the fresh air, the simple beauty of the day. She was beginning to feel that Golden Valley truly was the place for her to heal, to put down roots and build a life.

As she started down the steps, she heard a familiar voice calling her name. Turning, she saw Jimmy approaching, his face breaking into a grin as he came closer.

"Fayteen! Was hopin' I'd catch you," he said, his eyes bright with something she couldn't quite place.

She smiled, her heart fluttering at the sight of him. "What brings you out here?" She couldn't help noticing Jimmy had a blanket and a picnic basket in hand.

He looked at her, his gaze softening. "Mind if I steal you away for a bit? There's somethin' I've been meanin' to say, and I'd rather do it somewhere a little quieter."

Curiosity piqued, Fayteen followed him as they made their way to the edge of town, walking in comfortable silence until they reached a small grove of trees that overlooked the river. Jimmy stopped, turning to face her, a hint of nervousness in his expression. Jimmy cleared his throat, motioning for her to sit down on the blanket he provided.

"Fayteen," he began, rubbing the back of his neck. "I reckon I've been thinkin' about this for a while, and I figured it's about time I came out with it. I care about you, more than I can say. You've come to mean a lot to me, and I'd like to court you, proper."

She felt her heart swell, a warmth spreading through her chest as she looked up at him. "Jimmy, I've been waitin' for you to ask. Yes, I'd love that."

A smile broke across his face, and he took her hands, pulling her close. They sat in silence for a moment, the gentle rustle of leaves filling the air. Then, he leaned over, cupping her face as his lips brushed against hers in a soft, tender kiss filled with the promise of something new, something lasting.

When they pulled apart, she looked at him, a playful smile on her lips. "You sure took your time, didn't ya?"

Jimmy laughed, his eyes shining. "Reckon I wanted to make sure I did it right. You're worth takin' my time for, Fayteen. I want this to be somethin' that lasts."

"How 'bout we celebrate with a picnic?" he suggested, a twinkle in his eye. "Thought it'd be nice to watch the sun go down, just the two of us."

She nodded, smiling. "Sounds perfect, Jimmy. I'd love that."

They sat close on the blanket, the river murmuring softly beside them as they shared their simple meal. The golden light of the setting sun painted the world in warm hues, casting a gentle glow over the water and the tall grasses that swayed along the bank. Fayteen leaned back on the ground, closing her eyes as she breathed in the fresh, earthy scent of the evening, feeling a sense of peace settle over her.

Jimmy watched her, his gaze softening as he took in the relaxed smile that played on her lips. Unable to resist, he leaned down and kissed her, this time with more passion, more certainty. Fayteen responded without hesitation, her arms winding around him as her fingers tangled in his long hair, pulling him closer. When they finally parted, breathless, their foreheads rested together, and for a moment, the world seemed still. Jimmy couldn't help but marvel at how something so simple could feel so profoundly extraordinary. He cleared his throat, his hand slipping into hers, his voice low and earnest. "Fayteen, I gotta be honest... I never thought I'd feel somethin' like this again."

She opened her eyes, turning to look at him, curiosity shining in her gaze. "What way's that?"

He paused, collecting his thoughts, his thumb brushing lightly over her knuckles. "Content. Like I've finally found a place I can stay... and someone worth stayin' for."

She felt a flutter in her chest, a warmth that spread through her with every word he spoke. "I know what you mean. All my life, I felt like I was wanderin', lookin' for somethin' I couldn't quite name. But here, with you... it feels different. Like I'm right where I belong."

They shared a quiet smile, the understanding between them deepening as the silence settled comfortably around them. Fayteen looked out at the river, her thoughts drifting as she took in the beauty of the landscape, the simple joy of being in Jimmy's company.

"Tell me somethin'," she said softly, turning to him with a playful gleam in her eyes. "What made you decide to come out west and start buildin' a place like Golden Valley? I reckon it's not a dream most folks would take on."

Jimmy chuckled, his gaze turning thoughtful. "I suppose I never wanted a life that someone else planned out for me. My pa used to talk about makin' somethin' of himself, but he got lost chasin' dreams that weren't really his. I didn't want to end up the same way, so I set out to find somethin' real, somethin' I could be proud of."

He paused, a hint of vulnerability flickering across his face. "But even after buildin' The Golden Nugget, it still felt like somethin' was missin'. A place ain't worth much without good folks to share it with, and for a long time, I thought I'd be sharin' it alone."

Fayteen reached over, resting her hand on his arm. "You won't be alone, Jimmy. Not anymore."

He looked at her, his expression tender as he took her hand, holding it between his own. "I know that now. Reckon you've brought a light into my life that I didn't even know I was missin'. Just havin' you around makes everythin' feel... brighter."

She felt a blush rise to her cheeks, but she held his gaze, her voice barely a whisper. "You've done the same for me. I thought I'd buried my heart a long time ago, but you've helped me find it again."

For a moment, they simply looked at each other, the quiet intimacy of the moment stretching between them, rich with unspoken feelings. Then, almost on instinct, Jimmy leaned in, brushing a soft kiss against her forehead, his breath warm against her skin. She closed her eyes, savoring the gentle touch, the tenderness in his embrace.

"Fayteen," he murmured, his voice a low rumble, "I want to promise you somethin'. I know we're just startin' out, but I want you to know that I'm here for the long haul. Whatever comes our way, I'm gonna be right here by your side."

She opened her eyes, meeting his gaze, her heart swelling with a mix of joy and anticipation. "And I'll be right beside you, Jimmy. I don't know what the future holds, but I know I want to face it with you."

He smiled, a soft, happy sound escaping his lips as he pulled her into his arms, holding her close as they watched the sun sink lower, the sky painted in hues of pink and gold. They stayed like that for a while, wrapped in each other's warmth, the simple beauty of the moment filling them with a quiet contentment.

As the first stars began to twinkle above, Jimmy leaned down, capturing her lips in a kiss, deeper this time, filled with the promise of all they could be together. Fayteen felt her breath catch, her fingers curling into his shirt as she returned the kiss, letting herself be swept away by the rush of emotions that surged between them. She could feel his heart beating in time with hers, a rhythm that felt as natural as breathing, as timeless as the river flowing beside them.

When they finally parted, she rested her head against his shoulder, a soft sigh escaping her lips. "Reckon I could stay like this forever," she murmured, her voice a contented whisper.

Jimmy wrapped his arms around her, his voice low and tender. "Me too. There's no place I'd rather be."

They sat in comfortable silence, their fingers entwined, as the night deepened around them. Fayteen felt a sense of peace she hadn't known was possible, a quiet certainty that she was exactly where she was meant to be. The worries of the past, the uncertainties of the future—they all faded away, leaving only this moment, this connection that felt as solid as the ground beneath her feet.

Eventually, they rose, Jimmy gathering the picnic basket as they made their way back to the saloon, their laughter and soft whispers drifting on the night air. As they walked back through Golden Valley, their hands clasped tightly together, Fayteen felt a smile curve her lips, a smile that lingered as she leaned against Jimmy, her heart full.

She knew they had a long road ahead, challenges to face, and dreams yet to build. But in that moment, as they traveled under a sky filled with stars, she felt a quiet, unshakable belief that whatever lay ahead, they would face it together, side by side.

And that, she realized, was all she'd ever wanted.

15

A Community Forms

The Golden Nugget was bustling with excitement as Fayteen gathered her dancers on the saloon's polished stage. She'd spent the morning teaching the girls a few new routines, drawing from her years of experience and the popular dance crazes that had swept through the East. It had been a while since she'd led anything beyond the usual saloon routines, but she was eager to bring some of the more structured, elegant dances to the town, envisioning a place where people of all ages could come together for a bit of lighthearted fun.

"All right, ladies," Fayteen called, clapping her hands to draw their attention. "We've been workin' hard on this new routine, but tonight, I want to introduce a couple of dances that'll be a bit different from what you're used to."

The girls gathered around, their expressions a mix of curiosity and excitement. Lily Mae was especially eager, her eyes shining as she bounced on her toes. "What kind of dances, Fayteen? Are we gonna be learnin' somethin' fancy?"

Fayteen grinned, nodding. "Fancy, yes. But also somethin' folks can join in on. The polka and quadrille have been all the rage back East, and I reckon they'll be just as popular here. Tonight, we'll show the town how it's done."

She demonstrated a few steps, leading the girls in the lively hops and spins of the polka, her laughter echoing through the saloon as they caught onto the rhythm. The dance was easy to learn, full of energy and joy, and she could tell by the smiles on their faces that they were already envisioning themselves sweeping across the floor, drawing the townsfolk into the revelry.

Antonio, the saloon's pianist, watched with a bemused smile as he began to play a jaunty tune, his fingers moving nimbly over the keys. He had a knack for picking up new melodies, and Fayteen was grateful to have him along for the ride.

Next, she moved on to the quadrille, a more formal dance that involved precise steps and elegant formations. She walked the girls through the patterns, showing them how to pair off and move in sync, their steps guided by the music's ebb and flow. The dance was more challenging, requiring a bit more concentration, but Fayteen could see the pride in the girls' faces as they began to master the movements, their confidence growing with each practice.

Once they had the basics down, Fayteen took a step back, clapping her hands again. "You're doin' great, ladies! Now, tonight, we're gonna open up the floor. I want folks to feel welcome here, like this is a place where they can come together, celebrate, and make some memories. So, let's show them what we can do!"

Lily Mae grinned, her face flushed with excitement. "Reckon folks'll be talkin' about this night for a long time!"

Fayteen laughed, nodding in agreement. "That's the plan, Lily Mae."

As the afternoon wore on, the girls continued to practice, their laughter and chatter filling the saloon with a sense of anticipation. Fayteen couldn't help but feel a surge of pride as she watched them move with grace and energy, their camaraderie strengthening with each new step. They were more than just a dance troupe; they were becoming a family, a tight-knit group of women who looked out for one another and shared in each other's dreams.

By the time the sun began to dip below the horizon, Jimmy had made his way from his office, where he'd been overseeing the final touches on the saloon's new guest rooms. The ground floor now held a row of spacious rooms, each furnished with sturdy wooden beds, fresh linens, and washbasins. One of the rooms, a larger suite with two adjoining bedrooms, had been set up for families, and he felt a quiet satisfaction knowing he was creating a place where all sorts of folks could find a home, even if only for a night.

He made his way over to Fayteen, his gaze sweeping over the dancers as they finished up their practice. "Place looks lively," he remarked, a smile playing at the corners of his mouth. "Reckon we'll have ourselves a right good turnout tonight."

Fayteen wiped a bead of sweat from her brow, grinning up at him. "That's the idea. Thought I'd bring a bit of fancy footwork to Golden Valley, get folks movin' and sharin' in somethin' new. You ever danced the polka, Jimmy?"

He chuckled, rubbing the back of his neck. "Can't say I have, but I'm willin' to give it a shot. Long as I've got a good partner, that is."

She raised an eyebrow, offering him a playful smile. "Oh, I reckon I could teach you a thing or two. You just keep your wits about ya and follow my lead."

The crowd began to gather as dusk settled over the town, the townsfolk drifting into the saloon with a mixture of curiosity and excitement. Word had spread about the community dance, and families, couples, and groups of friends arrived in their Sunday best, eager to see what Fayteen and the dancers had in store.

Jimmy stood at the entrance, greeting the townsfolk as they filed in, a warm sense of pride swelling in his chest as he watched the saloon fill with laughter and conversation. It was a different crowd than usual, a mix of young and old, and he could feel the shift in the air, a sense of unity that brought a smile to his face.

As the evening progressed, Fayteen led the girls in a lively polka, her feet moving in perfect time with Antonio's spirited piano playing. She encouraged the townsfolk to join in, laughing as she guided a few hesitant couples onto the floor, showing them the steps and cheering them on as they found the rhythm.

Jimmy watched from the edge of the room, his heart swelling with admiration as he took in the joy on Fayteen's face, the way she moved with such confidence and grace. He hadn't felt this alive in years, and he knew, deep down, that it was her influence that had brought this sense of purpose, this sense of community, to Golden Valley.

The quadrille was next, and Fayteen paired off with Jimmy, her eyes sparkling as they took their places on the floor. She led him through the steps, guiding him with gentle nudges, her laughter ringing out as he stumbled a bit, his boots a little too heavy for the dainty footwork.

"You're doin' just fine," she teased, giving him a playful wink. "Just keep smilin' and folks'll think you're a natural."

He grinned, tightening his grip on her hand as they moved together in perfect sync, the music carrying them through the steps. He felt a surge of gratitude as they danced, a quiet sense of belonging that wrapped around him like a warm blanket.

As the dance ended, Fayteen caught her breath, her cheeks flushed, and turned to him with a smile. "Reckon you might have a hidden talent for this, Jimmy."

He chuckled, shrugging. "Well, I reckon I'd do just about anythin' if it meant spendin' time with you."

The evening continued with more dancing, more laughter, and the saloon buzzed with energy as folks mingled, sharing stories and making new friends. Jimmy watched the dancers, his mind already moving toward the practicalities of the business side of things. He'd worked hard to make The Golden Nugget a place for all, a respectable saloon where folks could come together, but he was also keenly aware of the saloon's other role—the one that took place behind closed doors on the second floor.

His girls entertained men upstairs, a part of the business that he'd always maintained a strict set of rules around. He prided himself on ensuring the safety and dignity of the women under his roof, but he knew that expanding the saloon's reach to families and travelers would require a delicate balance. He'd need to be savvy, keeping the two ventures separate yet cohesive, maintaining the saloon's reputation while providing a safe, welcoming space for all.

As the night wound down, Jimmy approached Fayteen, his gaze warm as he reached for her hand. "Thank you, Fayteen. You've turned this place into somethin' special tonight. Reckon you've given folks somethin' to remember."

She smiled, a soft glow in her eyes. "Golden Valley is special, Jimmy. It's full of good people, people who are lookin' for somethin' they can call home. I reckon we've just given 'em a reason to come back, to stay a while longer."

They shared a quiet moment, the satisfaction of a successful night settling over them. The dancers gathered their things, sharing hugs and laughter as they left, the townsfolk lingering in small groups, talking softly as they made their way back out into the night.

As the last of the guests trickled out of the saloon, Jimmy locked the front doors, casting a quick glance around the now-quiet room. The tables were still scattered with remnants of the evening—a few empty glasses, a forgotten handkerchief, a child's hat that someone had left behind. He smiled, feeling a deep sense of satisfaction. Tonight had been one for the books.

He turned to find Fayteen waiting at the bottom of the stairs, her gaze soft as she looked around the room. She caught his eye, giving him a gentle nod. "Shall we?"

He extended his hand, and she took it, their fingers entwining naturally as they made their way up to the third floor, where Jimmy's private quarters lay. The staircase creaked softly beneath their feet, the sounds familiar and comforting. This was his domain—a sanctuary he rarely shared with anyone, but tonight, it felt right having Fayteen by his side.

Once they reached the top, Jimmy led her to the small sitting area just outside his room, where a pair of well-worn armchairs and a sturdy table created a cozy spot to relax. The window beside them offered a view of the fields stretching out into the distance, bathed in the soft light of the evening. He gestured for her to take a seat, then stepped over to the table, where a bottle of wine and two glasses waited. Pouring the rich, dark liquid, he handed her a glass before settling into the chair beside her with a contented sigh. Beyond them, the balcony overlooked the wild plains, its table and chair inviting them to sit and take in the vastness of the land. Together, they sat in the stillness, the warmth of the wine and the quiet intimacy of the moment drawing them closer.

"Reckon we did somethin' real good tonight," he said, a note of pride in his voice. "Seein' the folks out there, smilin' and dancin'... well, it made this place feel more like a home than I ever thought possible."

Fayteen nodded, a soft smile on her lips. "It felt like a piece of somethin' bigger, didn't it?"

Jimmy studied her, his gaze thoughtful. "You're somethin' special, you know that? You got this way of makin' things better, just by bein' here. I reckon I don't say it enough, but I'm real grateful for you, Fayteen."

She reached over, resting her hand on his. "I'm grateful for you too, Jimmy. For givin' me a place to start fresh, to build a new life. And for lettin' me be part of yours."

They shared a quiet moment, the unspoken understanding between them deepening as they sat together, side by side. After a while, Fayteen spoke, her voice soft but steady.

"Jimmy," she began, her fingers tracing small circles on the edge of the table, "what are you hopin' for with this courtship of ours? I mean... where do you see us goin'?"

He took a deep breath, gathering his thoughts. "I reckon I've been thinkin' about that a lot lately. Never figured myself the marryin' type, but then... well, then I met you. You make me feel like maybe settlin' down wouldn't be so bad after all. Maybe it's somethin' we could build toward, if you're feelin' the same way."

Fayteen's heart fluttered, a warmth spreading through her as she nodded, meeting his gaze. "I never thought I'd want that either, but with you... it's different. I can see a future here, with you. A home, maybe even a family someday."

Jimmy reached for her hand, his expression tender. "Then let's take our time, do it right. I don't want to rush this, but I want you to know that if we decide to make it official, I'll be by your side every step of the way."

She squeezed his hand, feeling a surge of affection. "Me too, Jimmy. We'll take it slow, but we'll build somethin' real, somethin' worth holdin' onto."

They sat in comfortable silence for a while, the quiet companionship of the moment filling them with a shared sense of purpose. Fayteen leaned back, her mind turning to the events of the evening, the sense of community that had blossomed in the saloon.

"You know," she mused, "if we keep on hostin' these dances and bringin' folks in, it might be worth considerin' expandin' the business a bit. I mean, folks were hungry tonight, and if we had a chef on board, we could start servin' meals, maybe even do somethin' regular. Folks could come in for supper, stay for the dancin'... make a whole evenin' of it."

Jimmy tilted his head, clearly intrigued by the idea. "Haven't thought of that, but reckon it makes sense. Could draw in folks from all around, not just for the drinks and the dancin', but for a good meal too. We'd have to be smart about it, keepin' the family side of things separate from the other business we got goin' upstairs."

Fayteen nodded, understanding the delicate balance he was trying to maintain. "I reckon you could hire a chef who understands that. Set up regular mealtimes, nothin' fancy, just good hearty food. It'd give folks a reason to come back, make The Golden Nugget a place for all kinds of people, not just the usual crowd."

Jimmy leaned back, a thoughtful expression crossing his face. "Could be just what we need to keep this place growin'. I've always wanted to make somethin' more out of this saloon, somethin' that stands the test of time. Maybe we're onto somethin' here."

They shared a smile, the excitement of the idea sparking between them. Jimmy reached for her hand again, his fingers warm and steady against hers. "It means a lot, you know, havin' you by my side as we figure this all out. I reckon we make a good team."

She laughed softly, leaning into him. "I reckon we do. And I'll be right here, helpin' you every step of the way."

As they sat together, the moonlight casting a soft glow through the window, they both knew that they were beginning a journey, one filled with challenges and triumphs, with laughter and love. As they made their way to their respective rooms after a goodnight kiss, a quiet sense of hope settled over them, a hope that carried the promise of all they could be together.

16

A Gift Of Gratitude

The rhythmic clatter of hooves echoed softly against the quiet morning as Jimmy guided his horse out of Golden Valley. The town still lay in slumber, the streets empty and bathed in the pale light of dawn. He felt the familiar coolness of the early hour against his skin, a welcome contrast to the heat that would soon rise with the sun. He glanced back once more, his gaze lingering on the town that had become his home before turning his eyes to the path ahead—several days' journey to Montana.

Before leaving, Jimmy had spoken with Fayteen, the two of them standing by the front porch of the saloon. She'd insisted she could manage the saloon while he was away, her confidence giving him peace of mind, though a part of him still hated leaving her behind.

"You'll do just fine," he had said, pulling her into his arms. "Keep an eye on things, and if anyone gives you trouble…"

She'd smiled up at him, her sky-blue eyes bright with determination. "Don't you worry, Jimmy Hawthorne. I can handle it."

With a soft laugh, he'd kissed her, lingering in the moment, not wanting to let go. "I'll miss you every second."

"I'll miss you too," she'd whispered, her arms wrapping tighter around him. Then, with one last kiss and a warm embrace, she had watched him mount his horse and ride off into the morning, the unspoken promise between them carrying him forward.

As the open plains stretched out before him, Jimmy couldn't help but let his mind wander back to his younger days, back to when he'd first set out from his grandparents' farm. He had been so determined then, a boy with big dreams and a heart full of grit, eager to make a name for himself. Now, as he rode towards Montana, those same memories stirred once more.

Beneath him, his horse, a sturdy black gelding named Storm, moved with an easy, confident gait. Jimmy had chosen him specifically for this trip, knowing he'd need a horse with stamina and spirit. He patted the horse's neck, a quiet appreciation for the loyalty and strength that had already seen them through countless trails.

"Gonna be just you and me for a while, Storm," he murmured, the words lost in the morning breeze. "Hope you're ready for a bit of adventure."

As they made their way out of the valley onto the plains, Jimmy found himself captivated by the beauty of the land around him. The plains turned to rolling hills stretched out in every direction, painted in shades of green and gold. Wildflowers dotted the fields, their colors vibrant in the morning light, and the distant mountains stood tall, their peaks touched with the first rays of sunlight. The sight filled him with a quiet sense of peace, a reminder of the freedom he'd always found on the open road.

His thoughts drifted to Fayteen, to the way she'd smiled at him before he'd left, her eyes filled with a mixture of pride and encouragement. She'd given him a small bundle of provisions for the journey, wrapped with care and tied with a simple ribbon. He hadn't opened it yet, wanting to savor the thoughtfulness of her gesture, but just knowing it was there, tucked safely in his saddlebag, brought a warmth to his heart.

He imagined the future they might build together, the life that seemed to stretch out before them, filled with possibilities. Marriage... it was a thought he hadn't entertained in years, but with Fayteen, it felt as natural as breathing. She'd come into his life like a force of nature, stirring up dreams he'd long since buried, and he found himself wondering what it would be like to share a home with her, to create something lasting and true.

As the hours passed, memories of his childhood began to surface, memories of days spent on his grandparents' farm in Montana. He could see himself as a boy, wandering through the woods, the scent of cedar and pine thick in the air, his grandfather's voice calling him back when he strayed too far. Those were the days when he'd learned to whittle, to shape the wood into small animals and figures, a skill his grandfather had passed down with patience and care.

He remembered the evenings spent by the fire, his grandmother's laughter filling the room as she told stories of her own youth, tales of resilience and humor that had shaped his understanding of family and love. It was those memories that had driven him to build something real, something tangible in Golden Valley, and now he was returning, hoping to show his gratitude in a way that honored all they'd given him.

As dusk began to settle over the land, Jimmy found a sheltered spot near a small creek, where he could set up camp for the night. He dismounted, giving Storm a pat on the neck before unsaddling him, letting the horse graze nearby as he gathered a few pieces of firewood and built a small campfire. The flames flickered to life, casting a warm glow over the clearing as he settled down, his thoughts drifting to the journey ahead and the gift he was bringing to his grandparents.

It had taken months of planning, but he'd arranged for a new home to be built on their land, a sturdy house with cedar wood accents, crafted in honor of his grandfather's love for the forest. He'd chosen the finest materials, sparing no expense, and he could already picture the look on their faces when they saw it. It was a gesture of thanks, a way of giving back to the people who had shaped him into the man he'd become.

As he sat by the fire, the quiet sounds of the night surrounding him, he heard a soft rustle from the edge of the clearing. He looked up, his hand instinctively going to his side, but then he relaxed, recognizing the familiar figure emerging from the shadows.

"Ahanu," he greeted, a smile breaking across his face. "Didn't expect to see you out here."

Ahanu returned the smile, his movements smooth and deliberate as he joined Jimmy by the fire, settling down with a quiet grace. "The land has a way of bringing people together when they need it most," he replied, his voice calm and steady. "I thought I would pay you a visit, see how the journey is treating you."

Jimmy nodded, feeling a sense of calm settle over him. "It's been good, givin' me time to think. Headin' back to see my grandparents, givin' them a new home. I reckon it's been a long time comin'."

Ahanu studied him for a moment, his gaze thoughtful. "You have a strong heart, Jimmy, one that honors the past even as it looks to the future. But I sense there's more weighing on you than just this journey."

Jimmy sighed, running a hand through his hair. "It's Fayteen. I can't stop thinkin' about her, about what we could build together. She's got this way of bringin' light into my life, makin' me want things I never thought I'd want. It's like I'm seein' a whole new world through her eyes."

Ahanu nodded, a hint of a smile playing at the corners of his mouth. "Love has a way of transforming us, of opening doors we didn't know were there. But it also requires balance, a willingness to be vulnerable, to share your soul with another. Are you ready for that, Jimmy?"

Jimmy stared into the flames, the question resonating deep within him. "I reckon I am. I've spent so many years buildin' up walls, tryin' to prove somethin' to myself. But with her... well, it's like those walls don't matter anymore. I want to build a life with her, somethin' solid and real."

Ahanu placed a hand on Jimmy's shoulder, his gaze steady. "Then trust in that feeling. Let it guide you, but remember to honor the journey as much as the destination. You have the strength to create something beautiful, something lasting, if you stay true to yourself and to her."

They sat in companionable silence, the fire crackling softly as the night deepened around them. Jimmy felt a sense of peace settle over him, a quiet certainty that he was on the right path, that this journey was as much about finding himself as it was about giving back to his family.

After a while, Ahanu rose, his movements quiet and deliberate. "I will leave you to your thoughts, my friend. But remember, the land is always here to guide you, to ground you. Trust in its wisdom, and you will find your way."

Jimmy watched as Ahanu disappeared into the shadows, his presence fading into the night. He sat by the fire for a while longer, his mind filled with thoughts of Fayteen, of his grandparents, of the life he was building. He knew there would be challenges ahead, but he also knew he had the strength to face them, to build something true and lasting.

As he settled down to sleep, the stars stretched out above him, a silent promise of all that lay ahead. And as he drifted off, he felt a quiet sense of gratitude, a certainty that he was exactly where he was meant to be.

The next few days passed in a blur of open fields and rugged trails as Jimmy made his way to Montana. Each night, beneath the stars, he thought about his grandparents, how much time had passed since he'd last seen them, and the letters they'd exchanged over the years. He had always tried to keep them updated about his life in Golden Valley, but this trip was special. The new house, something he'd written to them about months ago, was now finished, and it was time for them to see the surprise he'd planned.

When Jimmy finally arrived, the sight of his grandparents' farm brought a mix of emotions flooding back. The small house they had lived in all these years sat in the distance, but what caught his attention was the larger, new house, standing proudly beside it. He couldn't help but smile. This was his gift to them, a way to thank them for everything they'd done for him.

As he rode up the familiar path, his eyes lingered on the details of the new home—the polished cedar wood, the wide porch that wrapped around the front, and the fresh paint standing out against the green fields. He knew the construction had been a constant presence in their lives for the last few months, and he could only imagine what they must have been thinking, watching it go up day by day. He hadn't visited often, but he'd kept in touch, and they'd written back expressing their excitement, gratitude, and humility. They'd never asked for something so grand, but Jimmy was determined to give it to them.

Just as he reached the porch, the door to their old house opened, and his grandmother, Mabel, stepped out. She spotted him immediately, her face lighting up with joy. Her silver hair shimmered in the sunlight as she hurried toward him, her eyes filled with a mixture of happiness and awe.

"Jimmy!" she called out, her voice trembling with excitement. "Oh, you've finally come! We've been watchin' that house go up for months, but I never expected you'd be here today to see it with us!"

He swung down from Storm and wrapped her in a warm embrace, his smile broad. "Had to come see it for myself, Grandma. And to make sure you two are really goin' to move in."

She pulled back, tears brimming in her eyes. "We weren't sure if we were worthy of somethin' so grand, Jimmy. You didn't have to do this, but my heart swells just knowin' it was built with your love."

Before Jimmy could respond, his grandfather Walter stepped out onto the porch, leaning on his cane but wearing a wide grin. "There he is," Walter called, his voice rich with warmth. "Come here and let me take a look at ya."

Jimmy walked over, taking his grandfather's hand in a firm grip, then pulling him in for a hug. "Good to see you, Grandpa," he said, his voice thick with emotion. "It's been too long."

Walter glanced at the new house, then back at Jimmy. "We've been watchin' that thing grow for months, wondering what the final outcome would be. I reckon you've built us a palace. It's humbling, Jimmy. We never imagined a life like this."

Jimmy smiled, placing a hand on his grandfather's shoulder. "You two gave me more than I could ever repay, so this house... it's my way of sayin' thank you. I wanted you to have somethin' built to last. Somethin' that shows how much you mean to me."

Mabel wiped away a tear and looked toward the new house. "We've been talkin' about it every night, wonderin' if we're fit to live in such a place. It's beautiful, Jimmy. But all we need is each other."

Walter chuckled, though there was a rough edge to his voice. "This house... it's more than we ever dreamed. We've been watchin' it go up with a sense of disbelief. But now that it's finished, I reckon we ought to settle in, don't you think, Mabel?"

Mabel nodded, her eyes sparkling. "I think it's time."

Jimmy smiled as he led them toward their new home, explaining the details he'd chosen for them. The cedar wood accents were a nod to the forest where he'd spent so many afternoons with his grandfather, learning to whittle. The wide porch was built for lazy evenings watching the sunset, and the stone hearth in the living room was for gathering around the fire on cold winter nights.

They walked through the house, each room carefully designed to be both cozy and functional. The kitchen was spacious, with a sturdy wooden table at its center—a place where they could share meals, just like they always had.

Walter and Mabel took it all in, clearly overwhelmed but grateful. Walter ran his hand along the smooth cedar beams, nodding slowly. "You've done right by us, Jimmy. This house is a blessing, and we'll be proud to call it ours."

But there was more. Jimmy smiled as he led them out to the barn where the wagons stood, packed with new furniture and supplies.

Mabel's eyes widened. "Oh, Jimmy, you didn't have to—"

"I wanted to, Grandma. You both deserve it," he said, his voice thick with emotion.

They spent the rest of the day settling into the new house, moving in the furniture and organizing the space. By evening, they sat together on the front porch, the golden light of the setting sun stretching across the fields.

After a long moment, Walter broke the peaceful silence. "You know, Jimmy, this house is somethin' special. But more than that, it's what you've become. A good man. A man we're proud to call family."

Jimmy's throat tightened, but he smiled, gazing out over the land. "I learned it all from you two. And now... well, it's my turn to make sure you're taken care of."

Mabel smiled softly, resting her hand on his arm. "You've given us more than we could ever repay, Jimmy. We'll cherish this home for the rest of our days."

As they watched the sun dip below the horizon, the warmth of the new house at their backs, Jimmy felt a deep sense of contentment. He had given back to the people who meant the most to him. His grandparents had everything they needed now—a new home, built to last, and a future bright with the promise of family and love.

"So," Walter began, his voice soft, "tell us about this girl you been seein'. Heard she's quite the woman, stirrin' up all kinds of talk back in Golden Valley."

Jimmy laughed, rubbing the back of his neck. "Fayteen. She's... well, she's somethin' else. Strong, smart, got a fire in her that lights up any room she walks into. Reckon I never thought I'd find someone like her, but now I can't imagine life without her."

Mabel smiled, her eyes twinkling. "Sounds like love to me, Jimmy. You take care of her, you hear? A woman like that's worth more than gold."

He nodded, a quiet determination filling him. "I will, Grandma. We're takin' it slow, but I reckon she's the one I've been waitin' for. Just want to make sure I do right by her, build somethin' real."

Walter leaned over, giving him a firm pat on the back. "You got a good heart, son. Just follow that, and you'll find your way."

They stayed on the porch long into the evening, sharing stories and laughter, the warmth of family wrapping around them like a blanket. As the stars began to appear, Jimmy felt a deep sense of gratitude, a certainty that he was exactly where he was meant to be, surrounded by the people who had shaped him, who had taught him what it meant to love and to live with purpose.

When it was time to say goodnight, he hugged his grandparents once more, feeling the strength of their love as they held him close. He knew he'd carry this moment with him, a memory he could draw on whenever he needed it, a reminder of the roots that had grounded him, that had given him the foundation to build a life he could be proud of.

As he lay down that night in the new guest room, the scent of cedar filling the air, he thought of Fayteen, of the life they were beginning to build together, a life filled with promise and hope. And as he drifted off to sleep, he felt a quiet certainty that this journey, this gift, was only the beginning of something beautiful, something lasting.

The next morning, as sunlight streamed through the window, Jimmy awoke to the smell of coffee and bacon wafting up from the kitchen. He took a moment to savor the warmth of the new house, feeling a quiet pride as he stretched and got dressed. Today, he had a few more surprises up his sleeve, and he could hardly wait to see the look on his grandparents' faces.

Downstairs, he found Mabel bustling about the kitchen, her face lighting up when she saw him. "Good mornin', Jimmy! Hope you're hungry—I made enough to feed an army."

He grinned, pulling out a chair at the kitchen table. "Mornin', Grandma. Smells like heaven in here. Can't remember the last time I had a breakfast this good."

As they ate, Walter joined them, his eyes twinkling as he looked between Jimmy and the hearty meal laid out before them. "So, what's on the agenda for today, son? You fixin' to head out already?"

Jimmy shook his head, a smile playing on his lips. "Not just yet. Figured I'd stick around a bit, lend a hand. Besides, I got a few more things planned."

After breakfast, Jimmy led his grandparents out behind the small barn, where another wagon laden with supplies sat. His grandfather raised an eyebrow, clearly surprised by the sight.

"Now, what's all this?" Walter asked, crossing his arms as he took in the wagon's contents.

Jimmy hopped up onto the wagon bed, starting to pull back the canvas tarp that covered the supplies. "Thought you two could use some things for the new house. Gotcha some quilts, extra kitchen wares, lamps, and even a few newer tools. Figured I'd make sure you're all set before I head back to Golden Valley."

Mabel clapped her hands together, her face lighting up with delight. "Oh, Jimmy, this is just wonderful! You really thought of everything, didn't you?"

He chuckled, hopping down to help unload the items. "Only the best for you two. Reckon we could spend the day settin' everything up, makin' the place feel like home."

They spent the morning arranging the new items throughout the house, filling the rooms with all the little comforts that made it feel lived-in. Mabel took particular joy in the quilts, spreading them across the beds with a satisfied smile. Meanwhile, Walter admired the sturdy tools, already planning how he'd put them to use.

After a quick lunch, Jimmy led his grandfather to the porch, where he'd set up a few pieces of cedar wood, nails, and a saw. "Thought we might spend the afternoon buildin' somethin' together," he said, his tone casual but his eyes filled with a hint of mischief.

Walter's face broke into a grin. "What've you got in mind, son?"

"A porch swing," Jimmy replied, pulling out a rough sketch he'd drawn the night before. "Figured it'd be nice for you and Grandma to have a spot to sit and watch the sun go down."

Walter's eyes softened, and he nodded, clapping Jimmy on the shoulder. "Reckon I'd like that, Jimmy. Let's get to work."

The two of them spent the afternoon cutting and shaping the cedar wood, working side by side just as they had when Jimmy was a boy. They shared stories and laughter, the rhythm of the work bringing back memories of long-ago summers. By the time they finished, the sun was beginning to dip below the horizon, casting a warm glow over the finished swing.

They mounted it on the porch, and Mabel joined them, settling onto the swing with a contented sigh. Jimmy watched them, a smile of satisfaction on his face as he saw how happy they looked, side by side, swaying gently in the evening light.

"Thank you, Jimmy," his grandmother said, her voice thick with emotion. "This is somethin' real special. You've given us more than we could ever repay."

He shook his head, taking her hand. "Ain't nothin' to repay, Grandma. You and Grandpa gave me everything, and this is just my way of sayin' thanks."

The next day, Jimmy surprised Mabel by leading her out to a small patch of land beside the house, where he'd prepared the soil for a garden. They spent the morning planting seeds—carrots, beans, potatoes, and a few herbs—working together in the warm sunshine. Mabel's face glowed with happiness as they dug side by side, her laughter echoing across the field.

Later, as they stood back to admire their work, she turned to him, a soft smile on her lips. "I reckon you've done more than enough, Jimmy. You've given us a new home, a fresh start. But most of all, you've given us you."

He hugged her, his heart full. "And I wouldn't trade it for the world, Grandma. You and Grandpa are the reason I've been able to build somethin' good. Every bit of it, I owe to you."

By the time he prepared to leave, his heart felt lighter, filled with the love and laughter they'd shared. He said his goodbyes, promising to return before too long, and as he mounted Storm, he looked back at the house one last time, his grandparents waving from the porch, framed by the swing they'd built together.

The journey back to Golden Valley stretched out before him, and he took it slowly, savoring each step. The landscape, the clear sky, and the scent of cedar all seemed to carry him forward, guiding him back to the town he'd come to call home.

And as he rode, his thoughts turned to Fayteen, the woman who'd opened his heart to new dreams, to the possibilities that lay ahead. He just wanted to get home, to the arms of the woman he was falling in love with.

17

Fayteen's Letter

The soft evening light filtered through Fayteen's window as she sat at her writing desk, the quiet of the room settling over her like a blanket. She'd been thinking about this moment for weeks, ever since her encounter with Silas Thornfield. The confrontation had left her shaken but strangely free, as though a weight she'd carried for years had finally been lifted.

She reached for a piece of paper, smoothing it out before her hands, and picked up the pen, hesitating as she thought of her parents—of her father, whose stern yet loving presence had once been her anchor, and her mother, who had filled their home with warmth and laughter. They were strangers now, separated by miles and years of silence. But she had to do this. She had to reach out and try to heal the wounds that had scarred her for so long.

With a deep breath, she dipped the pen into the inkwell and began to write.

Dear Mama and Papa,

It has been a long time since I last wrote to you, and for that, I apologize. I have often thought about you, about the life I left behind and the love we once shared. There are so many things I wish I could have told you, things I hope you will understand. My heart is heavy as I write this, but I feel it is time. Time to face the past, to let you know the truth, and to hope, perhaps, for a new beginning.

I am writing to you from a town called Golden Valley, here in Idaho. It is a small, bustling town, full of life and laughter. I have found work here as the leader of a dance troupe and singer at a saloon, The Golden Nugget, which has become something of a second home to me. It is a place of joy, of hard work, and of friendship. The owner, Jimmy, is a kind man who has become a dear friend, someone who has given me a place to heal and a sense of purpose. I never imagined I would find a home so far from Kansas, but life has a way of surprising us.

Recently, I came face to face with someone from my past—someone you might remember, though I know his name has not been spoken between us for many years. Silas Thornfield came to Golden Valley. I cannot express to you the fear I felt when I saw him, the memories that flooded back. But I knew I could not let him haunt me any longer. I confronted him in the middle of the street, right there in front of the whole town. I told him that he had taken my innocence, that he had broken the trust I had placed in him, and that I would not stay silent any longer.

I do not know if he came looking for me or if fate simply brought us together once more, but I saw something in him that I did not expect. Whilst he did not confess his wrongdoings, his shame was evident as he stood there, vulnerable for the first time. It was not the admis-

sion I had longed for, but it brought me a strange sense of closure. I feel as though I can finally move forward, as though I can breathe freely for the first time in years.

I know this must be difficult for you to read, and I am sorry if my words bring you pain. But I have carried this burden for too long, and I need you to understand what happened, to understand why I left as soon as I could. It was not because I did not love you. I did, and I still do. But I could not stay in a place where my pain was silenced, where I was made to feel as though my suffering was a stain to be hidden. I needed to find my own way, to build a life that was mine alone.

I do not know if you can forgive me for leaving, or if you can forgive yourselves for not hearing me then. But I want you to know that I am reaching out now, not to lay blame, but to seek understanding. I want to believe that we can find our way back to each other, that the love we shared as a family can be rekindled. You are my parents, and despite everything, I miss you. I miss the warmth of our home, the memories we made together, and the life we once shared.

If you are willing, I would like to hear from you. I want to know how you are, to hear your voices again. Perhaps someday we can see each other, and I can show you this town, this place that has given me a new sense of purpose and hope. There is still so much love in my heart for you, and I hope, with all my being, that you feel the same.

With all my love,

Fayteen

She folded the letter carefully, sealing it with a bit of wax, her hands trembling as she held the envelope in her lap. It felt like a piece of her heart, fragile and vulnerable, waiting to be sent out into the world. For a moment, she wondered if she was making the right choice, if reaching out after all these years would bring healing or simply reopen old wounds. But then she remembered the strength she had found in Golden Valley, the friends who had lifted her up, and the quiet assurance that she had done all she could to heal herself.

The next morning, she took the letter to the post office, placing it in the hands of the clerk with a quiet nod. As she walked back to the saloon, she felt a sense of peace settle over her, a feeling that, no matter what happened, she had taken a step toward healing, toward the future she wanted to build.

Two weeks later, as Fayteen was preparing for a night of dancing, a knock came at her door. She opened it to find a young boy from the post office, holding a letter out to her with a shy smile. "This came for you, miss," he said, tipping his cap before hurrying off.

She closed the door, her hands shaking as she looked at the envelope, recognizing her mother's familiar handwriting. Her heart pounded as she unfolded the letter, her eyes skimming the words as tears blurred her vision.

Dearest Fayteen,
Your letter reached us at a time when our hearts were heavy with regret, regret that has haunted us since the day you left. We have often wondered where you were, what had become of our beautiful girl, but we never knew how to reach you, how to mend the rift that had grown between us.

Your words have opened wounds that we have kept buried, but they have also brought a sense of clarity, a realization of the pain you must have endured. We failed you, Fayteen, and for that, we are deeply sorry. We were blinded by our trust in Silas, by our own fears, and we allowed you to carry a burden that no child should bear alone. There are no words that can undo the harm that has been done, but please know that our hearts ache for you, that we would give anything to take back those years of silence.

It brings us comfort to know that you have found a place where you are safe, where you have friends who care for you. And though we are far from you, please know that you are always in our thoughts, that our love for you has never wavered. We are grateful for the courage you have shown, and we are honored that you have allowed us the chance to seek your forgiveness.

If you are willing, we would like to see you again, to speak with you face to face, to hold our daughter in our arms once more. We have longed for this day, though we never dared to hope it would come. Thank you, Fayteen, for giving us this chance. We await your response, hopeful and ready to welcome you back into our lives.

With all our love,
Mama and Papa

Fayteen read the letter, tears slipping down her cheeks as she absorbed the words, the remorse and love that filled each line. It was not a perfect resolution, but it was a beginning, a chance to rebuild the bonds that had been broken.

As she folded the letter, she felt a sense of closure, a sense that her heart was finally beginning to heal. She placed it carefully in her trunk, a keepsake of the journey she had taken, and then she rose, ready to face the future, with hope and a love that stretched across the miles.

That evening, the saloon was alive with music and laughter, the warm glow of the lanterns casting a golden light over the bustling crowd. Fayteen moved through her routines with a practiced grace, her voice carrying through the room as she sang and danced, her presence a calming influence on the raucous crowd. But tonight, there was a heaviness in her heart that she couldn't quite shake, a sense of longing and sadness that clung to her, even as she gave her best to the crowd.

Jimmy noticed it, catching her eye from across the room as he moved through the tables, greeting patrons and keeping a watchful eye over the evening's festivities. Her smile was there, but it was distant, her gaze slipping away as soon as their eyes met. He sensed there was something weighing on her, something she wasn't ready to share, but he knew better than to press her just yet. Instead, he gave her a reassuring nod, letting her know that he was there, that he understood.

As the evening wound down and the last of the patrons began to file out, Jimmy made his way over to Fayteen, his heart softening as he took in the tired look in her eyes. "You did good tonight," he said quietly, resting a gentle hand on her shoulder. "But you seem a bit elsewhere. How 'bout we head up to the third floor? Got a bottle of wine waitin', thought we could take a moment to relax."

She hesitated, but his warm gaze and the softness in his voice put her at ease. She nodded, giving him a grateful smile. "That sounds perfect, Jimmy. Reckon I could use a quiet moment."

They made their way up the stairs, the saloon now quiet and empty, the echoes of the night's laughter fading into the stillness. Jimmy led her to the cozy sitting area outside his room, where two armchairs sat facing a small table. He poured them each a glass of wine, handing one to her as they settled in, the silence stretching comfortably between them.

Fayteen took a sip, savoring the warmth of the wine as she stared down into the glass, her thoughts turning to the letter she'd received, the words that had stirred so many emotions within her. She could feel Jimmy's gaze on her, patient and steady, and after a moment, she looked up, meeting his eyes.

"There's somethin' I need to tell you," she began, her voice soft, yet filled with a quiet determination. "Earlier today, I got a letter. From my parents."

Jimmy's eyes widened slightly, but he nodded, his expression encouraging. "That so? What did they have to say?"

She took a deep breath, gathering her thoughts. "I wrote to them a couple weeks back, tellin' them about what happened with Silas, about why I left all those years ago. I never knew if they'd even read it, let alone write back. But they did. They finally... well, they finally heard me."

She paused, her fingers tracing the edge of the wineglass as she tried to put her feelings into words. "They said they were sorry, that they'd been blind to what was goin' on, that they never meant to push me away. They asked for my forgiveness. They want to see me again."

Jimmy reached over, placing a hand over hers, his touch warm and grounding. "Fayteen, that's somethin' real powerful. Takin' that step, lettin' them back into your life. Reckon that took more strength than most people can imagine."

She looked down, her voice trembling slightly. "I never thought I'd hear those words, Jimmy. Part of me's been waitin' for them all my life, and now that they're here, I don't quite know what to do with 'em. It feels like a door's been opened, but it's also brought up things I thought I'd buried."

He nodded, understanding in his eyes. "Ain't easy to face the past, even when it's somethin' you've been longin' for. I'm proud of you, Fayteen. More than I can say. What you did... it's opened a path, not just for you, but for them too."

A tear slipped down her cheek, and she brushed it away, smiling faintly. "I suppose I feel lighter, somehow. Like I've been carryin' this weight around for so long, and now it's finally startin' to lift."

Jimmy's gaze softened, his own emotions stirring as he watched her. He felt a kinship in her struggle, a reminder of the wounds he still carried. His voice was thick as he spoke, the vulnerability surprising even himself. "I know a bit about carryin' those weights. As ya know, I left Montana as a boy, tryin' to find my pa after he went off chasin' gold. Spent years wonderin' if he ever thought about me, if he ever regretted leavin'."

Fayteen looked at him, a quiet understanding in her gaze. "Have you ever thought about tryin' to find him?"

Jimmy shook his head, the pain in his eyes evident. "Reckon I did at first, but after so many dead ends, I let it go. Focused on buildin' somethin' of my own. But sometimes, late at night, I wonder. Wonder if there's a part of me still missin', somethin' I left behind with him."

He paused, his gaze drifting as he took a deep breath. "But seein' you take that step, reachin' out to your parents... well, it's got me thinkin' about my own past, about the things I've left unresolved. Maybe one day, I'll have the courage to face it. Maybe."

She squeezed his hand, a warmth filling her as she looked at him, her voice soft but certain. "You will, Jimmy. I reckon you've got more courage in you than you realize."

He looked at her, a tear slipping down his cheek as he gave her hand a gentle squeeze. "Reckon I never thought I'd find someone who'd understand, who'd see me for who I am. But you do, Fayteen."

They sat in silence for a moment, the warmth of the wine and the intimacy of the moment wrapping around them like a blanket. Fayteen took a deep breath, feeling a sense of peace settle over her, a quiet assurance that it wasn't going anywhere now.

18

Golden Valley's Role

Golden Valley buzzed with life as Jimmy made his way through the well-worn streets. The town had grown considerably in the past few months, with new faces appearing almost daily, and the hum of commerce filling the air. Jimmy nodded to familiar faces, exchanging brief greetings as he passed. The saloon, now a thriving hub of activity, had solidified itself as the heart of the town, where friendships were forged over drinks, and the sound of laughter frequently spilled out onto the dusty roads. Each evening brought new patrons, and as Jimmy glanced toward the familiar structure, he couldn't help but feel a swell of pride for all they had built.

But as he looked out over the town, Jimmy felt a stirring in his chest, a sense of purpose that went beyond the walls of The Golden Nugget. He saw the potential in Golden Valley, the chance to make it into something more than just a stopover for miners and travelers. He wanted it to be a place that people sought out, a destination in its own right.

He'd been mulling over ideas for days, and this morning, he decided to act on them. With a determined stride, he headed over to the mercantile, where he knew he'd find Henry Wickham going over the morning stock.

As he entered, Henry looked up from his ledger, a smile breaking across his face. "Jimmy! What brings you by this fine mornin'?"

Jimmy returned the smile, pulling up a stool by the counter. "Mornin', Henry. Got somethin' on my mind, and I figured you'd be the man to talk to about it."

Henry raised an eyebrow, clearly intrigued. "Well, go on then. Let's hear it."

Jimmy leaned forward, his gaze serious. "I've been thinkin' about the future of Golden Valley. We've been seein' more folks comin' in from Boise, travelers and traders passin' through. But what if we did somethin' to make this town a place folks come to on purpose, not just on their way somewhere else?"

Henry nodded slowly, his interest piqued. "Reckon you're right about that. We got somethin' special here, but I'd never thought much about expandin' beyond what we got. You thinkin' of addin' more to the saloon?"

Jimmy scratched his chin, a spark of excitement in his eyes. "More to the whole town, really. Imagine if we had a regular market here, bringin' in merchants from all over. Folks could come to buy and sell, make connections, maybe even find a bit of entertainment while they're at it."

Henry's eyes lit up at the idea. "A market, you say? That'd be somethin' new for this part of the territory. Could bring in all sorts of people, maybe even make Golden Valley a bit of a hub."

Jimmy grinned, his excitement growing. "Exactly. I was thinkin' we could set up a fair once a month, start small and see how it goes. We'd have stalls for traders, a space for local farmers to sell their goods, and of course, The Golden Nugget could provide the entertainin' part."

Henry slapped the counter, his face breaking into a wide grin. "By golly, Jimmy, I think you're onto somethin'. I reckon Ada and I could start puttin' the word out, seein' if we can drum up interest. I know a few folks who'd be willin' to come down from Boise to take a look."

They spent the next hour hashing out the details, discussing the logistics of setting up a market and how they could attract merchants from surrounding areas. Jimmy's mind raced with ideas, envisioning a lively scene with vendors selling everything from fresh produce to hand-forged tools, musicians playing in the background, and crowds of people drawn by the prospect of a day's worth of excitement and commerce.

As he left the mercantile, his heart brimming with anticipation, he was struck by an unexpected sight. A pair of elegantly dressed men stood outside The Golden Nugget, their fine suits a stark contrast to the rough-and-tumble attire of most folks in Golden Valley. They spoke in low tones, examining the saloon with a critical eye.

Jimmy approached them, his curiosity piqued. "Mornin', gentlemen. Can I help you with somethin'?"

One of the men, tall with a neatly trimmed beard, extended a hand. "Mr. Hawthorne, I presume? My name is Samuel Latham, and this here is my associate, Edwin Carver. We represent a group of investors out of Boise, and we've been hearin' quite a bit about your establishment."

Jimmy raised an eyebrow, shaking Samuel's hand. "Good to meet you, Mr. Latham, Mr. Carver. So, what brings you out here to Golden Valley?"

Samuel exchanged a glance with Edwin, a faint smile on his lips. "We've been watchin' this town's growth, Mr. Hawthorne, and we're interested in expandin' our own investments in the region. Your saloon has garnered quite the reputation, and we believe Golden Valley has the potential to become a regional center of commerce and culture. If you're interested, we'd like to discuss the possibility of a partnership."

Jimmy crossed his arms, his gaze steady. "Go on, I'm listenin'."

Edwin took a step forward, his tone earnest. "We envision Golden Valley as a place where folks can come not only for entertainment but for quality goods, fine dining, and maybe even a bit of culture. We're willin' to invest in a few new businesses—shops, maybe even a theater. With the right backin', this town could rival Boise in terms of popularity."

Jimmy felt a surge of excitement mixed with caution. The idea of expanding Golden Valley into a bustling hub aligned with his vision, but he was wary of outside investors and the influence they might bring. He'd worked hard to make the town what it was, and he didn't want to lose control of his vision.

"What exactly are you proposin'?" he asked, his tone guarded.

Samuel's smile was calm, calculated. "We'd provide the capital to build additional businesses, while you maintain ownership and management of The Golden Nugget. In return, we'd take a percentage of the profits from the new ventures. It would be a mutually beneficial arrangement, one that allows you to retain control while we both profit from the town's growth."

Jimmy considered this, his mind racing with possibilities. A partnership like this could bring resources and connections that he couldn't secure on his own. But he also felt a pang of hesitation, a desire to protect the town's character and the close-knit community he had worked so hard to build.

"I'll need some time to think on it," he replied finally, his voice firm. "This town's important to me, and I want to make sure any expansion we do is right for the folks here."

Samuel nodded, a respectful look in his eyes. "Of course, Mr. Hawthorne. Take your time. We'll be stayin' in town for a few days, so feel free to reach out if you'd like to discuss it further."

They shook hands, and Jimmy watched as the two men walked away, their fine suits and polished manners a stark reminder of the world beyond Golden Valley. As he turned back to the saloon, he felt a surge of resolve, a determination to protect what he had built while embracing the possibilities of what it could become.

Later that evening, as he shared the news with Fayteen over a quiet dinner, her eyes lit up with interest. "A market, you say? And investors from Boise? Jimmy, that sounds like just the thing to put Golden Valley on the map!"

He nodded, a grin spreading across his face. "I reckon so, but I want to be sure we do it right. This town's got a heart, and I don't want to lose that in the name of expansion."

She reached across the table, taking his hand. "Then we'll make sure we hold onto it. We've already started somethin' special here, and if we do this together, we can build a town that folks are proud to call home."

Jimmy squeezed her hand, feeling a surge of gratitude and excitement. Together, they'd already turned The Golden Nugget into the heart of Golden Valley, a place where dreams could take root and grow. Now, with this new venture on the horizon, he felt a renewed sense of purpose, a belief that they could create something lasting, something that would shape the future of the town for generations to come.

As they finished their meal, he raised his glass, a quiet toast between them. "Here's to Golden Valley," he said, his voice filled with pride. "To the town we're buildin', and the dreams we're chasin'."

They clinked their glasses, a promise of all that lay ahead, their hearts bound by a shared vision and a love that had become the foundation of the town's future.

19

Unexpected Reunion

The warm afternoon sun cast a golden glow over Golden Valley, illuminating the busy streets and bustling storefronts. Jimmy had just finished overseeing some repairs to The Golden Nugget's porch and was about to head inside when he noticed a figure standing at the edge of the road, swaying slightly as though on the brink of collapse.

The woman looked like a ghost, her hair tangled and streaked with gray, her clothes threadbare and covered in dust. She clutched a small bag to her chest, her gaze darting around as though she were searching for something she couldn't quite name. There was something eerily familiar about her, a presence that sent a chill down Jimmy's spine.

As he took a hesitant step forward, she lifted her head, her eyes meeting his, and in that moment, he knew.

"Mama?" The word slipped from his lips, barely a whisper.

She staggered toward him, a flicker of recognition passing over her face before it vanished, replaced by confusion. "Jimmy... is it really you?"

He felt as if the ground had dropped out from under him, a mixture of anger, shock, and compassion surging within him. His mother, the woman who had vanished from his life so long ago, stood before him, frail and broken. He reached out, his hands steady even as his heart raced.

"It's me," he replied, his voice thick with emotion. "Come on, let's get you inside."

He guided her into The Golden Nugget, finding an empty corner where she could sit. As she sank into the chair, her shoulders slumped, and she let out a long, weary sigh. Jimmy watched her, his mind reeling, unsure of what to say or do. He had imagined this moment countless times, but never like this, never with her looking so lost and fragile.

He took a deep breath, steadying himself. "I'll be right back, Mama. Gonna fetch the doctor, alright?"

She nodded absently, her gaze drifting around the room as though she were seeing ghosts. He hurried out the door, his heart pounding as he made his way to Dr. Harper's clinic. He found the doctor and nurse Eliza just finishing up with a patient, their faces lighting up as he entered.

"Jimmy," Dr. Harper greeted him. "What brings you by?"

Jimmy hesitated, the words catching in his throat. "It's my mother. She's... she's here in town, but somethin' ain't right. She looks weak, like she's been on the road for days, and her mind... well, she's not all there."

Dr. Harper's expression grew serious, and he motioned for Eliza to join him. "We'll come with you, Jimmy. Let's see what we can do."

They returned to the saloon together, and Jimmy led them over to the corner where Eleanor sat, her hands trembling as she clutched the worn bag in her lap. Dr. Harper knelt beside her, speaking in a calm, soothing tone as he took her pulse and examined her.

"Mrs. Hawthorne, I'm Dr. Harper. I'm here to help you, alright? Can you tell me how you're feelin'?"

She looked at him, her eyes cloudy. "I'm so tired... I just kept walkin', lookin' for Jimmy. I thought... I thought I'd never find him."

"Jimmy, can you please pick her up and carry her back to the clinic. We need to assess her immediately and administer an IV to get necessary nutrients to her body."

Jimmy nodded and picked up his mother. "It's okay ma; Doc Harper and Nurse Eliza are goin' to take good care of ya. I promise." With tears welling in his eyes, he kissed her forehead and lay her on the examination table.

Dr. Harper nodded, glancing at Eliza. "We're gonna take good care of you. Jimmy, thank you. Would you mind giving us a moment? Eliza and I need to ask your mother a few questions."

Jimmy took a step back, his jaw clenched as he watched them work. The emotions swirling within him were nearly overwhelming—anger at the years she'd been gone, the pain of abandonment, and yet, beneath it all, a flicker of compassion for the woman who had brought him into the world.

After a few moments, Dr. Harper stood and motioned for him to join them. "Jimmy, I'd like to keep your mother here for a few days, if you're amenable. She's in a fragile state, physically and mentally. I suspect she's been wandering for quite some time, possibly without much food or rest."

Jimmy nodded, his throat tight. "Whatever you think is best, Doc. Just... help her."

Eliza placed a comforting hand on his arm. "We'll do our best, Jimmy. We'll give her a warm bed and some food, and I'll stay with her to keep an eye on things. There are some herbs we can use to help calm her mind and ease her sleep."

He took a deep breath, his gaze steady as he looked at her. "Thank you, Eliza. It means a lot."

As Dr. Harper and Eliza prepared Eleanor's room, Jimmy made his way outside, needing a moment to clear his head. He found himself wandering to the edge of town, where Ahanu was waiting, as though he'd known all along that Jimmy would seek him out.

"Trouble weighs heavy on your heart, my friend," Ahanu observed, his dark eyes steady and calm.

Jimmy nodded, running a hand through his hair. "It's my mother. She's here, but she's not the same. Her mind's gone... somewhere I can't follow. I don't know what to do, Ahanu. How do I help someone who's lost like that?"

Ahanu took a deep breath, his gaze thoughtful. "The mind is a complex thing, Jimmy. Sometimes it wanders, lost in shadows, but there are ways to bring it back to the light. The Shoshone believe in balance, in finding harmony with the spirit. We use herbs, ceremonies, songs... all these things help to center a person, to remind them of who they are."

Jimmy listened intently, a glimmer of hope flickering within him. "Would you help her? I know it might be a lot to ask, but she needs more than what the doc can offer. If there's anything you can do..."

Ahanu placed a hand on his shoulder, a quiet strength in his gaze. "I will help. Tonight, we will gather some herbs from the land, prepare a tea that will calm her spirit. And if she is willing, we can perform a ceremony, one that connects her to the earth, to the roots of who she is. It is not a cure, but it may give her peace."

Grateful, Jimmy returned to the clinic to find Dr. Harper and Eliza, who were discussing Eleanor's condition in low tones. Dr. Harper looked up as he approached, his expression serious.

"Jimmy, we've done what we can for now, but your mother is deeply troubled. I suspect there's a history of trauma, possibly even illness, that's been untreated for years. If she's open to it, Ahanu's methods might offer her some relief, especially in conjunction with the care we're providing."

Jimmy nodded, feeling a renewed sense of purpose. "Then let's do it. We'll use every resource we have."

That evening, Ahanu arrived with a small bundle of herbs, and they prepared the tea, its warm, earthy aroma filling the room. Jimmy brought it to his mother's bedside, watching as she sipped the tea, her hands steadying as the warmth spread through her. Ahanu began a low, melodic chant, the rhythm soothing, almost hypnotic, and Jimmy felt himself relax, the tension easing from his shoulders.

After a time, Eleanor's breathing slowed, her eyes growing heavy as the tea and Ahanu's chanting lulled her into a restful sleep. Jimmy watched her, a mix of relief and sadness in his heart. He wondered what demons haunted her, what memories lay buried beneath the surface, but for now, he was content to see her at peace.

Ahanu placed a hand on his shoulder, his voice low. "There is still much to be done, but tonight, she rests. In the days to come, we will continue this work, helping her find her way back. Healing is a journey, and she has only just begun."

Jimmy nodded, feeling the weight of the day settling over him. He looked at his mother, at the woman who had left him, but who had also brought him into the world, and he felt a sense of forgiveness begin to take root, tentative and fragile, but real.

"Thank you, Ahanu," he whispered, his voice thick with emotion. "I don't know if she'll ever be the same, but you've given me hope."

Ahanu smiled, a quiet strength in his gaze. "Hope is the beginning, Jimmy. With that, all things are possible."

After Ahanu's chanting faded and Eleanor drifted into a deep sleep, Jimmy stood by her bedside, watching her peaceful face, still processing the whirlwind of emotions that had overtaken him. His mother, the woman who had vanished from his life, lay here now, so close yet so distant, her mind a mystery he longed to solve. He felt a soft touch on his shoulder and turned to find Fayteen standing beside him, her expression gentle and compassionate.

"I saw Ahanu leaving," she said, her voice soft, "and I figured you might be needin' a friend right now."

He managed a tired smile, grateful for her presence. "I reckon you're right about that. Didn't know how much this'd shake me, seein' her again after all these years."

Fayteen slipped her hand into his, guiding him toward the chairs in the corner of the room. She pulled him down beside her, her hand warm in his. "It's gotta be strange, havin' her here after so long. You don't have to face this alone, Jimmy. I'm here for you, whatever you need."

He took a deep breath, his gaze fixed on his mother's sleeping form. "She left when I was just a kid, ran off and left me with more questions than I could ever answer. Spent years wonderin' what'd happened to her, why she'd go without so much as a word. And now, here she is, and I still don't know what I'm supposed to feel."

Fayteen nodded, her eyes thoughtful. "I know a bit about carryin' unanswered questions. I know what it's like to feel abandoned, even when the people who should've stood by you were right there. But seein' her now... maybe this is a chance to find some of those answers, to let yourself feel whatever comes up."

He looked at her, a mixture of pain and hope in his gaze. "She's not well, Fayteen. The doc and Ahanu are doin' what they can, but I don't know if she'll ever be the woman she was. Part of me wants to be angry, wants to ask her why she left, why she didn't come back. But lookin' at her like this... I can't help but feel sorry for her."

Fayteen gave his hand a gentle squeeze, her expression tender. "It's alright to feel both, Jimmy. You can be angry, and you can feel compassion. It doesn't have to be one or the other. Sometimes, the heart's got room for it all."

He let out a heavy sigh, leaning back in the chair. "How'd you get so wise, Fayteen?"

She smiled softly, resting her head on his shoulder. "Reckon I had to grow up fast, learn how to take care of myself. And I had some good people along the way, folks who helped me see that life's too short to hold onto hate. You got a chance here, Jimmy, to let go of some of that pain, even if you never get all the answers you're lookin' for."

They sat in comfortable silence, Fayteen's presence a balm to his troubled heart. After a while, she turned to him, her eyes warm. "Why don't you come with me for a walk? The night air might do you some good, clear your head a bit."

He hesitated, glancing back at his mother, but Fayteen gave him a reassuring nod. "Eliza's with her, and I reckon Ahanu'll check in again before long. You've done what you can for tonight. Let's step outside for a spell."

Jimmy nodded, allowing her to guide him out of the room and down the stairs. They stepped into the cool night air, the stars shining bright above them, casting a gentle glow over the quiet town. Fayteen led him to the edge of town, where they could see the open fields stretching out beneath the vast sky, the scent of earth and pine filling the air.

They walked in silence for a while, the soft crunch of their footsteps the only sound. Finally, Jimmy spoke, his voice quiet. "It's strange, feelin' like I'm bein' torn in two. Part of me's that little boy, desperate to have his mama back, and part of me's just... I don't know if I'll ever be able to forgive her for leavin'."

Fayteen stopped, turning to face him, her hands resting on his shoulders. "Forgiveness isn't about lettin' go of what happened. It's about freein' yourself from the weight of it. You may never understand why she did what she did, but maybe that's alright. Maybe this is your chance to find peace, not for her, but for yourself."

He looked into her eyes, feeling the truth of her words settle over him. "I reckon you're right. She may never be able to give me what I need, but that doesn't mean I have to carry this burden forever."

She smiled, brushing a stray lock of hair from his forehead. "You're stronger than you know, Jimmy. And you've got people here who care about you, who'll stand by you as you work through this. You don't have to do it alone."

They stood there for a moment, wrapped in the quiet comfort of each other's presence. He reached for her hand, pulling her close, his voice filled with gratitude. "I don't say it enough, but thank you, Fayteen. You've given me more than you'll ever know."

She rested her head on his chest, her arms wrapped around him. "We've both been through our own kind of hurt, Jimmy. That's what makes us strong, what makes us understand each other. And I'll be here, whatever comes next."

They stayed like that for a while, the world around them quiet and still, the stars a silent witness to the bond they shared. Finally, they made their way back to the clinic, their hearts lighter, their steps steady.

When they returned, they found Eliza waiting outside Eleanor's room, her face a mixture of relief and concern. "She woke up briefly," Eliza said, her voice low. "She was confused, asking for you, Jimmy."

He nodded, a quiet determination settling over him. "I'll sit with her for a while. She deserves that much."

Fayteen placed a gentle hand on his arm. "I'll be right here if you need me."

He entered the room, pulling a chair up beside the bed as Eleanor's eyes fluttered open. She looked at him, her gaze hazy but filled with a flicker of recognition.

"Jimmy," she whispered, her voice barely more than a breath. "I'm sorry... so sorry..."

He took her hand, his voice steady. "Rest now, Mama. We'll talk when you're stronger. I'm here, and I'm not goin' anywhere."

She nodded, a tear slipping down her cheek as she drifted back to sleep. He sat by her side, watching her, his heart filled with a strange mixture of sorrow and hope. He knew there would be no easy answers, no simple path to forgiveness. But for the first time, he felt a glimmer of peace, a sense that he could face this, step by step, with Fayteen and his friends by his side.

20

The Truth Unveiled

The morning sun filtered softly through the curtains, casting a gentle glow over Eleanor's room. Jimmy sat beside her bed, his gaze steady as he watched her slowly wake, her eyes flickering open to meet his. There was a clarity in her gaze today, a calmness that had been absent since she'd arrived in Golden Valley. He held his breath, hoping that this would be the moment when he could finally begin to understand.

She sat up slowly, smoothing the blanket over her lap as she gathered her thoughts. Her hands trembled, but she met his gaze with a quiet determination. "Jimmy, I've done you wrong, and I owe you an explanation. I reckon it's time you knew why I left."

He nodded, his voice steady but soft. "I've been waitin' for this a long time, Mama. Whatever you have to say, I'm here to listen."

She took a deep breath, her eyes drifting to the window as though searching for strength in the light beyond. "I wasn't always like this, Jimmy. When I was a girl, I was happy, carefree. But things changed when I was still young. My father was... he was a cruel man, always talkin' down to me, makin' me feel small. And when I grew older, his anger turned into something darker."

Jimmy's jaw tightened, but he remained silent, his heart aching as he listened.

"My ma, she died when I was quite young, but even before her death, she was a timid wee thing. It seemed she lived only to serve my pa, in fear and terror."

She continued, her voice barely above a whisper. "He'd yell at me, tell me I was worth nothin', that I was his to do with as he pleased. I tried to hide it, tried to be strong, but the pain... it settled deep in my heart. I never told a soul, Jimmy. I buried it, forced it down so far I thought it'd never come up again. But the pain was still there, hidden under the surface."

She paused, her eyes filling with tears. "When I met your father, it felt like a light breakin' through the darkness. He was so kind, so strong. He loved me in a way I'd never been loved before, and I thought... I thought I'd finally left all that behind. We built a life together, brought you into the world, and for a time, I was happy. Truly happy."

Jimmy felt a swell of emotion rise within him, a mixture of anger and sadness as he imagined his mother's pain. He reached for her hand, holding it gently as she spoke.

"But then... then the voices started," she continued, her tone trembling. "At first, I thought it was just my imagination, echoes of my past. But they grew louder, crueler, like shadows lurkin' in the corners of my mind. They'd tell me things, terrible things. That I wasn't good enough, that I didn't deserve to be a mother, that I'd never escape my past. And then they started talkin' about you, Jimmy. They said that if I didn't leave, you'd be taken from me, that they'd kill you just to punish me."

Her voice broke, a tear slipping down her cheek. "I know it sounds like madness, and maybe that's what it was. I couldn't tell what was real anymore. I'd hear them whisperin' at night, tellin' me I had to leave to keep you safe. And as much as it tore me apart, I believed them. I thought I was protectin' you by leavin'."

Jimmy's heart clenched, the anger he'd held onto for so long beginning to dissolve as he saw the depth of her pain. "Mama... why didn't you tell anyone? Why didn't you let someone help you?"

She shook her head, a faint, bitter smile crossing her lips. "Back then, there wasn't much understandin' for things like this. People would've said I was touched, maybe locked me away, and then where would you have been? I thought I was doin' the right thing. I thought if I left, the voices would leave you alone, and you'd grow up safe."

He took a shaky breath, struggling to find the words. "All these years, I thought you'd just... I thought you'd given up on me. But hearin' this, knowin' what you were goin' through... I wish I could've been there for you, wish I could've done somethin' to help."

Eleanor squeezed his hand, her gaze steady. "You were just a boy, Jimmy. There was nothin' you could've done. I made my choices, and they brought me here. But now, I have a chance to explain, to tell you the truth, and maybe find some peace in that."

Jimmy pulled his hand back gently, a storm of emotions roiling within him. He could barely breathe, the room felt too small, too confining, and he knew he needed air, space, anything to escape the torrent of emotions that threatened to overwhelm him.

Without a word, he stood and made his way to the door, his hands trembling as he pushed it open. "I need a moment," he muttered, barely glancing back as he walked briskly down the hall, out into the street, and toward the stable where Storm waited. The familiar scent of leather and hay hit him as he saddled up quickly, the tension in his body giving way to a burst of energy that carried him out of town and into the open expanse beyond.

He rode hard, his heart pounding in rhythm with the horse's hooves as he made his way to the river, the place he always went when he needed to think, to breathe. The trees blurred past him, and the cool air stung his face, grounding him as he rode on, each step taking him further from the weight of the conversation he'd left behind.

When he reached the river, he slid from the saddle, his legs shaky as he walked to the water's edge. He stood there, staring out over the rippling surface, his chest heaving as he fought to hold back the flood of emotions that had been building within him.

Finally, he let out a primal yell, a sound that echoed across the landscape, raw and filled with years of pain, confusion, and anger. He yelled until his throat was raw, each shout a release of the hurt he had carried for so long, the wounds that had festered in the absence of answers.

"How could you leave me?" he cried, his voice breaking as he spoke to the emptiness, his words torn from the depths of his soul. "How could you just walk away?"

He sank to his knees, the weight of his grief pressing him down as tears slipped down his cheeks. He had waited so long for this, dreamed of the day he would see her again, but the reality of it was almost too much to bear. He wanted to forgive her, to let go of the anger, but the little boy in him still ached for the mother he had lost, the mother he had searched for in every shadow, every quiet moment.

He closed his eyes, his heart pounding as memories flooded back—his grandparents' comforting arms, the quiet nights spent wondering where she was, why she had left. He remembered every unanswered question, every silent moment of longing, and the anger that had simmered just beneath the surface, waiting for a chance to be released.

He stood up slowly, his body trembling as he took a shaky breath. The boy in him wanted to run back to her, to wrap his arms around her and let her hold him, let her make up for the years she had been gone. But he knew that wasn't possible. Not yet.

As the anger began to subside, a sense of clarity washed over him. He realized that he needed to approach this with caution, to let himself feel everything without rushing to forgive, without rushing to forget. He had questions—so many questions—and he needed answers before he could even begin to consider what came next.

He walked to the edge of the river, splashing cold water on his face, letting the chill steady him, calm the tempest within. He stood there for a long time, watching the water as it flowed past, a reminder that life moved on, even when it felt like everything had been turned upside down.

By the time the sun had begun to set, Jimmy felt a strange sense of peace settle over him. He knew he wasn't done with this, that there would be more to confront, more to uncover. But he also knew that he was ready to face it, to find out who his mother really was, to understand the choices she had made—even if he couldn't understand why she had made them.

He climbed back onto Storm and rode slowly back toward town, the familiar landscape calming him as he let his thoughts drift, let the weight of the day settle. When he reached the saloon, he dismounted, leaving Storm in the stable before making his way back to the doctor's office.

The town was quiet, the lamps casting a warm glow over the streets as he approached the door. He felt a strange sense of apprehension, a mixture of dread and hope as he turned the handle and stepped inside.

Dr. Harper greeted him with a nod, his expression understanding. "She's been resting," he said quietly. "But I believe she's awake now, if you're ready."

Jimmy nodded, his throat tight as he made his way down the hall to his mother's room. He pushed the door open slowly, his gaze settling on her as she sat up in bed, her eyes meeting his with a mixture of fear and hope.

He walked over, pulling up a chair beside her, his voice quiet but steady. "I had to step away for a bit, had to clear my head.

There's a lot I don't understand, and I reckon it'll take some time for me to work through it all."

She nodded, her hands twisting together in her lap. "I understand, Jimmy. I've waited this long... I can wait as long as you need."

He took a deep breath, choosing his words carefully. "I want to take this slow, Mama. I need to ask questions, need to get to know you again. But I also want you to know that I'm willin' to try. I'm willin' to see where this takes us, one step at a time."

Her eyes filled with tears, and she reached out, her hand trembling as she took his. "Thank you, Jimmy. That's more than I could have hoped for. I never meant to hurt you, never meant for things to turn out like this."

He squeezed her hand, a flicker of hope rising within him. "We've both been hurt, both been broken. But maybe, just maybe, we can find a way forward. One day at a time."

They sat in silence, the weight of the past hanging between them, but the future—however uncertain—holding a glimmer of possibility. He knew there would be hard days ahead, that the path to healing would be long and filled with challenges. But he also knew that he wasn't facing it alone.

As he left that evening, a sense of quiet resolution settled over him. He wasn't ready to forgive completely, wasn't ready to forget. But he was ready to begin, to take the first steps toward a future that included his mother, however difficult it might be.

When he reached The Golden Nugget, he made his way up to the third floor, passing through the empty, quiet saloon. The chairs were stacked on tables, the bar wiped down, and the lanterns glowed softly, casting warm light across the polished wood. The place had become his sanctuary, the heart of the life he'd built, and tonight, it felt more like home than ever.

Out in the chairs on the balcony outside his room, he settled down with a glass of whiskey, staring out into the vast darkness that stretched beyond the town. The stars were faint tonight, the clouds heavy, but he found comfort in the quiet, the cool night air brushing against his face as he let his thoughts drift.

He wasn't alone for long. A soft sound behind him caught his attention, and he turned to find Fayteen standing in the doorway, her eyes searching his face with a mixture of concern and tenderness.

"Thought I'd find you here," she said softly, stepping out onto the balcony. She hesitated, as if unsure of her welcome, but he held out a hand, inviting her closer.

She took his hand, settling into the chair beside him, her presence steady and grounding. They sat in silence for a moment, her hand warm in his, and he felt the tension in his shoulders ease, the weight of the day lifting just a little as he breathed in the calm of her presence.

"Everything alright?" she asked, her voice barely more than a whisper.

He nodded, taking a sip of his whiskey, savoring the burn as it slid down his throat. "Reckon it will be. Just needed a moment to take it all in."

She nodded, understanding in her eyes. "Sometimes, it's the quiet that lets things settle, lets you see what's underneath it all."

He looked at her, his gaze softening as he reached out, brushing a strand of hair from her face. "I don't know what I'd do without you, Fayteen. You've been my anchor through all this, givin' me a reason to keep goin' when it feels like the world's fallin' apart."

She smiled, leaning into his touch, her hand coming up to rest on his cheek. "We've both been through our share of storms, Jimmy. But maybe that's what makes us strong, what makes us able to find a way through together."

He shifted closer, his hand sliding to the back of her neck as he pulled her toward him, his lips brushing against hers, tentative at first, then deeper, the need for connection filling the space between them. She melted into him, her arms wrapping around his shoulders as the kiss deepened, a warmth spreading through him, chasing away the shadows that had haunted him all day.

They pulled back slightly, their breaths mingling, their foreheads touching as they held each other, the intensity of the moment grounding them both. His fingers traced along her jaw, his voice a soft murmur. "I don't say it enough, but I love you, Fayteen. I reckon I've loved you from the moment you walked into that saloon."

She smiled, her eyes shining as she looked at him, her hand resting over his heart. "I love you too, Jimmy. More than words can say."

They stayed like that, wrapped in each other's arms, the world around them fading away as they found solace in the closeness, the shared warmth. He held her tightly, feeling her heartbeat against his, and in that moment, he felt as though he had found the strength to face whatever lay ahead.

After a while, she pulled back, her gaze soft but resolute. "It's late, and I reckon you need your rest," she said, a smile playing at the corners of her mouth. "But we've got tomorrow, and the day after, and every day after that."

He nodded, brushing a gentle kiss against her forehead. "Tomorrow, then," he murmured, his voice filled with quiet promise.

She slipped from his arms, pausing at the doorway to look back at him, her eyes lingering on his face. He watched her go, a sense of peace settling over him as she disappeared into the shadows, leaving behind a warmth that filled the emptiness in his heart.

He sat there for a long time, staring out into the night, the darkness stretching endlessly before him. He felt Fayteen's warmth lingering beside him, the faint scent of her hair still in the air, grounding him in a way he hadn't known he needed. His heart beat steady, but his mind churned with thoughts of the days ahead—of his mother, of the ghosts he was still learning to confront, and of the life he was building brick by brick, one uncertain step at a time. The night was vast, almost unsettling, but he welcomed it, knowing that within its shadows lay the echoes of his past—and somewhere, the faint promise of a future that might finally be his to shape.

21

The Saloon Festival

The sun had set over Golden Valley, casting the town in shades of amber and rose as its residents made their way toward The Golden Nugget. Tonight, the saloon held a festive air, with garlands of wildflowers woven around its polished cedar banisters and ribbons hanging from the rafters. The usual lively buzz was replaced by an even more vibrant energy, as families, miners, and merchants, dressed in their finest, filled the room with laughter and anticipation. The townsfolk marveled at the decorations, pleasantly surprised at how the already luxurious space had transformed into a warm and welcoming gathering place for all.

As Jimmy watched from the balcony, his gaze traveled over the crowd, catching sight of familiar faces, including Reverend Amos Thornton and Miss Cora Abernathy, who had joined a lively group near the bar. He couldn't help but smile as he saw Henry and Ada Wickham, the mercantile owners, laughing heartily with Gideon Grady, the blacksmith. Standing beside

Gideon was his wife, Martha, who was normally reserved but tonight wore a broad grin, clearly enjoying the camaraderie. Even Calvin Dodd, the town's usually solemn undertaker, had joined the crowd, his dark attire offset by a bright red pocket square, a subtle nod to the festive atmosphere.

Inside, Fayteen moved gracefully through the saloon, greeting each guest with a warm smile. Her flowing dress swayed as she welcomed folks by name, creating a sense of familiarity and belonging. She stopped to chat with Hattie and Lou McBride, the sisters who ran the town café, who were sitting with Cora and talking excitedly about the upcoming bake sale. Lou, ever the one to draw others into conversation, pulled Fayteen into their discussion.

"Fayteen, we need your advice," Lou began, grinning. "Cora here thinks that apple pie will be our biggest seller, but Hattie and I reckon it'll be our peach cobbler. What do you say?"

Fayteen laughed, her eyes twinkling. "Well, I reckon you're all right! Folks around here have a sweet tooth, and you can't go wrong with any of those. But I have a soft spot for peach cobbler myself."

The sisters exchanged triumphant looks, and Cora laughed, shaking her head. "You just gave them all the ammunition they needed, Fayteen. I won't live it down!"

With a playful wink, Fayteen continued on her way, stopping by the group of dancers gathered near the stage. Each woman wore a different-colored ribbon in her hair, which complemented the flowing dresses they had chosen for the night. Lily Mae Dawson, ever the flirt, had already captivated a small group of miners with her charming banter.

"Now, you boys look like you're ready to see some real dancin'," Lily Mae teased, twirling one of her ribbons with a sly smile. The young men blushed, stammering over their words as the other dancers joined Lily Mae, their laughter adding to the lively atmosphere.

As the dance troupe took their places around the room, Antonio, the saloon's pianist, sat at the grand piano and began to play a lively tune. Fayteen made her way to the stage, her voice cutting through the room with a warm, welcoming tone.

"Thank you all for comin' out tonight!" she called, her smile lighting up the room. "We're here to celebrate this town we've all worked so hard to build, and I hope you're all ready to sing, dance, and make some memories!"

Cheers erupted from the crowd, and Antonio transitioned into a familiar melody as Fayteen began to sing. Her voice, rich and soulful, filled the saloon, blending with the soft hum of conversation and laughter. Around the room, couples paired off, and the dance troupe guided others to the floor, leading them through lively steps that soon had everyone moving in time with the music.

In one corner of the room, Dr. Emmett Harper, who had recently begun treating Nell, watched the festivities with quiet amusement. Emmett, a kind man with a calming presence, exchanged a smile with nurse Eliza, who had been assisting him in caring for Nell as she continued her journey toward healing. They had recently moved Nell into one of the saloon's upstairs rooms, a temporary arrangement to ensure she had the support she needed during her recovery. Tonight, Nell sat with them, watching the crowd with a tentative smile, her shoulders relaxing as she absorbed the warmth of the community around her.

Jimmy noticed his mother from across the room and made his way over, pausing to exchange a few words with Emmett. "How's she doin' tonight, doc?"

Emmett nodded, his expression thoughtful. "She's made remarkable progress, Jimmy. Tonight's probably the most engaged I've seen her. I think being here, seeing all this—it's a good step forward."

Nell looked up at Jimmy, her gaze soft. "It feels like a dream, bein' here with you and watchin' all this. I never thought I'd find a place where I felt welcome again."

Jimmy placed a reassuring hand on her shoulder. "You've got a home here, Mama. You're part of this, same as anyone else."

As he spoke, Ahanu and Sahale joined them, each bringing small pouches filled with herbs and salves they'd prepared to aid in Nell's healing. Sahale, with her gentle demeanor, handed Nell a small bundle, explaining its use in her soft, melodic voice.

"This will help you sleep," she said, her words soothing. "We Shoshone believe that the earth has a way of healing us, if we let it. Use this with an open heart, and you will find peace."

Nell's eyes filled with gratitude as she accepted the bundle, her fingers tracing the soft fabric. "Thank you. You've all shown me more kindness than I deserve."

Ahanu smiled, his voice steady. "Kindness has a way of finding those who need it most, Nell. You are not alone anymore."

As they spoke, Fayteen's voice rose over the crowd, leading the group in another round of lively songs. The dance troupe continued to guide townsfolk onto the floor, teaching them steps to traditional dances like the polka and quadrille. Even Reverend Thornton, normally a more serious man, joined in, laughing as he attempted the lively footwork with surprising skill. The usually reserved Dr. Harper shared a dance with Eliza, who matched his steps with graceful precision, both of them letting go of the day's worries in the joyful movement.

Fayteen stepped down from the stage, giving her voice a rest as she wandered through the crowd, sharing smiles and laughter with the patrons. She found Jimmy by the bar, watching her with a quiet admiration that sent a warmth through her chest.

"Reckon you've done enough singin' for one night?" he asked, his tone playful.

She grinned, slipping her hand into his. "Only if you're ready to join me for a dance. I think it's about time you showed me those fancy footwork skills you're always hidin'."

Jimmy laughed, letting her lead him onto the floor as the music slowed. They moved together, swaying in time with the gentle melody, each lost in the other's gaze. Around them, the townsfolk continued to dance, the couples wrapped in their own quiet moments of connection.

As they danced, Fayteen noticed Nell watching them, a soft smile on her face as she sat surrounded by Dr. Harper, Eliza, Ahanu, and Sahale. Her motherly expression made Fayteen's heart swell, a reminder of the bonds that had formed in this place, the healing that had taken root in the most unlikely of circumstances.

As the evening drew to a close, Fayteen and Jimmy led the crowd in a final song, their voices blending with the townsfolk as the music filled the saloon one last time. When the song ended, a quiet peace settled over the room, the patrons lingering as they exchanged smiles and farewells.

Jimmy took Fayteen's hand, leading her to the balcony, where they could look out over the quiet town, the stars shining above them in the clear night sky. They stood together, their hands entwined, as the sounds of laughter and conversation drifted up from below, the remnants of a night that had brought the town closer together.

Jimmy looked at her, his gaze steady, his voice soft. "Tonight was somethin' special. I reckon we've built more than just a saloon here, Fayteen. We've built a place where folks can find a home, where we can all heal a little more every day."

She leaned into him, her head resting on his shoulder. "And we'll keep buildin' it, Jimmy. We'll keep addin' pieces, makin' this place stronger, together."

They shared a quiet kiss, a promise of the future they were building, the love that had grown between them as steady and enduring as the town itself. And as they stood beneath the vast Idaho sky, they felt the weight of the night settle over them, a reminder that, no matter what lay ahead, they would face it together, bound by the unbreakable ties they had forged in Golden Valley.

22

Langston's Threat

The morning dawned crisp and clear over Golden Valley, the warmth of the previous night's celebration still lingering in the hearts of its townsfolk. Jimmy was up early, as usual, already overseeing the saloon's cleanup alongside Antonio and the dance troupe, who had insisted on helping after the success of their community event. Though he didn't need to work another day in his life—his years in the mines had seen to that—he took pride in the saloon and the community it had fostered. He'd earned a substantial fortune during the Boise Basin gold rush, enough that he could have settled down in comfort anywhere he pleased. But instead, he had chosen Golden Valley, pouring his wealth into this town, building The Golden Nugget from the ground up, and helping others establish their businesses.

Jimmy's fortune was the kind that most men would flaunt, but he had little use for showiness. His satisfaction came not from the size of his bank account, but from the work of his hands, the cedar bar he'd polished until it gleamed, the laughter that filled the saloon every night. His wealth was a quiet one, evident only in the quality of the materials he used, the detail in the polished wood, and the meticulous upkeep of the saloon he had built to last. More importantly, his true wealth lay in the relationships he garnered and his evident care of people.

Around midday, the familiar clip-clop of horses' hooves echoed down the dusty street outside The Golden Nugget. Jimmy looked up as a shadow crossed the doorway, and there stood Bear Langston, a broad-shouldered man with a steely gaze and an air of entitlement that immediately set Jimmy on edge. Bear, with his finely tailored suit and expensive cigar, was the kind of man who enjoyed flaunting his wealth, the kind of man who thought everything could be bought—if the price was right. People all around the territory knew of Bear, and his intimidating business practices.

Jimmy put down his polishing cloth, squaring his shoulders as Bear strode into the room, his presence casting a chill over the warm, welcoming atmosphere. The saloon quieted, the workers and dancers falling silent as they took in the stranger's imposing figure.

"Mr. Hawthorne," Bear said, his voice smooth but carrying a hint of menace. "I trust the morning finds you well."

Jimmy nodded, his eyes never leaving Bear's. "Well enough. But I doubt you've come all the way from Boise just to make small talk."

Bear's mouth twitched into a smile, though his eyes remained cold. "Straight to business. I can respect that. You see, I've been watching this town, watching your little enterprise here, and I must say, you've done well for yourself. This place, this saloon—it's a diamond in the rough."

Jimmy crossed his arms, a wary expression on his face. "Appreciate the compliment, but I reckon you didn't come here just to tell me that."

Bear chuckled, pulling out a cigar and lighting it as he leaned against the bar. "You're sharp, Hawthorne. I'll give you that. No, I came here with a proposal." He exhaled a cloud of smoke, letting it drift lazily around him. "I want to buy The Golden Nugget."

Jimmy stiffened, his hands clenching at his sides. "The Nugget's not for sale," he replied, his voice firm.

Bear raised an eyebrow, unfazed. "Everything's for sale, Hawthorne. You name your price, and I'll make sure you're well compensated. I'm offering you a chance to walk away from this place with more money than you'll ever need."

Jimmy met Bear's gaze, his voice steady. "I already got more than I'll ever need, Langston. You might think everything's got a price, but I've got all the money I want. This place, it's worth more to me than any dollar amount you could offer."

Bear's eyes narrowed slightly, a hint of irritation flickering across his face. Men like him didn't understand someone like Jimmy, who could choose wealth without flaunting it, who could walk away from luxury simply because he valued hard work and the quiet satisfaction of honest labor. But Bear recovered quickly, masking his frustration with a slick smile.

"Is that so? Well, let me put it this way—refusing me could prove costly. Golden Valley is still a new town, after all. Accidents happen. A fire, perhaps. Or an unfortunate incident with the law. I've got connections, Jimmy. I can make things very uncomfortable for you and everyone in this town if I don't get what I want."

At that, Jimmy's eyes narrowed, a dangerous edge creeping into his voice. "You threatenin' me, Langston?"

Bear smiled, his tone smooth as silk. "Not at all. Just offering you a friendly reminder of how... unpredictable things can be. I wouldn't want anything to tarnish this fine establishment of yours. But if you were to accept my offer, well, I'd make sure Golden Valley thrived under my protection."

Jimmy clenched his fists, struggling to keep his composure. He knew Bear wasn't bluffing—the man had a reputation for making life difficult for those who stood in his way. But Jimmy also knew he couldn't give in, couldn't let a man like Bear take control of what he had built.

"I'm not interested in your so-called protection," Jimmy said, his voice low and sharp. "Now, I suggest you take your offer and get out before I decide to throw you out myself."

Bear Langston's eyes narrowed with a flicker of anger, but his smirk never faltered. "Very well, Hawthorne. But you'd do well to think this over. I'll be back soon enough. Maybe then you'll be more... cooperative."

Without waiting for a response, Bear turned on his heel and strode out of the saloon. Jimmy stood rigid, the tension lingering like a bad storm on the horizon. He knew men like Bear didn't make idle threats, and Golden Valley wasn't ready for what was coming. His gut churned. The morning crashes, the broken glassware, and the shattered windowpane—they weren't accidents. Trouble was already brewing.

Fayteen, who had been watching from the balcony, hurried down the stairs, her face set with concern. She crossed to Jimmy and laid a hand on his arm.

"What did he want?" she asked, though she already knew.

"He wants The Nugget," Jimmy replied grimly. "And when I told him no, he promised to make things difficult. Said he could ruin us—everything we've built."

Fayteen's eyes darkened with anger. "That man doesn't belong here, Jimmy. Golden Valley's not gonna roll over and let him stomp through. The townsfolk will stand with us."

Jimmy nodded, though his mind raced. "I'll talk to some folks tonight. This isn't just about us, Fayteen. Bear's not bluffing. We'll need everyone ready."

Later that night, Jimmy gathered some of the town's most trusted citizens in the saloon. Henry and Ada Wickham, Gideon and Martha Grady, Reverend Thornton, and Calvin Dodd sat around the bar, listening as Jimmy laid out Bear's threats.

"We've got a problem," Jimmy said, eyes scanning the group. "Bear Langston's not gonna stop. He's got money, men, and he's planning something. I don't know when, but it'll be soon."

Henry's voice cut through the tension. "We're with you, Jimmy. You know that. This town isn't gonna let some outsider waltz in and take what isn't his."

Martha spoke up, her expression fierce. "There are folks around here who won't stand by and let him get away with this. We'll fight if we have to."

Reverend Thornton placed a hand on Jimmy's shoulder, his tone somber but resolute. "We'll watch out for each other. I'll spread the word quietly and make sure everyone's prepared. But we need prayer and we need to be smart."

Jimmy straightened, eyes hard. "We'll need more than that. I'm talking guns. I want every able man and woman carrying a weapon. We've got no marshal, no jail, no real law here. We're our own defense. So we're gonna act like it."

Gideon nodded, his one good eye narrowing. "We'll keep our horse saddles at the ready, too. If something happens, we need to be able to ride—fast."

Ada spoke softly but firmly. "We'll be ready, Jimmy. This town's got grit. And if Bear thinks we're gonna just roll over, he's in for a surprise."

The resolve in the room was palpable. Jimmy looked around, knowing these people weren't just townsfolk. They were family, a community willing to defend what they'd built. But even as they laid plans, he couldn't shake the unease creeping over him.

Later, as Jimmy and Fayteen locked up the saloon, the night stretched quiet around them. The streets of Golden Valley were still, but it was a stillness that felt too fragile, like the calm before a storm. Jimmy scanned the horizon, his hand instinctively brushing the pistol on his hip.

"You're on edge," Fayteen said quietly, watching him.

"I don't trust this quiet," Jimmy muttered. "Bear's not gonna just let this go. And I can't shake the feelin' that he's already started whatever he's got planned."

Fayteen squeezed his arm. "You're not alone, Jimmy. Whatever comes, we'll face it together. This town's more than just you and me—it's all of us. And we won't let Bear Langston or anyone else tear it apart."

Just as they were about to turn in for the night, the saloon doors swung open, and Antonio rushed in, breathless. His usual calm was gone, replaced by a look of urgency.

"Jimmy, you need to know somethin'," Antonio said, lowering his voice. "I was at the livery stable earlier. Overheard some men talkin'. They mentioned Bear Langston—said he's hired some folks to stir up trouble."

Jimmy's eyes narrowed. "What kind of trouble?"

Antonio glanced around, checking that no one else was listening. "Didn't hear specifics, but it sounded bad. Thought you ought to know."

Jimmy's jaw tightened. "Thanks, Antonio. If you hear anything else, you come to me right away."

Antonio nodded, then turned to leave, casting a worried glance back at Fayteen before heading out into the dark.

Jimmy turned to Fayteen, his voice grim. "Bear's already makin' his move."

Fayteen's face hardened. "Then we'll make ours. We've got the townsfolk behind us. Let's talk to them, organize a plan. We're not gonna sit back and wait for him to strike."

Jimmy nodded. "I'll talk to Gideon and Reverend Thornton tomorrow. We'll set up patrols. But we've gotta be ready for anything. Bear's men won't play fair."

That night, as Jimmy and Fayteen finally closed up the saloon, the tension hung thick in the air. Jimmy made a point to check every lock, every window, his pistol close at hand. He couldn't afford to relax, not with Bear lurking in the shadows.

***

The next few days passed with a nervous energy that spread through Golden Valley. People carried their weapons more openly, kept their horses close. Conversations were hushed, eyes lingered on strangers a little too long, and no one stayed out past dark unless absolutely necessary. Everyone knew something was coming. They just didn't know when.

Jimmy kept his patrols discreet, checking with Gideon, Reverend Thornton, and Calvin Dodd regularly. But despite the tension, there was an unspoken resolve that ran through the town. They wouldn't let Bear Langston take what they'd built. Not without a fight.

And as Jimmy watched from the balcony of the saloon one quiet night, he felt that resolve solidify into a promise. No matter what came, they were ready.

***

The saloon had emptied out earlier than usual, leaving only a few of the regulars playing cards or quietly finishing their drinks. The night air outside had a chill to it, but inside, the lamps cast a warm glow across the tables and polished bar. Jimmy stood behind the counter, wiping down glasses with a rag, but his mind was elsewhere.

Bear Langston was making his move, Jimmy could feel it in his bones. Every time the door creaked open, he felt his hand twitch closer to the gun at his hip, his muscles tightening with the instinct to protect everything he'd worked so hard for.

But the saloon was quiet tonight. Too quiet.

Fayteen, noticing the tension in his stance, came over to him, resting her hand on his arm. "Jimmy, you're restless tonight."

He gave her a tired smile, but his gaze kept drifting to the door.

She reached for his hand, her grip firm and steady. "We're all with ya, Jimmy." She planted a kiss on his cheek.

Her words calmed him, just for a moment, and they shared a brief, intimate glance before Fayteen excused herself to check on something upstairs. Jimmy watched her go, her blonde hair catching the light as she disappeared up the staircase.

A few more patrons trickled out of the saloon, tipping their hats to Jimmy on their way. He nodded back, but his mind was on Fayteen, upstairs, the woman who had stood beside him through every storm.

A creak echoed through the saloon, the sound of a door swinging open. Jimmy tensed, hand instinctively reaching for his gun—but when he turned, it was just Antonio, coming in with an armful of supplies. Jimmy let out a quiet breath, chuckling at his own nerves.

"Sorry, Jimmy," Antonio said sheepishly. "Didn't mean to startle ya."

Jimmy waved him off. "Don't worry 'bout it, Antonio. We're all on edge lately."

Antonio set the supplies down, but his face grew serious. "You got every right to be. Word's spreadin' that Bear's up to somethin'. He's brought in some rough-lookin' men. I saw 'em myself near the livery earlier."

Jimmy's expression darkened. "How many?"

"Four or five, maybe more. They're not here to be friendly, I can tell ya that."

Jimmy clenched his jaw. He couldn't let this drag out any longer. "Thanks for lettin' me know, Antonio. Keep your eyes and ears open. If you hear anything more, come straight to me."

Antonio nodded and left, leaving Jimmy alone in the saloon, his mind racing. He needed to gather the rest of the townsfolk, but first, he wanted to check on Fayteen.

Jimmy turned to head upstairs. "Fayteen?" he called. Silence. The uneasy feeling in his chest flared again.

"Fayteen?" he called louder, his voice echoing in the empty saloon. His heart began to pound as he climbed the stairs two at a time. When he reached the top, the hallway was empty. He checked his room. Empty. The small sitting area. Empty. He went down to the second floor, checked her room. Empty. He knocked on the girls' doors, asking if they'd seen Fayteen, to which they all responded no. Even Nell hadn't seen her.

A cold knot of fear twisted in his gut. He quickly scanned the rooms, calling her name louder with each step. Nothing.

Jimmy raced down the stairs, panic clawing at him. His mind raced, thinking of all the places she could've gone. But she wouldn't have just left, not without telling him.

He burst through the saloon doors and into the street, calling her name into the quiet night. Only the empty street answered back, shadows stretching across the ground beneath the dim lantern light. His chest tightened, and his breath came faster.

As he turned to go back inside, something caught his eye—a small piece of paper, pinned to the door with a knife. His heart pounded in his chest as he crossed the room and yanked it free.

The note was scrawled in jagged handwriting, hurried and menacing.

'Hawthorne—if you want the girl back, you'll reconsider my offer. We're watching, and this is only the beginning.'

The note slipped from Jimmy's fingers as the weight of Bear's threat crashed over him like a tidal wave. His hands shook, his mind racing.

Bear had taken Fayteen.

A cold rage burned through him, fierce and unrelenting. Jimmy's hands clenched into fists as he stood frozen for a moment, the enormity of the situation slamming into him. Bear wasn't after just the saloon—he was after the one thing that mattered most to Jimmy.

Jimmy didn't waste time. He stood outside the saloon and yelled into the darkness, "They've taken Fayteen!"

23

The Rescue Mission

The news of Fayteen's kidnapping spread through Golden Valley like wildfire. Within minutes, the saloon was filled with familiar faces—each marked by worry and determination. Jimmy stood at the center, his face a mixture of fear and fury. Ahanu stood beside him, calm and focused, his presence a grounding force amidst the chaos.

Jimmy clenched his fists, his voice hoarse as he addressed the group. "Langston and his men took Fayteen last night. I found this," he said, holding up the note Bear had left on the door. "He's usin' her to get to me, and I'll be damned if I let him get away with it. We need to move fast—every minute counts."

Ahanu stepped forward, placing a hand on Jimmy's shoulder. "Then we will move fast, brother. But we will move with wisdom too." His voice was steady, his gaze intense. He turned to the crowd, his eyes sweeping over the faces of their friends and neighbors. "We will need strong men to come with us, those who know the land and are willing to risk their lives. This is not just about one person. This is about all of you—about protecting what you have built here."

Henry Wickham, the mercantile owner, stepped forward, his jaw set with determination. "I'm with you, Jimmy. That scoundrel came here once, he'll come again. Let's make sure he learns a lesson he won't forget."

Gideon Grady, the blacksmith, nodded in agreement. "Count me in too. I know these trails better than most. If Bear thinks he can waltz into this town and start throwin' his weight around, he's got another thing comin'."

Jimmy looked around at the gathered men, a sense of fierce gratitude swelling within him. "Thank you, all of you. We leave now. Ahanu's got a plan, and we'll need to follow it carefully."

Ahanu nodded, gesturing for the group to gather around as he spread a map of the area on the bar. He pointed to a dense patch of forest west of town. "Bear and his men likely took her somewhere remote, where they would not be disturbed. This area here—there is a cave system I used to explore as a boy. It is hidden, and it is close enough for them to have reached by now."

The men listened intently as Ahanu laid out the plan. "I will go ahead with Jimmy, using paths only I know. The rest of you will circle around, creating a diversion. We will need to be quick, silent, and precise. And once we reach them, let me handle the first approach. My people have ways of moving unseen, of drawing out information without violence."

Jimmy nodded, his gaze unwavering. "Let's go get her back."

The rescue party moved swiftly through the forest, Ahanu leading the way with a keen sense of direction, his movements silent as a shadow. Jimmy followed closely, his heart pounding with anticipation and dread, every fiber of his being focused on getting Fayteen back. Behind them, Gideon and Henry led the rest of the men, spreading out as Ahanu had instructed, ready to create the distraction that would allow Jimmy and Ahanu to slip inside unnoticed.

Ahanu stopped suddenly, raising his hand. "We are close," he whispered. He motioned for the men to hold back, and with silent gestures, he explained the rest of the plan. "Jimmy, stay close. We will scout ahead and look for any signs of her."

As they moved forward, Ahanu bent low, examining the ground. He pointed to faint imprints in the earth—footprints, slightly disturbed foliage, a discarded piece of rope. "They came this way, and recently. Bear's men are not skilled at covering their tracks."

The two men continued, slipping between the trees, Ahanu's movements almost ghost-like as he scanned the area. They soon came upon a small clearing, and there, nestled against the side of a rocky hill, was the entrance to a cave, half-hidden by overgrown shrubs. Two guards stood at the entrance, rifles in hand, their expressions bored but alert.

Ahanu glanced at Jimmy, his voice a mere breath. "I will create a distraction, drawing them away from the entrance. Once they are gone, you get inside and find Fayteen. Move swiftly, and trust your instincts."

Jimmy nodded, his jaw set. He felt a surge of adrenaline as he gripped his pistol, ready for whatever came next.

Ahanu slipped into the shadows, his steps soundless as he circled around the guards. From somewhere nearby, a sharp bird call pierced the air, startling the men. One of the guards frowned, raising his rifle. "Did you hear that?"

The other nodded, peering into the trees. "Sounded strange. Might be a signal. We should check it out."

They moved cautiously toward the sound, leaving the entrance unguarded. Jimmy seized the opportunity, slipping inside the cave, his heart pounding. The air was cool and damp, the passage narrow and winding. He followed the faint echoes of voices, his footsteps light as he made his way deeper into the darkness.

Finally, he saw a faint glow ahead—a small lantern hanging from a makeshift hook, casting a weak light over the cavern. Bear Langston stood beside it, his arms crossed, a smug expression on his face. Fayteen was there too, tied to a chair, her face pale but defiant.

Bear looked up as Jimmy entered, his expression shifting to one of surprise, then amusement. "Well, well, Hawthorne. I didn't think you had the nerve to come after her yourself. I figured you'd send your lackeys while you hid back in town."

Jimmy took a step forward, his voice cold. "You made a mistake, Langston. You thought you could take what's mine, but you're about to learn you can't just waltz in here and take whatever you want."

Bear laughed, his eyes gleaming with malice. "I'm a man of business, Hawthorne. I take what I need, and right now, I need you to understand that everything has a price. Including her."

Jimmy's hand tightened around his pistol, his gaze flicking to Fayteen, who met his eyes with a fierce look. "Don't worry about me, Jimmy," she said, her voice steady despite the fear in her eyes. "Just do what you have to."

At that moment, Ahanu slipped into the cavern, his presence undetected as he took position behind Bear. He moved with the grace of a predator, his eyes focused and intent. Bear, oblivious to the danger, kept his attention on Jimmy, unaware that the tables had just turned.

Without warning, Ahanu struck, locking his arm around Bear's throat, pulling him backward. Bear struggled, his face turning red as he clawed at Ahanu's arm, but Ahanu held firm, his voice a low growl. "You do not belong here, Langston. This land does not want you, and neither do we."

Bear gasped for breath, his hands flailing. Jimmy took the opportunity to rush forward, untying Fayteen, his hands moving quickly over the ropes that bound her. She slumped against him, her relief palpable as she clung to him.

"Are you alright?" he asked, his voice filled with concern.

She nodded, swallowing hard. "I am now. Let's get out of here, Jimmy."

They moved swiftly, Ahanu keeping a firm grip on Bear as they made their way out of the cave. Outside, the rest of the rescue party was waiting, and Gideon and Henry quickly moved forward, taking Bear off Ahanu's hands and binding him securely.

Henry looked at Jimmy, a satisfied grin on his face. "Guess he didn't count on us comin' after him, did he?"

Jimmy shook his head, his gaze hard. "No, he didn't. But he'll soon learn that Golden Valley takes care of its own. Let's get him back to town and make sure he knows he's not welcome here anymore."

The men escorted Bear back to Golden Valley, the townsfolk gathering in the street as they brought him into town, his hands bound and his mouth gagged, his face a mask of fury. Reverend Thornton stepped forward, his voice strong as he addressed the crowd.

"This man came here with ill intentions, seeking to destroy what we've built. But we stand united, and we will not be swayed by greed or threats."

Jimmy looked at Bear, his voice firm. "You're not welcome here, Langston. And you'll be held accountable for what you've done. We'll be takin' you to a place where the law can deal with you properly."

Bear glared at him, but Jimmy met his gaze with quiet strength, his resolve unshaken. The crowd stood behind him, their faces reflecting their loyalty and trust, their unity a silent promise that Golden Valley would remain strong, no matter who tried to tear it down.

Gideon Grady and Henry Wickham stepped forward, taking Bear by the shoulders. Gideon nodded at Jimmy, a reassuring glint in his eye. "We'll take him to the next town over, where there's a marshal and a jail to keep him locked up tight. Golden Valley may need its own lawman sooner than we hoped."

Jimmy nodded, feeling a pang of disappointment that their peaceful town would have to employ such measures, but knowing that this was necessary for its future.

The townsfolk watched as Gideon and Henry led Bear down the road, his struggles futile against their firm grip. As they disappeared from sight, Jimmy let out a long breath, the tension in his shoulders easing. He turned to Fayteen, his voice gentle.

"Let's get you to the doc, Fayteen. You've been through enough."

She nodded, the strength she had shown earlier giving way to visible exhaustion. Jimmy wrapped an arm around her, guiding her down the street to Dr. Emmett Harper's clinic. As they entered, the doctor looked up from his desk, his face filled with concern.

"Fayteen!" Dr. Harper exclaimed, ushering them inside. "Sit down, sit down. Tell me what happened."

Jimmy gave him a quick summary, his voice tight as he recounted the events of the past day. Dr. Harper listened intently, his gaze flicking over Fayteen as he took stock of her condition. He led her to the examination table, speaking softly as he checked for any injuries.

"You're safe now, Fayteen," he murmured, his touch gentle as he examined her arms, noting the bruises left by the ropes. "No broken bones, thankfully. Just some bruising and a few scrapes. I'll give you something for the pain and help you get cleaned up."

Fayteen nodded, managing a small smile. "Thank you, Dr. Harper. I've had worse, but... it feels good to know I'm safe again."

Jimmy stood by her side, his hand resting on her shoulder, his expression a mixture of relief and fierce protectiveness.

"She'll be safe as long as I have any say in it. Thank you, Doc, for lookin' after her."

Dr. Harper nodded, his gaze warm. "That's what I'm here for. And Fayteen, if you experience any lingering pain or need anything else, you come see me. Don't hesitate, alright?"

She nodded, reaching for Jimmy's hand. He helped her to her feet, and together, they walked out of the clinic, the cool evening air washing over them as they stepped back into the street.

The townsfolk were still gathered outside, their faces filled with relief and quiet joy as they watched Jimmy and Fayteen emerge. Hattie and Lou McBride, who had heard what happened, ran over, wrapping Fayteen in a fierce hug.

"Thank the good Lord you're alright, Fayteen!" Hattie exclaimed, her voice thick with emotion. "You had us all worried sick."

Fayteen hugged them back, her eyes welling up as she realized just how much this town, these people, had come to mean to her. "Thank you," she whispered, her voice filled with gratitude. "You all came for me, risked so much. I don't know how I'll ever repay you."

Lou grinned, wiping her eyes. "You already have, Fayteen. You've brought us all together, shown us what it means to belong to a family. And we'll always be here for you—every single one of us."

As they walked back to the saloon, Jimmy held her close, his heart swelling with love and gratitude for the people who had come to their aid, for the town they were building, for the life they were crafting together.

They climbed the steps to The Golden Nugget, and as they entered, Jimmy turned to Fayteen, his voice filled with quiet resolve. "Whatever happens next, we'll face it together. This town—it's ours, and no one's gonna take it from us."

She looked up at him, her gaze filled with warmth and admiration. "I know, Jimmy. I see now just how much you mean it, how much you love this place. And... how much you love me."

He pulled her close, his lips brushing her forehead, his voice soft. "More than I can ever say. More than I'll ever be able to put into words. You're everything to me, Fayteen. And I'm not gonna let anything— or anyone—take you away from me."

They stood there, wrapped in each other's arms, the saloon quiet around them, a sanctuary from the dangers outside. And as the first stars appeared in the night sky, they knew that whatever challenges lay ahead, they would face them side by side, their hearts bound by the unbreakable ties they had forged in the heart of Golden Valley.

24

A New Foundation

The morning light filtered softly through the curtains in Fayteen's room at The Golden Nugget, casting a warm glow over the cedar furniture and the delicate lace she had hung by the window. She had just finished dressing when a soft knock echoed from the door. Opening it, she found Eliza Wakefield, the town's nurse, standing there with a warm smile and a basket of herbs and bandages.

"Good morning, Fayteen," Eliza greeted her, stepping inside. "I thought I'd check in and see how you're feeling after all you went through. I brought some herbs that should help with any bruising or soreness."

Fayteen smiled, her eyes lighting up. "Thank you, Eliza. I'm feelin' better, though a bit sore. But thanks to everyone, I feel more grateful than anything else. Please, have a seat."

Eliza settled herself by the window, setting the basket down and beginning to prepare a poultice. As she worked, she glanced up at Fayteen, a gentle curiosity in her gaze. "You're a strong woman, Fayteen. Not everyone could handle what you went through with such grace."

Fayteen shrugged, though a smile played at the corners of her lips. "I reckon I've had my fair share of hardships. But this town—it's been a gift. And Jimmy..." She trailed off, her cheeks flushing slightly.

Eliza chuckled, catching the look in Fayteen's eyes. "Yes, and Jimmy." She finished mixing the herbs, placing the poultice in Fayteen's hand. "Use this a few times a day. It'll help with the soreness and ease any swelling."

Fayteen thanked her, placing the poultice on the small table beside her bed. "Eliza, you've been so kind. Not just today, but always. You and Dr. Harper both. I can't tell you what it means to have people who care."

Eliza reached over, giving Fayteen's hand a squeeze. "That's what we're here for. And I think this town's only getting started. Dr. Harper and I were talking earlier this morning about the changes we'll be seeing soon. Did you hear about the telegraph office?"

Fayteen raised an eyebrow, intrigued. "A telegraph office? Here in Golden Valley?"

Eliza nodded. "They're building one now, just down the street from the mercantile. Henry and Ada Wickham are overseeing it, making sure it's done right. And they've been talking about bringing in a marshal too, to keep the peace. With the way the town's growing, it seems like the right time. That will also mean a jail!" Eliza herself was flummoxed at the thought.

Fayteen smiled, the news sparking a sense of pride in her heart. "Golden Valley's becoming a real town. With its own telegraph office, a marshall, and even a jail. Who would've thought?"

Eliza laughed, standing up and gathering her things. "Well, with the way things are going, it won't be long before we're a bustling center of trade. You take care, Fayteen. And don't hesitate to come see me if you need anything more. I'm always happy to spend time with you, my dear friend."

With a tender hug goodbye, Eliza left, and Fayteen felt a sense of hope settle over her, knowing the town was moving forward, building something strong and lasting. She leaned by the window, watching as a group of men gathered where the telegraph office would be.

A few evenings passed, and Jimmy knocked on Fayteen's door, his expression unusually serious. She invited him in, and he closed the door behind him, taking a deep breath as he turned to face her.

"There's somethin' I need to tell you, Fayteen," he began, his voice soft but steady. "After all that's happened, I've been thinkin' on the future. On what this town means to me, what *you* mean to me. I know we've been takin' things slow, but I'm not sure I can wait any longer."

Her heart fluttered, a sense of anticipation rising within her as she took his hand. "Jimmy, you know how I feel about you. I'm not goin' anywhere."

He smiled, a spark of excitement flashing in his eyes. "I know. And I want you to know that you're the most important person in my life. I want to build a life with you, a future here in Golden Valley. But before I say anythin' else, there's somethin' I need to show you."

Taking her hand, he led her through the saloon and out into the cool evening air. They walked down the quiet street, the stars beginning to twinkle above, casting a gentle glow over the town. He led her to the edge of town, to a small hill overlooking the valley. A fire was crackling there, and beside it, a small table covered with a cloth, two glasses, and a bottle of her favorite wine.

Fayteen's eyes widened in surprise as she took in the scene. "Jimmy, what is this?"

He grinned, his hand slipping around her waist as he led her to the table. "I've been plannin' this for a while. I wanted to do it right, somethin' memorable."

They sat down, and Jimmy poured them each a glass, the firelight flickering over his face, casting his features in a warm glow. He took a deep breath, setting his glass aside as he reached into his coat pocket and pulled out a small, ornately carved wooden box. Fayteen's breath caught as he opened it, revealing a delicate gold ring with a single, glistening sapphire—a blue as deep as the Idaho sky.

"Fayteen Everhart," he said, his voice filled with a raw vulnerability she had never seen in him before. "I've loved you from the moment I met you. And I know we've both been through hard times, had our share of pain. But I believe we're stronger together. I want you by my side for the rest of my life. Will you marry me?"

She looked up at him, her eyes brimming with tears, a soft smile playing on her lips. "Yes, Jimmy," she whispered, her voice trembling with emotion. "Yes, I'll marry you."

Jimmy let out a laugh, his eyes shining as he slipped the ring onto her finger. He pulled her into his arms, spinning her around, their laughter echoing over the valley as he held her close. They stood there together, wrapped in each other's embrace, the fire crackling beside them, the stars shining above.

As they held each other, Jimmy's voice softened. "There's one more thing I have for you." He pulled out a folded piece of paper from his pocket, handing it to her. She opened it, her eyes widening as she read.

"It's a deed," he explained, smiling at her astonished expression. "To this patch of land which goes to just beyond that hill. It's yours, Fayteen. I want us to build a home there, a place where we can watch this town grow, where we can build a family. I want you to know that this isn't just about a ring, or a promise. It's about buildin' a life together."

Tears slipped down her cheeks as she looked up at him, her heart overflowing with love and gratitude. "Jimmy, I never dreamed... You've given me more than I ever thought I'd have."

He kissed her gently, his arms wrapping around her as they looked out over the town, the place they had chosen to make their own. And as they stood together, with the promise of their future laid out before them, they knew that whatever challenges lay ahead, they would face them together, side by side, their hearts bound by an unbreakable love.

The next morning, the news of their engagement spread quickly through Golden Valley, filling the townsfolk with excitement and joy. Plans for the telegraph office continued, and a few men set to work on a small jail, each structure a symbol of the town's growth and progress. With each passing day, the town felt more like a community, each person contributing to the vision they had begun together.

As Jimmy and Fayteen walked down the street, hand in hand, they felt the warmth of the community surrounding them, a sense of belonging that went deeper than they had ever imagined. They were no longer just building a town—they were building a future, one they would share with the people who had stood by them, who had fought beside them, and who would continue to be part of their journey.

And as the first foundation for the new jail was laid, and the telegraph lines began to take shape, Fayteen looked at Jimmy, a spark of mischief in her eyes. "You realize, we're going to be the talk of this town for quite some time, Mr. Hawthorne."

Jimmy laughed, pulling her close. "Then let 'em talk, Miss Everhart—soon to be Mrs. Hawthorne. I reckon we've earned it."

They shared a kiss beneath the morning sun, the town bustling around them, each moment a testament to the love, resilience, and dreams that had brought them together. In the heart of Golden Valley, they had found each other, and together, they would build a life as enduring as the mountains and as vast as the Idaho sky.

Jimmy and Fayteen continued strolling down Golden Valley's main street, their hands entwined, as they took in the progress happening all around them. The telegraph office was being constructed, the wooden structure standing proudly next to the mercantile. Hammers rang out, and voices filled the air as the townsfolk busied themselves with construction, each person contributing to the town's new era of growth. They waved to Eli Thorne and his small crew, who were doing the building.

As they approached the telegraph office, they noticed a young man directing a couple of workers as they hoisted the telegraph lines into place. He was tall and lean, with a wiry frame and a sharp, attentive expression. His dark hair was slightly tousled, and he wore a simple but neatly pressed vest and shirt. He turned as Jimmy and Fayteen approached, giving them a friendly nod.

"Good morning, folks! Name's Caleb Morgan," he said, extending his hand. "Just arrived in town to run your new telegraph office here. Pleasure to meet ya."

Jimmy shook his hand, smiling. "Welcome to Golden Valley, Caleb. I'm Jimmy Hawthorne, and this here's Fayteen Everhart."

Caleb's eyes lit up with recognition. "Ah, the owners of The Golden Nugget! Heard about your saloon all the way back in Boise. I've got a feelin' I'll be spendin' a few nights in there myself, once things are up and runnin' here." He chuckled, casting a glance at the telegraph lines as they were secured to the building. "This place is growin' fast—I've set up a few telegraph offices in my time, but I've never seen a town expand quite like this one."

Fayteen smiled, intrigued. "You've set up other telegraph offices? Seems like you're a bit of a wanderer."

Caleb shrugged, a sheepish grin spreading across his face. "You could say that. I've seen my fair share of towns—mostly workin' out west, though I got my start in St. Louis. There's somethin' about bein' the first to bring folks a way to reach out, to connect with the rest of the world, that makes the job feel worth it."

Jimmy gave a nod of approval, appreciating the man's sense of purpose. "I reckon you'll find yourself right at home here. This town may be small, but we're connected to folks all over. You'll be the bridge, keepin' us in touch with the outside world."

Caleb's face grew serious, a hint of pride in his eyes. "That's the plan. I take my job seriously—there's no faster way to spread news than by telegraph, and I aim to make sure Golden Valley stays informed. If there's trouble brewin', I'll be the first to let folks know, and if there's good news, well, I'll be the one to share that too."

Fayteen exchanged a glance with Jimmy, both of them reassured by Caleb's confidence. As they bid him farewell, he tipped his hat and returned to his work, his focus unwavering as he oversaw the final touches on the telegraph lines. The sight of the new office filled them with a renewed sense of excitement for Golden Valley's future.

As they walked further down the street, they noticed a man on horseback approaching the town from the east. He rode tall in the saddle, his presence commanding attention even from a distance. Dressed in a long duster coat with a wide-brimmed hat shading his face, he looked like a man who had seen more than his fair share of action. His horse, a sturdy bay with a glossy coat, moved with the same calm confidence as its rider.

The man reined in his horse as he reached the center of town, dismounting with a fluid motion that spoke of years spent in the saddle. He stood well over six feet, with a rugged, sun-worn face framed by a well-trimmed beard and piercing blue eyes that seemed to take in everything at once. He glanced around, his gaze settling on Jimmy and Fayteen as he approached.

"Afternoon, folks," he said, his voice a low rumble. "Name's Marshal Hank Slater. I've been sent from Boise to keep an eye on things while you get your own marshal's office up and runnin'. Word is, Golden Valley's in need of a lawman."

Jimmy shook his hand, feeling the strength in the man's grip. "You heard right, Marshal Slater. We've had a few run-ins lately that reminded us this town could use someone like you around."

Slater nodded, a hint of a smile crossing his weathered face. "Heard about the trouble with that fella Langston. You folks handled it well, but it's my job to make sure that sort of thing doesn't become a habit." He glanced around the bustling town, his eyes sharp and appraising. "You got a lot of good people here. We'll make sure they stay safe."

Fayteen smiled, sensing a reassuring presence in the marshal. "Thank you, Marshal Slater. I reckon folks will feel a lot safer knowin' you're around."

Slater tipped his hat to her. "It's what I'm here for, ma'am. I've been workin' as a lawman for over a decade, movin' from one place to the next, but I've always believed that a town's only as strong as the folks who protect it. I aim to keep things peaceful here, if that's alright with you."

Jimmy nodded, relieved to have someone with Slater's experience on their side. "That's exactly what we're hopin' for. Let us know if there's anythin' we can do to help you get settled."

Slater nodded, glancing over at the men working on the new jail across the street. "I'll be settin' up shop near that new jail of yours. I'll make my rounds and get to know the folks here. And if anyone needs a reminder to stay in line, well, they'll get it soon enough."

As the marshal moved toward the jail, Jimmy and Fayteen watched, feeling a renewed sense of security knowing they had someone so capable watching over their town. They continued down the street, taking in the sights of their thriving community, their hands still clasped together.

As they walked back toward the saloon, Jimmy stopped suddenly, his gaze softening as he turned to Fayteen. "I'm glad you're here with me, Fayteen. This town, these people—they're all a part of what we're buildin'. But none of it would mean anythin' without you by my side."

Fayteen's eyes shone with warmth as she leaned into him, wrapping her arms around his waist. "I wouldn't want to be anywhere else, Jimmy. This is our home, and I'm grateful every day for what we've built together."

He leaned down, capturing her lips in a tender kiss, a promise of the life they had only just begun to build. And as they stood there, surrounded by the town they loved, they knew that no matter what challenges lay ahead, they would face them together, their hearts bound by an unbreakable love.

Golden Valley was growing, its foundation stronger than ever, with new faces and new allies joining the ranks. And with the telegraph office connecting them to the world, and Marshal Slater protecting their streets, they felt a sense of peace, a promise that the life they were building would endure.

25

Preparing For Forever

Golden Valley buzzed with excitement as Jimmy and Fayteen's engagement news spread. Around town, friends and neighbors shared well-wishes, and the promise of new beginnings seemed to fill the air. Fayteen found herself frequently blushing as she navigated congratulations and advice from townsfolk, but she couldn't help feeling a deep sense of belonging, knowing the town was just as invested in their love story as they were.

One sunny afternoon, Jimmy took Fayteen's hand, a mischievous glint in his eye, and led her up to the third floor of The Golden Nugget. They paused at the door to his quarters, and he turned to her, his expression warm.

"There's somethin' I want to show you," he said, opening the door to reveal his spacious room. "Now that we're gettin' married, I figured it was about time you helped make this place feel a little more like home—our home."

Fayteen stepped inside, taking in the room. The space was filled with Jimmy's practical but well-made furnishings, including a sturdy bed, a couple of leather chairs by a fireplace, and a small bookshelf near the window. The room exuded a rugged charm, but there was no doubt that it had the unmistakable touch of a bachelor.

She smiled, looking up at him. "I reckon you're right, Jimmy. I think this room could use a bit of softenin' up for the time bein'. At least until we're ready to build that house on the land you bought me." She gazed out the window, her eyes dreamy as she thought of the piece of land Jimmy had gifted her. "We'll have our place out there soon enough. But this'll do just fine for now."

Jimmy grinned, his heart swelling with love. "Good, 'cause I got plans for this place. I want you to have your own space here, so I thought I'd get some of the men to help me build an extension—maybe put in a proper bath too. Whatever you want."

Her face lit up, and she took his hand. "I'd love that, Jimmy. I've always wanted a copper bath, one big enough to soak in after a long day. And I was thinkin'... maybe a bigger bed, with some new linens. Somethin' that feels like it belongs to both of us."

He nodded, clearly excited. "Consider it done. I'll make sure we get the best copper we can find for that bath of yours. And as for the bed, I'll see what I can do to make it big enough for two." He winked, pulling her close for a kiss, lingering as if to savor the warmth of her smile.

The following day, Jimmy gathered a few of the men in town to help with the renovations. Gideon Grady, ever the practical blacksmith, agreed to oversee the structural work, while Eli brought a load of lumber from his sawmill, personally choosing each plank for its quality. Henry and Caleb, the new telegraph operator, even offered a hand, his lean frame surprisingly strong as they hammered and sawed, transforming Jimmy's quarters into a comfortable living space.

As they worked, the men traded stories and laughter, the camaraderie easing the hard labor. Jimmy took every opportunity to share his ideas for the space, and the others listened with genuine interest, adding suggestions of their own.

"Jimmy," Henry said, wiping his brow as he paused from hauling timber, "you're settin' this place up right. I reckon Fayteen's goin' to be as happy as a lark once she sees it all finished."

Gideon chuckled, testing the strength of the new support beams. "You're a lucky man, Jimmy. Most folks here would give anything to find a woman like her. Just make sure you take good care of her, alright?"

Jimmy smiled, glancing toward the saloon below, where he knew Fayteen was busy preparing for the evening. "Believe me, Gideon, I intend to. She's got my heart, and that's no small thing."

Eli, who typically was quiet, looked at the men then cleared his throat. "I reckon ya'll are lucky. I miss my Bessie like mad, so take it from me, look after your womenfolk and do your best to make 'em happy. Life's too short to worry about fussin' over nothin'." He grinned and carried on working.

By the end of the week, the new extension took shape. The men added a small bathing area, complete with a raised platform for the copper tub Jimmy had ordered from Boise. The new bath gleamed in the afternoon sunlight, a work of art in itself, and Jimmy imagined Fayteen's delight when she first laid eyes on it. The room also featured a wider bed, dressed with fresh linens in rich, earthy colors, and a few extra shelves for the small touches she planned to add.

When the work was finished, Jimmy stood back, a look of satisfaction on his face. He could already envision the two of them making memories here, spending their evenings by the fire, planning their future, until the day came when they would build a home on the land just outside of town.

Later that afternoon, Fayteen was helping Lou McBride behind the bar when Eliza arrived with a letter in hand, a knowing smile on her face.

"This came for you, Fayteen," Eliza said, handing her the envelope. "It looks like it's from back east. The young lad at the post office was busy, so I offered to bring it over."

Fayteen took the letter, recognizing her mother's handwriting. Her heart skipped a beat, and she stepped into a quiet corner, Jimmy by her side as she opened it. Her eyes widened as she read aloud, a joyful smile spreading across her face.

Dearest Fayteen,

We are overjoyed to hear from you. Your letter has brought us so much happiness, and we cannot wait to see you. We're eager to meet Jimmy, the man you've chosen, and to be part of this new life you've built in Golden Valley.

We'll be arriving in two weeks, just as soon as we can gather a few things for the journey. Expect to see us soon, and know that we carry nothing but love and excitement in our hearts for you.

With all our love,
Mama and Papa

She looked up, tears glistening in her eyes, her heart brimming with happiness. "They're comin'. They're really comin'." Leaving the ladies at the bar, she went and found Jimmy to give him the good news.

Jimmy wrapped her in a tight embrace, the warmth of his love surrounding her. "That's wonderful news, Fayteen. I want them to see just how special you are, and I'll make sure they feel right at home here in Golden Valley."

Over the next few days, Jimmy and Fayteen focused on adding the final touches to their quarters, transforming the space into a home that reflected both their personalities. Fayteen chose a vibrant quilt for the bed, and Jimmy surprised her with a hand-carved cedar chest at the foot of it, filled with soft blankets and pillows. They shared quiet moments by the fireplace, talking late into the night, envisioning their future and dreaming of the home they would build together on their land.

The townsfolk, equally invested in their happiness, began offering their assistance for the upcoming visit from Fayteen's parents. Hattie and Lou McBride promised to prepare a feast for their arrival, which the couple eagerly accepted.

On the day of their arrival, the entire town seemed to hum with anticipation. Jimmy stood beside Fayteen at the edge of town, waiting with a mixture of excitement and nerves. As the wagon appeared on the horizon, she squeezed his hand, her eyes filled with emotion.

"There they are," she whispered, a tremor in her voice. "It's been so long."

He pulled her close, his voice a gentle murmur. "No matter what, I'm here for you. We'll make this a day to remember."

As the wagon rolled to a stop, Fayteen felt her breath catch, her heart pounding as she caught sight of her parents. She hadn't seen them in so long that for a moment, it was as though she were dreaming. Charles and Caroline Everhart climbed down, their faces a mixture of joy, relief, and disbelief as they looked upon their daughter.

Her mother, Caroline, rushed forward, tears streaming down her cheeks as she pulled Fayteen into a tight embrace. "Oh, Fayteen, my sweet girl!" She held her back just long enough to look her over, her gaze softening as she took in Fayteen's radiant smile, her long blonde hair cascading down her shoulders, and the brightness in her eyes. "Look at you," Caroline whispered, brushing her hand over Fayteen's hair. "You're so beautiful. You look happy. Happier than I've ever seen you."

Fayteen hugged her mother tightly, a laugh escaping as tears pricked at her eyes. "I am, Mama. I truly am."

Her father, Charles, approached slowly, his steps heavy with emotion. He looked at her, his eyes brimming with unshed tears, and opened his arms. Fayteen rushed to him, feeling the strength of his embrace as he held her close, gently pressing his lips to her forehead.

"My little girl," he whispered, his voice cracking. "I've missed you so much, Fayteen. I'm so sorry...for all of it." He held her tightly, his body trembling as he let his tears fall. "I didn't know what to say back then, how to fix it. But I'm so grateful to see you, to know you're safe, and to see you smile."

She stroked his back, her voice soft. "Papa, it's alright. I'm so glad you're here now. That's all that matters."

After a moment, they pulled apart, and Fayteen turned to Jimmy, her eyes filled with joy as she took his hand, drawing him into the circle.

"Mama, Papa," she said, her voice brimming with pride, "this is Jimmy Hawthorne, my fiancé."

Charles extended his hand, his grip firm as he shook Jimmy's hand, a look of approval in his eyes. "Thank you, young man. Thank you for lookin' after our Fayteen. I can see she's in good hands."

Jimmy gave a respectful nod, his own voice thick with emotion. "I love your daughter very much, sir. She's changed my life, and I'll do everything in my power to keep her safe and happy."

Caroline took Jimmy's hand, her eyes filled with curiosity and warmth. "I've heard so much about you, Jimmy. I look forward to getting to know the man who's stolen my daughter's heart."

He smiled, glancing down at Fayteen with a look of pure love. "It's my honor, Mrs. Everhart. You raised an extraordinary woman."

They spent the next few minutes catching up, and as they walked towards The Golden Nugget, Fayteen eagerly pointed out the sights of Golden Valley. She shared stories about the friends she had made, the plans she and Jimmy had for the town, and how much the people here had come to mean to her.

Her parents listened intently, marveling at the life she had built and the joy that radiated from her.

When they reached the saloon, Jimmy led them to one of the best rooms he had prepared for their stay. It was warm and inviting, with a freshly made bed, a small writing desk, and a cozy sitting area by the window.

"I hope this suits you," Jimmy said, motioning toward the room with a smile. "It's the best we've got until we can build Fayteen and me a proper place on the land just outside of town."

Caroline looked around, clearly impressed. "This is lovely, Jimmy. You've made a fine home here." She paused, casting a glance up the stairs to the second floor. "Though I must admit, I was a bit surprised when I heard about the...entertainment offered here."

Fayteen's face fell slightly, sensing her mother's apprehension. She reached for Jimmy's hand, drawing strength from his presence. "Mama, I know it's different from what you're used to. But Jimmy treats the girls with respect, and he's made sure that everyone here is safe and looked after."

Caroline's eyes softened as she looked at her daughter. "I see that you're happy, Fayteen. And I trust you. It's just that, well..." She glanced at Jimmy, a hint of uncertainty in her gaze. "Forgive me, Jimmy. It's just a bit of a shock to imagine my daughter living above a place where such... activities take place."

Jimmy cleared his throat, his voice steady but understanding. "I understand, Mrs. Everhart. When I built this saloon, I wanted it to be a safe place, where folks could enjoy themselves without worry. And I've made sure that the girls are treated with dignity. They're under contract, and no one's forced to do anything they don't choose. I protect them like family."

Charles put a comforting hand on his wife's shoulder. "We raised Fayteen to think for herself, Caroline. If this is the life she's chosen, then I reckon we ought to be open to it."

Caroline nodded, taking a deep breath as she looked from Jimmy to Fayteen. "I appreciate your honesty, Jimmy. And I can see that you've built somethin' special here, a place where people can come together. It's just takin' a moment to sink in."

Fayteen stepped forward, holding her mother's hands. "I know it's not what you imagined for me, Mama. But I've found a place where I'm loved and respected. And Jimmy... he's given me the freedom to be myself, to follow my dreams. I wouldn't change a thing about this life we're buildin' together."

Her mother sighed, her expression softening as she looked into her daughter's eyes. "I can see that, my love. And I'm proud of you—for your courage, and for followin' your heart. If this is what makes you happy, then I'll do my best to understand."

Jimmy stepped forward, his voice warm. "Mrs. Everhart, Mr. Everhart, I know it's a lot to take in. But I want you both to know that Fayteen's happiness is my first priority. We're buildin' a life together, and that includes havin' her family close, if you'll allow us that privilege."

Charles gave a nod of approval, a quiet strength in his voice. "We'd be honored to be part of your lives, Jimmy. I've seen enough to know that you're a man of character. And Fayteen, I can see you've chosen well."

The tension eased, and they spent the rest of the evening enjoying a sumptuous meal together, prepared by Hattie and Lou, exchanging stories of Fayteen's childhood and the journey she had taken to get here. Jimmy found himself enchanted by the tales her parents shared, each one revealing a side of Fayteen he had yet to discover.

As the night wore on, Fayteen felt a deep sense of gratitude, knowing that her family had come to accept the life she had chosen. She squeezed Jimmy's hand, their eyes meeting in a shared moment of understanding and joy. They had come so far, and with her parents' acceptance, they could now begin the next chapter with open hearts, free from the shadows of the past.

And as they said their goodnights, Fayteen knew that the love she had found in Golden Valley was stronger than anything she had ever imagined—a love that would continue to grow, with the blessing of family, friends, and a future as bright as the morning sun.

26

Flames Of Foe And Friendship

With Fayteen's parents settled in, excitement buzzed throughout Golden Valley as the townsfolk prepared for the upcoming wedding. Every day, new details were discussed and decided, each choice bringing the vision of their special day closer to reality. Fayteen's heart soared, filled with joy as she and Jimmy, hand-in-hand, planned a ceremony that would celebrate not only their love but also the life they had created in Golden Valley.

As they finalized the guest list one evening, Fayteen turned to Jimmy, her eyes filled with a mixture of curiosity and tenderness. "Jimmy, now that my parents are here, there's someone I'd like them to meet. I know it might be hard, but I think it would mean a lot to them—and to you too."

Jimmy met her gaze, understanding immediately. He nodded, a quiet resolve in his eyes. "You're talkin' about my mother, Nell."

She reached out, taking his hand. "I am. I think it could be good for you, and for her, to have the chance to share this moment as a family. And I know my parents would like to meet the woman who raised you."

With a deep breath, Jimmy agreed, and the next morning, he brought Fayteen, along with her parents, Charles and Caroline, to visit Nell in the small room she now occupied on the saloon's second floor. As they stepped inside, Nell rose from her chair, her face lighting up with a tentative smile as she saw them enter.

Fayteen spoke softly, guiding her parents forward. "Mama, Papa, this is Nell, Jimmy's mother."

Caroline stepped forward, her own eyes filled with warmth and understanding. "It's a pleasure to meet you, Nell. Fayteen's told us so much about you. I can see where Jimmy gets his strength from."

Nell smiled, a faint blush coloring her cheeks. "Thank you, ma'am. I'm mighty proud of the man he's become. And I reckon it's good to finally meet the parents of the young woman he loves so much."

Charles nodded, extending a hand to her. "It's a pleasure, Nell. I can see that you and Jimmy are cut from the same cloth. You've both got a resilience about you—something rare and admirable."

As they spoke, Nell's gaze softened, and she turned to Jimmy. "I can't help but think of your father, Jimmy. He'd be proud to see the life you've built here, the love you've found."

Jimmy stiffened slightly, his face clouding. "I've wondered about him, Ma. Wondered what drove him away all those years ago."

Nell sighed, her voice trembling with emotion. "Your father... he was a complicated man. He wanted more than what we had, and he thought that leaving would be the best way to find it. I don't know where he ended up, but I know he loved you in his own way. I just wish I could have given you the family you deserved."

Fayteen placed a gentle hand on Nell's shoulder, a look of empathy in her eyes. "You're here now, Nell, and that's what matters. We're building a family together, all of us. And I know that whatever struggles lay in the past, we can face the future as one."

Jimmy wrapped an arm around Fayteen, a smile touching his lips as he glanced at his mother. "You're right. We've got a future to build, and I'm grateful to have you all by my side."

As the conversation shifted to lighter topics, they spoke of the upcoming wedding, the details of the ceremony, and the excitement that filled the air. But as the day drew to a close, a dark shadow loomed over Golden Valley.

***

The night before the wedding, the town seemed unusually quiet. The saloon was empty, with the usual laughter and music replaced by the soft crackling of the fire in the hearth. Fayteen was finishing some final touches on the decorations with the help of her mother, while Jimmy and Charles made plans for the ceremony. The air was calm, almost too calm, as if the town itself was holding its breath.

Then, suddenly, there was a faint smell of smoke. Jimmy paused, his brow furrowing as he sniffed the air. "Do you smell that?"

Fayteen's face fell, her eyes widening with alarm. "Jimmy, what is it?"

He ran to the back of the saloon, where the scent was stronger, a thin plume of smoke curling up from the small outhouse attached to the back of the property. The old structure, which hadn't been used much since the indoor latrines had been installed, was ablaze, flames licking up the sides and threatening to spread to the main building.

Jimmy's voice rang out, commanding and urgent. "Fire! There's a fire out back! We need water—quickly!"

Henry and Gideon, who were nearby, heard the call and rushed over. They quickly formed a line, passing buckets of water from the nearby well. Other townsfolk gathered, adding their strength to the effort, each one determined to protect The Golden Nugget from harm.

Gideon splashed a bucketful of water against the flames, his face set with grim determination. "Looks like Langston's men were here, after all. Thought they could scare us by settin' this ol' shack on fire."

Caleb, the telegraph operator, worked beside him, grabbing bucket after bucket. "Let's show 'em that this town stands together. If they think a bit of fire's gonna make us back down, they're in for a surprise."

Ahanu appeared, moving swiftly to join the line. He grabbed a large blanket and, with Jimmy's help, began beating back the flames, the thick smoke swirling around them as they worked. The fire hissed and sputtered, struggling against the steady assault of water and effort, until finally, with a last cloud of steam, it died out.

A cheer rose from the group, relief and satisfaction evident on every face as they surveyed the damage. The outhouse was charred, a blackened shell, but the flames had not reached the saloon itself. The Golden Nugget remained untouched, a testament to the strength and unity of Golden Valley's people.

Jimmy exhaled, brushing soot from his hands. He turned to the gathered townsfolk, a grateful smile breaking across his face. "Thank you, everyone. Without you, we might've lost more than an old shed. I don't know who's responsible, but I reckon they'll think twice before tryin' this again."

Henry clapped him on the shoulder, a glint of pride in his eyes. "We'll keep our eyes open, Jimmy. This town's got your back."

As the townsfolk drifted back to their homes, Fayteen ran to Jimmy, wrapping her arms around him. "Thank heavens you caught it in time," she said, her voice thick with emotion. "I was so afraid..."

He held her close, resting his cheek against her hair. "It's alright, Fayteen. The saloon's safe, and thanks to everyone, the fire didn't spread. We'll rebuild that shack if we need to, but nothin' is gonna stop us from havin' the weddin' tomorrow."

Charles stepped forward, placing a reassuring hand on Jimmy's shoulder. "You've built somethin' special here, Jimmy.

And it's clear that this town stands with you. We'll be ready if Langston tries somethin' like this again."

Fayteen's mother, Caroline, glanced at the smoldering ruins of the outhouse, a shiver running down her spine. "Whoever did this doesn't know the kind of people they're dealin' with. Golden Valley won't be easily cowed."

Jimmy, Fayteen, and their friends assessed the damage. The small outhouse was beyond repair, but its loss was minimal compared to what might have happened had the fire reached the saloon. They worked quickly to clear the debris, sweeping away the ashes as they prepared to move forward.

Standing together, Fayteen looked up at Jimmy, her eyes bright with determination. "No matter what happens, we're goin' to get married tomorrow. This fire won't scare us off."

Jimmy smiled, wrapping an arm around her. "You're right. Tomorrow, we'll celebrate, and we'll show everyone that Golden Valley is stronger than any threat."

And as they prepared for their wedding, surrounded by the unwavering support of their community, they knew that their love—and their town—would endure, their strength forged in the flames that could not consume them.

27

Golden Valley Unites

The day of the wedding dawned clear and bright, the golden sunlight casting a warm glow over the entire town of Golden Valley. The townsfolk had been up early, bustling about as they prepared for the biggest celebration the town had ever seen. Long tables stretched across the square outside The Golden Nugget, covered in bright checkered cloths, decorated with freshly picked wildflowers from the fields surrounding the town. A banquet had been laid out, brimming with roasted meats, fresh bread, baked pies, and, of course, the centerpiece—a beautifully crafted wedding cake made by Hattie and Lou at the café, adorned with fresh flowers and cream.

In her room, Fayteen stood before a tall mirror, staring at her reflection with a sense of awe. She wore an off-the-shoulder white gown that Caroline, Cora, and Eliza had helped her into. The delicate lace skimmed along her collarbone and trailed down her arms. The skirt flowed around her in soft waves, each movement whispering with an ethereal grace. Her hair was woven with sprigs of lavender and small white flowers, cascading over her shoulders in gentle waves. She looked like something out of a dream, and as she stared at herself, she felt an unexpected surge of emotion well up in her chest.

Her mother, Caroline, stepped back, dabbing at her eyes with a handkerchief. "Oh, Fayteen," she whispered, her voice thick with emotion. "You're the most beautiful bride I've ever seen."

Fayteen's cheeks flushed, and she took her mother's hands, pulling her close for a hug. "Thank you, Mama. I couldn't have done this without you. It means the world to me that you're here today."

Just then, Nell entered the room, her eyes filling with tears as she took in Fayteen's appearance. She reached out, clasping Fayteen's hands. "You look like an angel, Fayteen. Jimmy is a lucky man to be marrying such a wonderful woman. I know you're goin' to make him the happiest man alive."

A soft knock sounded at the door, and Charles stepped inside, his gaze softening as he looked at his daughter. He moved forward, cupping her face in his hands, his eyes glistening with pride and a touch of sadness. "My little girl," he murmured, his voice cracking. "You've grown into a beautiful woman. I couldn't be prouder of you, Fayteen."

Fayteen's heart swelled, and she wrapped her arms around him, holding him tightly. "Thank you, Papa. I love you."

The moment felt suspended in time, as if the world around them had slowed, and Fayteen savored every second, every glance, every embrace. This was her family, and on this day, they had come together to celebrate not only her marriage but also the unbreakable bonds that held them all together.

The ceremony was held in the small church at the center of Golden Valley. Reverend Thornton stood at the front of the modest but beautifully adorned space, with wildflowers placed carefully along the aisle and the altar, creating a scene of rustic charm and simplicity. As the church bells rang, Fayteen, with her father by her side, stepped through the doors.

The gathered crowd let out a collective gasp. She walked down the aisle with her father, each step echoing softly against the wooden boards beneath her feet. Her heart pounded in her chest, but as she raised her eyes, she saw Jimmy waiting for her at the end of the aisle, his expression one of pure, unfiltered love.

Jimmy stood tall in a finely tailored dark grey suit, his broad shoulders filling it out with ease. His hair was neatly combed, but a few strands fell loose, giving him that familiar, rugged charm that made her heart flutter. His eyes were locked onto hers, a warmth and depth in his gaze that sent a thrill through her.

As Fayteen reached the end of the aisle, Charles placed her hand in Jimmy's, his voice barely a whisper as he addressed his soon-to-be son-in-law. "Take care of her, Jimmy. She's more precious than anything in this world."

Jimmy nodded, his grip firm as he took Fayteen's hand. "You have my word, sir. I'll cherish her all the days of my life."

Reverend Thornton stepped forward, his voice resonant and warm as he began the ceremony. He spoke of love and loyalty, of faith and unity, reminding everyone gathered that marriage was a promise, a commitment to stand by one another through all of life's joys and sorrows.

As they exchanged vows, Jimmy's voice trembled, his words filled with raw emotion. "Fayteen, you've shown me a love I never knew was possible. I promise to stand by you, to protect you, and to love you with all my heart. You are my light, my reason, my forever."

Fayteen's eyes filled with tears, her voice soft but steady as she responded. "Jimmy, you are my home, my heart, my everything. I promise to love you fiercely, to stand by you in all things, and to build a life filled with joy, laughter, and love."

Reverend Thornton's smile widened as he raised his hands. "By the power vested in me, I now pronounce you husband and wife. Jimmy, you may kiss your bride."

Jimmy leaned forward, his hand gently tilting her chin as he pressed his lips to hers. The world seemed to fall away, the crowd's cheers fading into the background as they lost themselves in the moment. They had shared so much, overcome so many challenges, and now they stood together as one, bound by a love that was as fierce as it was enduring.

The celebration that followed was nothing short of magical. After the ceremony, the banquet tables stretched out under the open sky, where the townsfolk gathered to feast on roasted meats, fresh bread, pies, and the grand wedding cake. The air was filled with laughter, and the smell of delicious food, mingled with the sweet scent of wildflowers.

As the evening descended, the guests moved inside The Golden Nugget for dancing and more finger foods. The band played lively tunes as Jimmy and Fayteen twirled around the dance floor. Their steps were in perfect harmony as they moved together, their eyes never leaving each other.

Henry proposed a toast, his voice booming as he raised his glass. "To Jimmy and Fayteen! May your love be as strong as the mountains and as endless as the sky!"

The crowd cheered, lifting their glasses in unison, and Fayteen felt her heart swell with gratitude. She glanced at Jimmy, his eyes reflecting the same sense of awe and wonder that she felt. This was their life, their love, and it was surrounded by a community that stood with them, supporting them in every way.

As the moon rose, casting a warm glow over the town, Jimmy led Fayteen toward the front of the saloon. They stood together at the entrance, watching as the townsfolk gathered their belongings, bidding them goodnight with words of blessing and joy. Slowly, the town grew quiet, leaving them alone beneath the stars.

* * *

In the privacy of their quarters, Jimmy took Fayteen's hands, guiding her gently to the center of the room. He gazed at her, his eyes filled with love and a hint of nervousness. "I'll be honest, Fayteen. I've never done this before. I don't know much, but I know I want it to be perfect for you."

Fayteen smiled, her heart fluttering as she brushed her hand along his cheek. "Me neither, Jimmy. But I reckon we'll figure it out together. We've got all the time in the world."

They stood there, looking at each other, their smiles shy but filled with anticipation. Slowly, they began to undress, their movements careful and tender, each touch sending a thrill through their bodies. They laughed softly, fumbling with buttons and ties, the sound of their laughter mingling with the gentle crackling of the fire.

As they lay together, exploring each other with a sense of wonder, they shared whispered words and quiet laughter, their hands tracing gentle paths across each other's skin. There was no rush, only the soft, steady beat of their hearts, each moment a testament to the love they had found, the life they were building.

They took turns leading, guiding one another with tenderness and patience, their touches both hesitant and bold, discovering new depths of intimacy with each caress. They giggled at their awkwardness, reveling in the freedom to be themselves, to embrace this new chapter with open hearts and unguarded souls.

When at last they lay entwined, their breathing soft and steady, Fayteen rested her head against Jimmy's chest, her eyes drifting closed as a sense of profound peace washed over her. She felt his arms tighten around her, his lips pressing a gentle kiss to her forehead.

"Thank you, Fayteen," he whispered, his voice filled with emotion. "For everything. For this life, this love. You're my heart, my soul, my forever."

She smiled, a tear slipping down her cheek as she held him close. "And you're mine, Jimmy. I never thought I'd find someone like you, someone who makes me feel so complete."

As they drifted off to sleep, the room was filled with the warmth of their love, a glow that seemed to light the very air around them. And as they lay together, wrapped in each other's arms, they knew that this was only the beginning of a lifetime of shared dreams, of quiet moments, and of a love that would last forever.

28

The Final Confrontation

The days following the wedding were a blur of happiness for Jimmy and Fayteen. They had planned a honeymoon, but decided to wait until Fayteen's parents, Caroline and Charles, returned to Kansas. The Everharts had found comfort in Golden Valley, enjoying the peace of seeing their daughter thriving and happy.

One afternoon, Fayteen and her parents were sitting together in the saloon, reminiscing over stories from her childhood. Jimmy was in the back with Gideon, inspecting some of the recent renovations. Suddenly, the warm laughter and gentle hum of the room were interrupted by heavy footsteps and a cold, familiar voice.

"Well, well, if it isn't the happy family," the voice sneered.

Fayteen looked up, her blood running cold as she locked eyes with Silas Thornfield. He stood just inside the doorway, his face twisted in a menacing grin, his clothes dusty and disheveled. Though years had worn him down, his presence was just as threatening as ever.

Charles's face turned pale, and Caroline's hand flew to her mouth, her expression a mixture of shock and rage. "Silas Thornfield..." she breathed, horror dawning on her face. She remembered him all too well from her many visits to the bank and the evenings he had spent in their home, dining as a family friend.

Silas's gaze shifted to Caroline, and his lips curled into a smirk. "Ah, Mrs. Everhart," he said, his tone mocking. "It's been too long. I trust you've been well?"

Caroline took a step forward, her voice filled with anger and disbelief. "How dare you show your face here, Silas? You betrayed our trust and hurt our daughter, and you walk in here as if you've done nothing wrong!"

Charles's face darkened, and he took a protective stance beside Fayteen. "You're not welcome here, Thornfield," he said, his voice deadly calm. "You've done enough damage, and we're not about to let you hurt her again."

Silas laughed, his eyes flashing with a sick sort of amusement. "Oh, come on, Charles. I just wanted to pay my respects. After all, your little girl's done well for herself, hasn't she?"

Charles clenched his fists, anger radiating off him. "You vile coward," he snarled. "You've ruined lives, and you think you can waltz in here as if you own the place?"

Before anyone could react, Charles's fist shot out, landing squarely on Silas's jaw and sending him staggering back. Silas straightened, his face twisted with rage, but before he could retaliate, Jimmy appeared, his eyes blazing.

In one fluid motion, Jimmy drew his gun, leveling it at Silas with a steady hand. "Not another word, Thornfield," he said, his voice calm but filled with deadly intent. "I'd suggest you start walkin' now, because I've got every reason to end this right here."

Silas's bravado faltered, and he raised his hands slightly, sneering but taking a cautious step back. "Big man, aren't you, Jimmy? You think you can scare me with that gun?"

Jimmy took a step closer, his expression unyielding. "This isn't about scarin' you. This is about makin' sure you understand that if you ever come near Fayteen again, I won't hesitate. You're finished, Thornfield. You're nothin' but a stain on her past, and I won't let you taint her future."

Just then, Marshall Clayton stepped through the doors, his eyes narrowing as he took in the scene. "What's goin' on here, Jimmy?"

Jimmy didn't lower the gun, but his gaze shifted to the marshal. "Marshall, this is Silas Thornfield. He's the man who hurt Fayteen, back in Kansas. He's got no business bein' here, and he sure as hell doesn't deserve to walk free."

The marshal's face hardened as he looked at Silas. "Thornfield, I think it's time for you to come with me. You've got some questions to answer, and if what I'm hearin' is true, we'll be takin' you straight to the city for a trial. There's a jail cell there with your name on it."

Silas sneered, his eyes flashing with desperation. "You can't do this! I've got rights. This is a setup!"

Jimmy lowered the gun slightly, his expression unyielding. "Oh, you've got rights, alright. But they won't protect you from the law, and they sure won't protect you from the truth. Your reputation's finished, Thornfield. By the time this reaches court, the world will know exactly what kind of man you are. And Fayteen won't need to waste another second on you."

The marshal moved forward, pulling a set of handcuffs from his belt. He grabbed Silas's arms, locking the cuffs around his wrists with a sharp click. "You're under arrest, Thornfield. And I'd suggest you keep quiet on the way to the jail. I reckon you've done enough talkin' for a lifetime."

Charles stepped forward, his eyes blazing as he looked Silas in the eye. "You're goin' to pay for what you did to my daughter, Thornfield. You took somethin' precious from our family, and we're not goin' to let you get away with it."

Silas struggled against the cuffs, his face twisted in fury. "This isn't over, Charles! I'll ruin you all, you hear me? I'll—"

The marshal cut him off, dragging him toward the door. "That's enough outta you. I'll be takin' him back to the city," he said to Jimmy and Charles, nodding respectfully. "There, he'll face trial, and I'll make sure his reputation is as good as gone. He won't have any chance to harm anyone else."

Fayteen felt a wave of relief wash over her as she watched Silas being hauled away, his threats fading into the distance. She turned to Jimmy, who was still gripping the gun, his expression softening as he looked at her.

"It's over," he said, his voice filled with quiet conviction. "He won't be comin' back, and you're finally free of him."

She moved into his arms, her head resting against his chest as she let out a shuddering breath. "Thank you, Jimmy. Thank you for standin' by me, for protectin' me. I couldn't have faced him without you."

Charles placed a hand on Jimmy's shoulder, gratitude and admiration in his gaze. "You've done more for my daughter than I could ever repay, Jimmy. You've given her a new life, a safe one. I'm proud to call you my son-in-law."

Jimmy nodded, his voice steady. "I'll always be here for her, Mr. Everhart. And for you and Mrs. Everhart, too. This is our family now, and I won't let anyone threaten it."

Charles looked at Jimmy, "Son, please call us Charles and Caroline. You're family now." Jimmy nodded his head and smiled.

Caroline stepped forward, embracing Fayteen with tears in her eyes. "I'm so sorry, Fayteen. We should have believed you from the start. But I'm so proud of you—of the strength you've shown, and the life you've built here."

Fayteen hugged her mother tightly, her voice soft. "We're together now, Mama. That's all that matters. Silas is gone, and he's not comin' back. We can finally put this behind us."

They spent the rest of the afternoon together, the weight of the confrontation slowly giving way to a sense of peace. As evening fell, Jimmy and Fayteen took a quiet walk through the town, reflecting on the events of the day. They spoke of the future, of their dreams, and of the life they were building together, free from the shadows of the past.

Jimmy paused, looking down at Fayteen with a tenderness that filled her heart. "You've overcome so much, Fayteen. I'm honored to stand beside you, to be part of this life with you."

She smiled, reaching for his hand. "Thank you, Jimmy. For protectin' me, for givin' me a reason to believe in a better future. I don't think I could have faced him without you."

They shared a quiet embrace, the stars beginning to twinkle above them. The road ahead stretched before them, filled with hope and promise. And as they walked back to The Golden Nugget, hand in hand, they knew that their love—and the strength they shared—was the foundation of a new chapter, one free from the pain of the past, and filled with the possibilities of all that lay ahead.

29

Dreams In The Making

With Silas Thornfield out of their lives for good, Fayteen and Jimmy could finally breathe deeply, knowing that they were free from his shadow. Now, with the dust settling in Golden Valley, they were ready to set off on a honeymoon—a journey that would take them beyond anything either of them had ever imagined.

One morning, as they sat together over breakfast, Jimmy laid a newspaper on the table in front of Fayteen. She looked up at him with a curious smile, her eyes lighting up as she saw the words Steamship to Europe in bold print.

"Jimmy," she gasped, her hand flying to her mouth, "are you serious?"

He nodded, a grin spreading across his face. "I am. I thought it'd be the perfect way for us to start our lives together—seein' the world, experiencin' places we've only heard about. And if you're up for it, I'd like to take you to Paris."

Fayteen's eyes widened, her breath catching in her throat. "Paris? I'd never dreamed..." She reached for his hand, squeezing it tightly. "Jimmy, that's beyond anything I ever imagined. I'd love it."

With the decision made, they began to plan the journey. It would take nearly two weeks by steamship to reach Europe, but the adventure and the romance of the journey only added to the excitement. They made arrangements for a ship departing from New York, which meant they'd first travel there by train, allowing the couple to see even more of the world along the way.

The townsfolk were thrilled for them, gathering to see them off with well-wishes and gifts. Hattie and Lou made them a basket of travel-friendly treats, and Cora presented them with a hand-bound journal, encouraging them to write down their adventures along the way.

As they bid farewell to their friends and family, Fayteen's parents held her close, tears of joy in their eyes. "We're so happy for you, my dear," Caroline said, holding Fayteen's hands. "You deserve every happiness, and we know Jimmy will make sure you have it."

Charles hugged Jimmy, his voice warm with gratitude. "Thank you for takin' such good care of our girl, Jimmy. And for bringin' such happiness into her life. I know you'll make wonderful memories on this journey."

Jimmy smiled, giving Charles a firm handshake. "I promise, sir. I'll do everything I can to make her happy. Thank you for trustin' me with her heart."

With a final wave, Jimmy and Fayteen said their bittersweet goodbyes to her parents, knowing that by the time they returned from their Parisian honeymoon, Charles and Caroline would have already made their way back to Hays, Kansas. Fayteen felt a pang of sadness but consoled herself with the thought that it wouldn't be too long before they were reunited. She took comfort in knowing they'd see each other again soon, and the next visit would be filled with even more stories to share.

They arrived in New York with time to spare before boarding the steamship bound for France. The city's bustling streets and towering buildings were a marvel to Jimmy, who had never seen anything so grand. But the real wonder awaited them aboard the steamship—a vessel so vast that they could hardly believe their eyes.

As the ship set sail, Jimmy and Fayteen stood on the deck, watching the coastline fade into the distance, their hearts full of excitement and anticipation. They spent their days exploring the ship, dining in elegant salons, and taking in the beauty of the open sea. Every night, they would return to their cozy cabin, where they would talk about their dreams, their plans, and the life they wanted to build together. And of course, enjoy each other thoroughly.

The streets of Paris were unlike anything Jimmy and Fayteen had ever seen. As they strolled hand-in-hand through the wide boulevards newly built by Baron Haussmann, they marveled at the grandeur of the architecture. The elegant Parisian buildings, with their wrought-iron balconies and large windows, towered above them, casting soft shadows on the cobbled streets below.

At the Louvre Museum, they wandered through galleries filled with masterpieces by da Vinci, Michelangelo, and Raphael. Fayteen's breath caught as she stood before "The Mona Lisa," marveling at the enigmatic smile of the woman in the painting. Jimmy, though less versed in art, couldn't help but be drawn to Fayteen's enthusiasm and passion as she explained the importance of each work of art they saw.

After their time in the Louvre, they ventured to Notre-Dame Cathedral, its Gothic spires soaring into the sky. Inside, the light filtered through the stained-glass windows, casting rainbow hues on the stone floor. Fayteen, raised in a religious household, lit a candle for the blessings they had received. Jimmy, too, felt a deep sense of reverence, though it was the awe of the craftsmanship that moved him most. They stood in silent prayer, hands clasped together, feeling the sacred energy of the place.

One warm afternoon, they decided to take a boat ride along the Seine River, which cut through the heart of Paris. As they glided gently along the water, they passed under picturesque bridges, each one an architectural marvel, and saw the city's most iconic landmarks. With her head resting on Jimmy's shoulder, Fayteen pointed out the Palais de Justice and Sainte-Chapelle. The gentle rocking of the boat, the cool breeze on their faces, and the sight of Paris unfolding around them felt almost magical. The river seemed to whisper secrets of the city's history, and for a moment, it was just the two of them, surrounded by beauty and love.

After their river tour, they spent an afternoon lounging in one of the charming Parisian cafés that lined the streets.

Seated at a small round table outside Café de la Paix, they sipped on cups of hot chocolate—rich, velvety, and like nothing they'd ever tasted back home in Golden Valley. Around them, Parisians bustled by in the latest fashions, and Fayteen was entranced by the elegance of Parisian women in their tailored dresses and wide-brimmed hats.

Jimmy, ever the pragmatist, leaned back in his chair, surveying the bustling Parisian café. "I reckon we'll need to build ourselves somethin' like this back home. Maybe serve evening meals at The Golden Nugget. People like to gather, and I've been thinkin'—it's more than just the drink. It's community."

Fayteen chuckled, giving him a playful look. "Always thinkin' of the next step, aren't you?"

He grinned, nodding toward the lively tables around them. "We've talked about bringin' a chef into the saloon for a while now. After seein' how folks come together here in Paris, it's settled—we'll do it. We won't compete with Lou and Hattie—they've got the café crowd well handled. But supper, now that's a different story. Evenin' meals, with a proper chef. We could offer something new, something that'd bring folks in after a long day's work, or when they're lookin' for somethin' special."

Fayteen's eyes lit up. "That's perfect. We could create an atmosphere, maybe with a little music, a good meal... a place where people can relax."

Jimmy nodded, already picturing it. "Exactly. They come for a meal, stay for the company. It's somethin' we could do that'd make The Golden Nugget more than just a saloon."

He grinned, but his smile faded slightly as he gazed at her, his expression softening. "Just thinkin' of how I'll never have enough time to love you the way I want."

She reached across the table, gently caressing his hand. "You've got all the time in the world, Jimmy. Right here, right now."

Jimmy surprised Fayteen with tickets to the Opera, where they experienced a performance in the newly built Palais Garnier. The lavish interior, with its gold detailing, velvet seats, and grand chandelier, took their breath away. They watched in awe as the performers sang with such emotion that it seemed to reach deep into their souls. During the intermission, they mingled with Paris's elite, though Jimmy, always humble, remarked he preferred the simplicity of their Golden Valley saloon to such extravagance.

Later that night, after an evening filled with the beauty of music and the city, they returned to their small but charming hotel in the Marais district. Their room had large French windows that overlooked the bustling street below, the sounds of Paris faint and soothing.

Jimmy kissed her softly as they stood by the window, their silhouettes framed by the moonlight streaming in. "I never imagined a place like this," he murmured against her lips. "But I never imagined you, either."

Fayteen smiled, her hands slipping into his hair as she kissed him back, their kisses growing deeper, more urgent. "Paris is beautiful," she whispered, "but it's only because I'm here with you."

They moved slowly to the bed, the soft sheets rustling beneath them as they undressed each other, their movements unhurried, savoring the moment. There was an intimacy between them now that ran deeper than ever before. Their hands explored each other's bodies, tender and full of affection. The flickering light from the gas lamps outside cast a warm glow across the room, bathing them in golden hues.

They made love slowly, gently, their breathing becoming one as they whispered each other's names. It was a night filled with passion and love, the magic of Paris weaving itself into their every touch. The city, the romance, and the love they shared—it all came together in that moment, a perfect union.

The next morning, as the sun rose over the city, they visited Montmartre. At the top of the hill, they reached the Basilica of the Sacred Heart (Sacré-Cœur), where the view of the city stretched out before them. They sat together on the steps, watching as the city woke up. Fayteen rested her head on Jimmy's shoulder, and in that quiet moment, they both knew that the memories they were creating in Paris would last a lifetime.

Jimmy smiled, pulling her close. "So, what do you think? Should we come back to Paris someday?"

Fayteen chuckled. "I reckon we've got plenty to see back home first, but yeah, Jimmy... someday."

They sat there in silence, holding each other as the city of Paris stretched before them, filled with love, history, and the promise of adventures yet to come.

***

When they returned to Golden Valley, they were welcomed back with open arms. The townsfolk had been busy in their absence, preparing a small celebration to mark their return. But as Jimmy and Fayteen settled back into their routines, they found their thoughts turning to the future—to the home they would build and the life they would create.

One afternoon, as they sat on the porch of The Golden Nugget, Jimmy unrolled a set of plans he had drawn up with the help of a local carpenter. It was a blueprint for a large, two-story home with five bedrooms, spacious enough to grow with their family and to host friends and relatives whenever they came to visit.

Fayteen traced her fingers over the lines of the drawing, a smile spreading across her face. "It's beautiful, Jimmy. You've thought of everything—a big kitchen, a parlor, even a library. And the nursery... it's perfect."

Jimmy wrapped an arm around her, his voice filled with pride. "This is the home I want to build for us, Fayteen. A place where we can make new memories, where we can welcome the family we've dreamed of. I want every part of it to reflect the life we're buildin' together."

They decided to build on the plot of land just outside town, a piece Jimmy had purchased for Fayteen shortly before their wedding. It was the perfect spot for their new venture, and Jimmy knew exactly who to call for the job—Jack Monroe, an old friend from his mining days. Jack was renowned for his craftsmanship and integrity, having left the mines years ago to start his own successful construction business. When Jimmy reached out to him, Jack was eager to take on the project.

There was just one condition: Jimmy insisted that Eli, the town's master carpenter, handle the carpentry work. Jack, knowing about Eli's skill, readily agreed, confident that the two of them would build something truly special. With the plans settled, the project was ready to move forward.

Within a week, Jack arrived in Golden Valley with a crew of skilled workers, ready to begin the construction. He greeted Jimmy with a hearty handshake and a laugh. "Jimmy Hawthorne, you old dog! I'd heard you'd made somethin' of yourself, but I didn't expect this. A saloon, a town, and now a home! You've done well for yourself."

Jimmy grinned, clapping Jack on the back. "It's good to see you, Jack. And I'm glad you're here to help me build this place. We've got big plans for it."

Jack looked over the blueprints, nodding with approval. "You've got a good eye, Jimmy. This'll be a fine home. And with the wood and supplies you've got here, we'll make it somethin' special."

The crew wasted no time in getting to work, clearing the land and laying the foundation. Fayteen loved watching the progress, marveling at the skill and precision of the workers as they brought her dream home to life. She and Jimmy spent hours discussing every detail, from the type of wood to be used for the floors to the color of the walls.

Together, they chose cedar for the framework, a nod to the trees that had surrounded Jimmy in his youth. For the exterior, they selected stone and timber, blending rustic charm with elegant craftsmanship. The home would have wide windows to let in the light and a wraparound porch where they could sit in the evenings, watching the sun set over the hills.

The townsfolk watched the construction with keen interest, excited to see their beloved couple build something so lasting. Hattie, Lou, and Cora stopped by often, offering suggestions and bringing treats for the crew.

As the foundation took shape, Jimmy and Fayteen stood together, hand-in-hand, watching the workers lay the stones that would form the base of their home. They knew it would be a long process, but they were ready for it, excited to build something that would stand the test of time, a testament to their love and the life they had chosen together.

30

Realities Of Frontier Life

The Golden Nugget was buzzing with life, as it often was on a Saturday night. The air was filled with laughter, music, and the clinking of glasses, a joyful blend of sound that spilled out into the streets of Golden Valley. Inside, the dance troupe took turns on stage, each woman bringing her own style and charm, their performances setting the crowd ablaze with excitement.

Lily Mae, though not performing tonight, sat off to the side with Ethan McGraw, the young miner who had been courting her for the past month. She wore a soft smile, her hand resting on his as they spoke in quiet tones, lost in their own little world.

"It's a shame you can't dance tonight, Lily Mae," Ethan said, his eyes warm with admiration. "I'd love to see you up there again. You light up the whole room."

Lily Mae blushed, glancing down with a shy smile. "Well, maybe next time. I'm not performin' tonight, but I wouldn't mind dancin' with you, just the two of us, sometime soon."

Ethan grinned, squeezing her hand. "I'd like that. Real soon." They shared a quiet laugh, their connection clear to anyone who glanced their way, and for a moment, the noise of the saloon faded into the background as they focused on each other.

Nearby, Ruby was on stage, her vibrant red dress swirling around her as she performed a lively dance with Belle and Anna. Their movements were graceful and synchronized, the energy between them palpable as they twirled and spun, the crowd cheering them on. But as the dance came to an end, Ruby noticed a familiar patron watching her with a glint in his eye that made her uneasy. She brushed it off, smiling politely as she moved to the bar to catch her breath.

Josie, who only occasionally entertained men in the saloon, sat at the bar sipping a glass of water. She was different from the other women—while some enjoyed the dance and entertainment as their full-time profession, Josie kept a lower profile. She rarely entertained men, and when she did, it was always on her own terms. Despite her quiet demeanor, she had a steel resolve that Fayteen admired.

Fayteen had noticed the respect the girls held for Josie, especially since her choices were clear—she wouldn't take any man unless she wanted to. Fayteen saw Josie's independence as both a source of strength and a quiet rebellion against the expectations placed on women like her. It was something she wanted to support as Josie found her way within the tight-knit family of The Golden Nugget.

Later that evening, Fayteen found herself in Jimmy's office, curiosity and concern etched on her face. She had been meaning to ask him something that had been on her mind for a while, but the right moment had only now presented itself.

"Jimmy," she began, her voice soft but steady, "I've been wonderin'...why is it alright with you for some of the girls to entertain the men here? I know it's their choice, but it just doesn't seem to match up with the kind of man you are. I know you to be kind, protective—someone with a strong sense of what's right."

Jimmy looked at her thoughtfully, leaning back in his chair as he considered his response. "I get where you're comin' from, Fayteen. And you're right—it doesn't sit easy with me sometimes. But I made a promise to myself that I'd protect these women, and part of that means respectin' their choices. They're here because they feel safe, and I've made it clear that I'll look after 'em. Some of these girls...they come from rough pasts. This is the best way they know to survive and to have some control over their lives."

Fayteen nodded, understanding dawning on her face. "You've created a place where they're respected and looked after. I can see that now. But you've also shown them that they have choices—that they're worth more than just the money they bring in. I admire that about you, Jimmy."

He smiled, leaning into her touch. "Sometimes I wonder if I'm doin' enough. If maybe I could find a way to help them move on, give 'em a chance at a different life if they want it. But for now, this is the best I can offer. And I'll protect 'em as long as they're here." This sparked an idea within Fayteen.

Their conversation was interrupted by a sudden shout from upstairs, a noise that sent a chill through Fayteen. She exchanged a glance with Jimmy, her heart pounding as he shot to his feet, his expression shifting instantly from warmth to fierce protectiveness.

Without another word, Jimmy moved swiftly through the saloon and up the stairs, Fayteen close behind him. As they reached the second floor, they could hear raised voices coming from Ruby's room. Jimmy didn't hesitate, bursting through the door to find Ruby backed against the wall, her face pale, while a burly miner loomed over her, his hand gripping her arm.

"Get your hands off her," Jimmy's voice was deadly calm, but the menace in his tone was unmistakable.

The man turned, his eyes narrowing as he faced Jimmy. "What's it to you, Hawthorne? I paid for her company tonight, and I'll take what I'm owed."

Jimmy took a step forward, his hand resting on the handle of the revolver at his hip. "You didn't pay for the right to lay a finger on her without her say-so. Now, I'm givin' you one chance to let go, or you'll be leavin' here in a way you won't soon forget."

The man hesitated, glancing from Jimmy's hand on his gun to Ruby, who was staring at him with a mixture of fear and defiance. He scowled, loosening his grip, but his expression was full of contempt.

"You think you can run this town, Hawthorne? You think these women are anything more than—"

He didn't get to finish. In one swift motion, Jimmy had him by the collar, dragging him toward the door with a strength that belied his calm demeanor. "I don't care what you think," Jimmy growled, pushing him out into the hallway. "Get out of here, and don't come back. If I see your face around here again, you'll be answerin' to me."

The man stumbled, cursing under his breath, but the cold look in Jimmy's eyes told him he was outmatched. He turned, slinking down the stairs and out of the saloon, the other patrons watching as he disappeared into the night.

Jimmy turned back to Ruby, his face softening as he approached her. "Are you alright?"

Ruby nodded, her hands trembling slightly as she pushed her hair back from her face. "Thank you, Jimmy. I thought he was gonna...well, I'm just glad you showed up when you did."

Jimmy reached out, placing a comforting hand on her shoulder. "You don't need to worry. I won't let anyone hurt you or any of the girls here. You're safe as long as you're in The Golden Nugget."

Fayteen stepped forward, wrapping an arm around Ruby, offering her a comforting smile. "You're stronger than you think, Ruby. You stood your ground, and you've got all of us here to look after you. We're a family, remember?"

Ruby managed a small smile, her shoulders relaxing as she looked from Fayteen to Jimmy. "Thank you, both of you. I couldn't ask for better people to work for—or to be friends with."

Later, as the saloon began to empty, the dancers gathered together on the stage, sharing stories and laughter as they unwound from the night. Lily Mae told them about her latest outing with Ethan, her cheeks flushed as she spoke of the simple joys they'd shared—a picnic by the river, a walk through the fields, and the quiet, unspoken promise that lingered between them.

"I think he's serious about me," she admitted, a shy smile spreading across her face. "He's different from the others. Gentle, like he's got nothin' to prove."

The women teased her good-naturedly, their voices filled with warmth as they shared in her happiness. Ruby sat beside her, smiling as she listened, her heart lightened by the laughter and camaraderie of her friends.

When the last patron had left, Jimmy approached the stage, addressing the dancers with a quiet smile. "Thank you all for another fine night. And remember, you're always safe here. If any man gives you trouble, you come to me, and I'll take care of it."

The women nodded, gratitude in their eyes as they looked at Jimmy, their respect for him evident. He was more than their employer—he was their protector, a man who had given them a home when the world had offered them little else.

Fayteen joined Jimmy as he closed up the saloon, slipping her hand into his as they stood together in the quiet. "Thank you for protectin' them, Jimmy," she said softly. "For keepin' them safe, even when it's not easy."

Jimmy smiled, pulling her close, pressing a gentle kiss to her forehead. "They deserve a place where they're respected, Fayteen. And I'll do whatever it takes to make sure they have it."

She leaned against him, looking up with a mischievous grin. "I think that's somethin' I admire about you, Mr. Hawthorne.

But don't think I haven't noticed how serious you've been lately. You're supposed to be enjoyin' married life, you know."

Jimmy chuckled, sliding his arm around her waist and leaning in close. "Oh, I intend to enjoy it plenty, Mrs. Hawthorne," he replied, his voice low. With a wink, he pressed a lingering kiss to the side of her neck, making her laugh softly as she squirmed in his embrace.

She swatted at him playfully, but he only held her tighter, landing a light slap on her backside that made her gasp, her laughter filling the quiet saloon. "Now, don't go gettin' fresh with me down here in front of all these empty chairs," she teased, trying to stifle her grin.

"Empty chairs don't care, darlin'," he replied, his blue eyes twinkling. "Besides, I'm not done with you yet." He took her hand, leading her toward the stairs.

They walked back upstairs, arm in arm, stealing kisses along the way, their laughter trailing behind them. The quiet of the night settled around them, but in each other's arms, they felt only warmth, love, and the sense that whatever lay ahead, they would face it together, side by side.

Tonight, their thoughts weren't on the responsibilities or the challenges of running The Golden Nugget. Tonight was theirs—a moment of shared joy in the life they were building, filled with laughter, love, and the promise of all that was yet to come.

31

Dreams Beyond Golden Valley

The office was dimly lit, the flickering lantern casting shadows across the walls as Jimmy and Fayteen sat close, discussing the future of the saloon and the dancers. They'd just finished another bustling night, and the energy from the evening still hummed through the walls, even as the saloon quieted in the late hours.

Jimmy's voice echoed a thought he'd previously spoken, "Sometimes I wonder if I'm doin' enough. If maybe I could find a way to help them move on, give 'em a chance at a different life if they want it. Like givin' up entertainin' the menfolk and building themselves a life that isn't based around that anymore. I know that's where they're at, Fayteen, but I want them girls to see they are so much more than that."

Fayteen's eyes lit up, and she leaned forward, a glimmer of excitement sparking within her. "Jimmy, I think you're right," she replied, her voice soft but brimming with enthusiasm. "I've been thinkin' about how well the troupe's been doin' lately. They've drawn big crowds, night after night. What if we took 'em on a tour? Not across the whole country, but maybe just around the Idaho Territory?"

Jimmy's brow furrowed slightly, caught off guard. "A tour?" he echoed, a hint of surprise in his tone. "You mean, packin' everyone up and takin' the show on the road?"

Fayteen nodded, her excitement growing as she spoke. "Yes! We could perform in other towns, bring a bit of Golden Valley to folks out there who don't get to see much entertainment. The girls could dance, and I could sing. It'd be a chance for them to feel like stars, like they're part of somethin' bigger. When I traveled with my troupe, I got to see so much. There's a kind of freedom that comes with it."

Jimmy let out a low chuckle, rubbing his hand across his jaw as he considered the idea. "It's a grand notion, I'll give you that. And I reckon they'd love it—maybe more than I'd care to admit. But..." His voice trailed off, his expression thoughtful as he weighed the implications.

Fayteen watched him carefully, sensing the conflict in his gaze. "What's worryin' you?" she asked gently, reaching out to place a reassuring hand on his arm.

He sighed, glancing down at her hand, then back up, meeting her gaze. "It's just... we'd be apart for months. And, to be honest, I don't like the thought of not seein' you for that long." He managed a smile, but the look in his eyes was serious. "We've barely had time to settle into this life we're buildin'. I don't want us to spend our first months as newlyweds apart."

Her smile softened as she leaned closer, pressing a gentle kiss to his cheek. "I feel the same way. I'd miss you somethin' fierce, Jimmy. But maybe there's a way we can make it work. What if the troupe went on their own? Antonio could lead them, and I could stay here with you, maybe sing a couple of nights a week. We could bring in a temporary pianist, someone just for the nights I perform."

Jimmy considered this, his gaze thoughtful as he mulled over the possibility. "That might be doable. Antonio's a good man, and I trust him to look after the girls. But would they be alright without you, Fayteen? You're their leader—you keep 'em together, give 'em purpose. I'm not sure if they'd feel as safe without you."

Fayteen sighed, her enthusiasm tempered by the reality of his words. "That's true. I'd hate for them to feel abandoned, especially after all we've been through together. But this could be an opportunity for them to see a bit of the world, to grow and find themselves. It doesn't have to be a long tour, maybe just a couple of months. And we could always join them for the last few performances."

Jimmy's mouth quirked into a smile, the corners of his eyes crinkling as he looked at her. "You sure know how to make a man feel torn, Fayteen," he teased, though his tone held a note of seriousness. "You've got me dreamin' about possibilities I hadn't considered. But the truth is, I've grown mighty used to seein' you every day. And I'm not sure I'd fare well with you out on the road while I'm stuck here."

She leaned in, resting her head on his shoulder. "Well, it's just an idea. Nothin's set in stone. But it could give the girls a taste of somethin' different, a chance to be part of somethin' bigger than this town. I know it's a lot to think about, but I couldn't keep it to myself—I had to tell you."

Jimmy wrapped an arm around her, pulling her close. "I appreciate that, darlin'. And I see where you're comin' from. I'll think it over, see if there's a way we can make it work without bein' apart for too long." He paused, his voice softening. "I guess what I'm sayin' is, I'd like to make you proud, to help you build somethin' that'll last. But I don't want to lose you in the process."

Fayteen smiled, her heart swelling with affection for the man who'd given her a place in his world, a place that felt more like home with each passing day. "You already make me proud, Jimmy Hawthorne. And I'm not goin' anywhere. I'm right here, by your side."

They sat together in the quiet of the office, the sounds of the saloon fading as the last of the patrons trickled out. The idea lingered between them, an unspoken possibility that held both excitement and apprehension. For now, it was just a dream, but one that seemed within reach—a chance for the dancers to step into a new world, to bring a bit of Golden Valley to the hearts of others.

Later, as they made their way upstairs, Jimmy mulled over the potential impact of the tour. He'd built The Golden Nugget into a successful business, and the troupe's performances were a key part of its charm. If they were gone, even for a couple of months, he'd have to find ways to keep the saloon lively, to ensure that folks still came in for the music, the drinks, and the sense of community he'd worked so hard to create.

He voiced his concerns to Fayteen as they climbed the stairs. "Without the troupe, the saloon's gonna feel different. Folks come here for the dances, the music—it's what keeps the place alive. If they're gone, even for a short time, we're gonna need somethin' to fill that space."

Fayteen nodded, understanding the weight of his words. "Maybe we could bring in local performers, give them a chance to step into the spotlight. Or what if we set up themed nights—something that draws folks in for the unique experience? I could sing a couple of nights a week, and we could offer different styles of music."

Jimmy smiled, a glint of admiration in his eyes. "You're full of ideas tonight, aren't you? I like it. Themed nights could work—we could do a mix of dances, maybe even invite local musicians to join us. It'll keep things fresh, and folks will know there's always somethin' new to look forward to."

They reached the third floor, and Jimmy paused, pulling her close as they stood in the hallway. "We've got a lot to think about, but I reckon we're up for it. Whatever happens, we'll make it work."

Fayteen wrapped her arms around him, resting her head against his chest. "Together, we can do anything, Jimmy. We've built somethin' special here, and it's only goin' to grow. Whether we're here, or out there, I know we'll find a way to make it work."

Jimmy kissed her forehead, then leaned down, his voice a playful murmur in her ear. "You're somethin' else, you know that? Keep talkin' like this, and I'll be ready to follow you anywhere."

She laughed softly, tilting her head up to meet his gaze. "Good. Because I'm not lettin' you out of my sight, Mr. Hawthorne."

They shared a lingering kiss, their laughter echoing down the hall as they made their way to their room. For now, the idea of the tour remained just that—an idea. But the dreams it stirred within them were real, a testament to the life they were building, the adventure they were creating together. And as they settled into the quiet of the night, they knew that whatever lay ahead, they would face it hand in hand, dreaming of all the possibilities that awaited them in the vast, wild world beyond Golden Valley.

32

A Ghost From The Past

The new house stood proudly on the edge of Golden Valley, its freshly cut timber beams and wide windows capturing the morning sunlight. Jimmy and Fayteen had spent the past several weeks watching as it took shape, slowly becoming the home they had envisioned—a symbol of the life they were building together. It was nearly finished now, with just a few final touches to add, and it brought a sense of pride and satisfaction that words couldn't express.

Jimmy stood with his arm around Fayteen, gazing at the nearly complete structure. "It's comin' along real nice, isn't it?" he murmured, a hint of pride in his voice. "Just a few more days, and we'll finally be able to move in."

Fayteen nestled against him, her smile soft. "It's more than nice, Jimmy. It feels like home already."

They shared a quiet moment, letting the breeze carry their dreams across the open field. But the peace was broken as a lone rider appeared at the edge of the property. The man dismounted, tipping his hat respectfully, urgency plain in his expression.

"Mr. Hawthorne," he greeted, his voice tentative. "I've got some news for you, sir. It's about your father... Tom Hawthorne. He's been found, just a few towns over near Twin Falls."

Jimmy's arm dropped from around Fayteen, his face a storm of emotions—surprise, anger, and disbelief mingling as he processed the man's words. "My father?" he echoed, barely able to believe it. "After all these years?"

The man nodded, sympathy softening his gaze. "Yes, sir. Apparently, he's in poor health, and they say he's been askin' for you."

Jimmy took a step back, feeling the weight of the revelation settle heavily on his shoulders. His father—the man who had left him behind so many years ago—was alive, asking for him. The memories he'd buried, memories of a young boy's abandoned hope, surfaced with painful clarity. He looked to Fayteen, her eyes filled with concern, and he felt a mixture of anger and confusion.

"I don't know what to make of this," he admitted, his voice low.

Fayteen reached out, taking his hand. "Whatever you decide, Jimmy, I'll be with you. But maybe you should go and see him, for closure if nothin' else."

Jimmy let out a long, shaky breath, memories he had tried to forget surfacing against his will. He remembered sitting by the window as a boy, waiting for his father to come back, hoping against hope that he'd see his father's silhouette on the horizon.

His grandparents had filled the void as best they could, but that emptiness had never fully healed.

He turned to Fayteen, his voice almost a whisper. "I used to sit there for hours, watchin' the road, hopin' he'd come back. But he never did. I told myself I didn't need him, that I'd make my own way without him. But a part of me's always wondered... why he left, and why I wasn't worth stayin' for."

Fayteen wrapped her arms around him, her embrace a comforting anchor. "You've carried that pain for a long time, Jimmy. Maybe it's time to find out the truth, whatever it is. You don't have to forgive him if you're not ready, but you deserve to know."

He nodded, his gaze distant, haunted by memories of the boy he had been, the man he had become. "I'll go. I don't know what I'll find, but I have to know."

As they rode back to town that evening, Jimmy's thoughts churned, and he found himself wanting to share the news with his mother. Nell had been a part of his healing, her reappearance in his life reawakening memories he had long suppressed. Later, he found her in one of the saloon's rooms, where she was resting, and he knocked softly on the door.

Nell looked up, a smile breaking over her face as she saw him. "Jimmy, my boy. Come in."

He entered, sitting beside her, and took a steadying breath. "I have some news, Ma. It's... it's about Pa. He's been found."

Her face froze, her hand reaching instinctively to clutch at her chest. "Your father? After all this time?"

Jimmy nodded, watching her expression shift from shock to sorrow, old wounds resurfacing in her eyes. "I haven't decided what I'm gonna do yet, but... I thought you should know. I wanted you to hear it from me."

Nell reached out, taking his hand. "You'll do what's right, Jimmy. I always knew that about you. And if you find it in your heart to forgive him... know that you'll find peace, too."

Jimmy nodded, squeezing her hand. Her words stayed with him as he prepared for the journey ahead, knowing that his mother understood the weight of his decision.

They returned to their third-floor quarters, Jimmy's mind still heavy with the news. He paced in the office, his thoughts racing, memories surfacing that he had long buried. Fayteen watched him, giving him space, knowing that he needed time to process.

Finally, he turned to her, a mixture of resolve and vulnerability in his eyes. "I don't want to face this alone, Fayteen. If I go, you're comin' with me."

She nodded without hesitation, stepping toward him. "Of course I am. We're a team, Jimmy. I wouldn't have it any other way."

He pulled her close, the familiar warmth of her presence calming the storm within him. "I'm not sure what I'll find, or if I'll even want to hear what he has to say. But I have to know."

She rested her head against his chest, her voice soft. "And no matter what, you'll have me right there with you. We'll face this together."

They spent the evening packing, their plans for the troupe's tour set aside, the excitement over the house dulled by the gravity of the journey ahead. Jimmy's mind was filled with memories, fragments of a childhood he had tried to forget—the sound of his father's laughter, the way he'd lift him onto his shoulders, the scent of the cedar trees where they used to walk together. He remembered the day his father had left, the empty promise that he'd be back soon, a promise that had never been fulfilled.

As they prepared to leave, Jimmy found himself slipping into a quiet reverie, lost in the fragments of his past. Fayteen joined him, wrapping her arms around him, offering a comforting presence as he reflected on the boy he had been, the man he had become, and the father he would finally confront.

The journey to Twin Falls took a few days, the landscape unfolding around them, vast and unchanging, a reminder of the distance between his past and present. They rode side by side, the silence between them filled with unspoken thoughts, the shared understanding that this journey was as much about healing as it was about finding answers.

One evening, they camped by a river, the stars stretching across the sky like a blanket of light. Jimmy sat by the fire, his gaze fixed on the flames, memories stirring within him.

"Tell me about him," Fayteen said softly, breaking the silence. "What do you remember?"

Jimmy sighed, rubbing a hand over his face. "He was a big man, strong. I remember how he'd lift me up onto his shoulders, how safe I felt up there. I used to think he was invincible, that nothin' could ever take him away. But then one day, he was just... gone."

He paused, his gaze distant as he continued. "My grandparents tried to fill the void, and they did their best. But there was always that part of me that wondered... if I'd done somethin' wrong, if I wasn't enough for him to stay. It took me years to let go of that feelin'."

Fayteen moved closer, resting a hand on his shoulder. "It wasn't your fault, Jimmy. You were just a boy."

He nodded, a flicker of pain crossing his face. "I know that now. But back then, it was hard to understand. I spent a long time tryin' to be the man he never was, buildin' a life for myself, tellin' myself I didn't need him. But seein' him now... it's stirrin' up things I thought I'd buried."

They sat in silence, the crackle of the fire filling the quiet as Jimmy grappled with the emotions that had lain dormant for so long. He knew that facing his father would bring closure, but it would also mean confronting the pain of his abandonment, the wounds that had shaped him.

As they rode into Twin Falls the next morning, Jimmy felt a knot of tension tighten in his chest. He could see the small, unassuming building where his father was staying, a place that held none of the grandeur he had imagined. He dismounted, turning to Fayteen, his gaze steady but uncertain.

"Whatever happens in there," he said, his voice low, "thank you for bein' here. I don't think I could do this alone."

She reached for his hand, her grip firm, her eyes filled with quiet strength. "You're not alone, Jimmy. We'll face this together."

Jimmy's steps were slow and heavy as he and Fayteen walked through the small hallway. The building had an air of neglect, with peeling paint on the walls and creaking floorboards beneath their feet. Each step felt like a journey back in time, and with every passing second, Jimmy felt the weight of old wounds pressing down on him, tightening his chest.

They paused outside the door, and Jimmy took a deep, steadying breath, his hand hovering just above the worn doorknob. He looked back at Fayteen, his eyes shadowed with uncertainty, anger, and a vulnerability he rarely let show.

Fayteen offered him a gentle smile, her hand resting lightly on his arm. "I'm right here," she said, her voice a soft anchor in the storm of emotions swirling within him.

He nodded, swallowing hard before finally turning the knob and stepping inside. The room was dimly lit, with only a narrow window letting in the weak morning light. And there, lying on a bed that looked as worn as the man himself, was Tom Hawthorne, Jimmy's father.

Tom was gaunt, his skin pallid, his hair graying and thin. He looked older than his years, as if life had taken more from him than he could afford to give. Jimmy felt a surge of anger, a bitter resentment rising in his throat as he took in the sight before him. This was the man who had left him behind, who had disappeared without a word, who had carved a hole in his heart that had never quite healed.

Tom looked up, his gaze cloudy but unmistakably aware. His eyes widened slightly as they met Jimmy's, recognition flashing in the depths of his weary stare. "Jimmy..." he croaked, his voice weak and raspy. "Is it really you?"

Jimmy crossed his arms, his face hard, refusing to soften. "Yeah, it's me," he replied, his tone cold, almost unfamiliar to his own ears. "Not that you'd know, seein' as how you left me all those years ago. Left me wonderin' what I'd done wrong, why I wasn't worth stickin' around for."

Tom's face twisted with something like regret, a shadow passing over his features. "I didn't... I never meant to hurt you, Jimmy. I thought I was doin' what was best. I wanted to find somethin' better for us, somethin' that would make you proud."

Jimmy's jaw clenched, his fists tightening at his sides. "You wanted to make me proud?" he repeated, his voice laced with bitterness. "By leavin' me with nothin' but questions? By abandonin' me, by lettin' me grow up without a father? You think that's what I needed?"

His father closed his eyes, a pained expression crossing his face. "I was young, Jimmy. I made mistakes. I thought I could find gold, make a fortune, and come back for you... but things didn't go as planned."

"You never came back," Jimmy shot back, the words like a wound reopened, raw and bleeding. "You never even tried. You just left me there, wonderin' what happened, wonderin' if you'd died, if you'd forgotten me, if I wasn't enough."

Fayteen moved closer, resting a comforting hand on his arm, but Jimmy barely felt it. The anger burned too brightly, the years of pain and loneliness fueling the fire that had been simmering inside him since he was a boy.

Tom's voice broke, filled with a sorrow that seemed to age him even more. "I... I know. I've carried that guilt every day. I thought about you, every single day. I imagined you growin' up, wonderin' what kind of man you'd become. I wanted to reach out, but I was ashamed. I couldn't face you, knowin' I'd failed."

Jimmy's laugh was harsh, cold. "You're right about that—you failed. You failed me, you failed yourself. You left me with nothin' but a hole where a father should've been. You think sayin' you feel guilty makes it better? You think it undoes the years I spent lookin' out that window, waitin' for you?"

He turned away, tears stinging his eyes, but he made no effort to hide them. They fell, hot and unchecked, down his cheeks, the long-buried hurt flooding to the surface.

"I left Grandma and Grandpa's place as a teenage boy, lookin' for you, Tom! I went to all the mines I could think of, but I never found ya. I lost so much of my youth, a time when I could've been doin' all kinds of things, but instead, I had to grow up and find my way." Jimmy wiped his face, gaining some composure.

"The irony is, Tom, I struck it real big early this decade just outta Boise, and now I'm helpin' build a town with the proceeds from that mine. I don't ever have to work if I don't want to, but I choose to. Maybe I oughta thank you for that. I never gave up; I kept goin', and now we've got a good thing goin' back in Golden Valley." Jimmy paused, steeling himself for what he would say next, something he knew would hit Tom with the weight of truth.

"Ma's now with us. She turned up in town one day, bedraggled and a mess, but we've got her some good folk who are helpin' her, and she's been able to tell us, in time, what happened with herself."

Tom's face registered shock, his eyes widening. "My Nell... she's with you?" he gasped, his hands trembling as a few tears trickled down his face. "Oh, how I missed her so dearly." He closed his eyes, as if remembering something precious. "Please tell her I loved her so. I never moved on from her, never got over her. Never will. She's the love of my life, son. Along with you. I know that means nothin' to you now, but it's the truth. God as my witness. I'm just glad she's found some peace now."

Jimmy felt a strange pang of sympathy watching his father crumble under the weight of his words, his own heart stirring with something almost like forgiveness. It wasn't there yet, not fully, but he could feel its roots forming, deep beneath the layers of pain.

He took a step back, looking out the window, breathing in deeply as he felt Fayteen's steady hand on his shoulder. Her presence was a balm, grounding him.

Finally, Fayteen spoke up, her tone firm but compassionate. "Mr. Hawthorne, I'm Jimmy's wife. We just got married some months back. I'm glad I finally got the chance to meet you, but I think Jimmy and I need to find some room for the night. We'll be back in the mornin'. See you then, Mr. Hawthorne."

Jimmy gave a small nod, unable to say more. He turned, his hand finding Fayteen's, and they walked toward the door together, not turning back. But as they stepped out into the hallway, Jimmy took a deep breath, a small, tentative step toward the peace he hadn't known he needed.

Inside, Tom lay back, a look of gratitude softening his worn features. He felt a weight lift, a quiet peace settling over him. He knew he might never truly deserve forgiveness, but in that moment, he found a glimmer of it in his son's eyes. And it was enough to bring him peace, even if only for a moment.

The next morning, Jimmy and Fayteen made their way back to the small building, the dawn mist still hanging in the air. The events of the previous day weighed on Jimmy, but he felt lighter now, the anger and resentment he had carried for so long finally beginning to dissolve. He didn't know exactly what he would say, but he knew forgiveness had a place in this conversation. It was time to move forward.

They reached the door to Tom's room, and Jimmy paused, taking a steadying breath before he knocked. Tom's voice, weak but welcoming, answered from inside, and Jimmy stepped through the door, Fayteen at his side.

Tom was sitting up in bed, a faint, hopeful smile breaking over his face as he saw them. "You came back," he murmured, gratitude and disbelief mixing in his gaze.

Jimmy nodded, pulling a chair close to the bed. "Yeah, I did. I had to settle some things with you."

Tom looked down, shame flickering in his expression. "I know I don't deserve your forgiveness, Jimmy. I know what I did left you with nothin' but hurt, and I'll carry that with me for the rest of my days. But I'm grateful you're here... more than I can say."

Jimmy sat quietly, studying his father, seeing the frailty and regret that had aged him well beyond his years. He let out a long breath, his voice steady but soft. "I spent a lot of years angry, wonderin' why you never came back, why I wasn't worth stayin' for. But I see now... maybe you were just as lost as I was."

Tom's brow furrowed, his hands twisting together as he fought to keep his composure. "I wanted to be there for you, Jimmy, more than anything. I wanted to make somethin' of myself, to come back with somethin' more for you and your mother. But I lost my way, and I couldn't find it back in time."

Jimmy nodded, letting the words settle in the space between them. "I needed to hear that. And I needed to say this—I forgive you, Pa. I can't hold onto the anger anymore. I've got my own life now, a family, and I don't want the weight of the past to hold me back."

Tom's face crumpled as tears began to fall, his shoulders shaking with quiet sobs. "Thank you, son. Thank you. I never thought... I never thought I'd get the chance to hear those words."

Jimmy reached over, placing a hand on his father's shoulder, feeling the weight of old wounds easing as he spoke the truth that had been buried for so long. "You're still my father, Tom. We can't change what happened, but we can find some peace with it."

Fayteen stepped forward, her touch gentle on Jimmy's arm, her presence a steadying comfort. "You've both carried this for a long time. Now's the time to let it go and move forward."

Jimmy looked around the rundown room where his father, Tom, was staying, and a wave of unease washed over him. This wasn't a place where anyone could recover or even be properly cared for. Tom needed more than this. After everything Jimmy had done for his Ma, Nell, it didn't sit right to leave his father in such a state.

Determined, Jimmy set out into Twin Falls, searching for a place where Tom could get the care he truly needed. After some time, he found a well-kept facility, a boarding house known for its attentive staff and its connection to the local doctors' clinic. It had clean rooms, reliable meals, and trained staff to help with daily care—everything Tom would need for his recovery.

Jimmy met with the owners and the local doctor to ensure everything was in order, paying in advance for Tom's lodging, meals, laundry, and medical care. It wasn't just about easing his conscience; it was about doing what was right, as he had done for his Ma. Jimmy felt a weight lift from his shoulders as he finalized the arrangements, knowing that at least now, Tom would be looked after properly.

As they rode back to Golden Valley, he thought about his mother and the journey she, too, had been on since returning.

When they arrived back at the saloon, they found Nell sitting in the parlor, a blanket over her lap, her hands still as she looked up, a tentative smile breaking across her face.

Jimmy took a seat across from her, his gaze steady. "Ma, we saw him," he said softly. "We saw Pa."

Nell's eyes widened, surprise and a flicker of fear passing over her features. "You... you saw him? He's alive?"

He nodded, reaching across to take her hand. "He's alive, Ma. He's not well, but he's holdin' on. And he... he still loves you. He asked me to tell you that. He never stopped."

Nell looked down, her hands trembling as tears filled her eyes. "After all I did... after the way I left? I thought he must hate me, thought he'd have moved on by now."

"Ma, he never moved on," Jimmy said, his voice steady. "He told me he never stopped lovin' you, that he never found anyone else. And I could see it in his eyes. He meant it."

Nell closed her eyes, a tear slipping down her cheek. She took a shuddering breath, as though the weight of her past had finally caught up to her. "All these years, I've carried the guilt of leavin' you both. I thought if I stayed, I'd ruin your lives, that the voices would come back, that I'd hurt you. I thought I was doin' what was best, but it broke me every day."

Jimmy reached over, squeezing her hand gently. "He forgives you, Ma. I can see that now. And I think... I think maybe it's time you forgave yourself too."

Nell looked up, a hesitant hope shining in her eyes. "Do you think... do you think he'd want to see me? After everything I put him through?"

Fayteen stepped in, her voice warm and reassuring. "He does, Nell. He deserves to know the truth, and you deserve the chance to say what you need to say. You've both lived with this pain for so long. Maybe it's time to put it to rest."

Nell nodded, wiping her tears away, her face resolute. "Then I'll go. I'll face him. I owe him that much, and I owe it to myself. I've hidden from my past for too long, and if he can still find it in his heart to love me, then maybe... maybe I can find a way to forgive myself."

Jimmy smiled, a flicker of pride shining in his eyes. "We'll go with you, Ma. You don't have to do this alone."

Nell gave a shaky nod, her smile filled with gratitude. "Thank you, Jimmy. And thank you, Fayteen. You've both given me the courage I never thought I'd find again. I don't know what I'll say, but I'll say what's in my heart. It's time to put the ghosts to rest."

They shared a quiet moment, the silence filled with the unspoken promise of healing and reconciliation. And as they prepared to journey back to Twin Falls, each of them knew that the past, though painful, no longer held them captive. They were moving forward, together, as a family bound by forgiveness and the strength to embrace the future.

In that moment, Jimmy felt a deep sense of peace, knowing that they had not only confronted the ghosts of their past but had also found the courage to move beyond them. With Fayteen and Nell by his side, he knew that together, they were building a life filled with resilience, love, and the quiet strength that came from facing one's deepest fears.

And as they set out, he knew that whatever lay ahead, they would face it together, bound not just by blood, but by the healing power of forgiveness.

33

Past Made Whole

Nell sat beside Tom's bed, her hands trembling slightly as she clasped them in her lap. It had been years since she'd seen his face, and though time had taken its toll on him, there were moments when she could still see the young man she'd fallen in love with—the man she'd once shared dreams with before everything changed.

Tom watched her, a mixture of wonder and sorrow in his gaze. He reached out, his hand tentative, his voice barely a whisper. "Nell, I... I never thought I'd see you again."

Nell looked down, her fingers knotting together. "I didn't think you would want to, after what I did," she replied softly. "I left you both. I thought I was protectin' you... I thought if I stayed, I'd make everything worse. The voices, the confusion... it all got so bad, and I didn't know what else to do."

Tom's face softened, a deep sadness in his eyes. "You didn't ruin anything, Nell. I would've done anything to help you if I'd known. I spent years tryin' to understand why you left, but I never stopped lovin' you."

She swallowed hard, tears pooling in her eyes. "I couldn't face it, Tom. I was so scared of what I might do... of what those voices made me think I would do. I thought that by leavin', I was sparin' you both. I've lived with that decision every day, wonderin' if I made the right choice or if I should have fought harder."

Tom's hand found hers, their fingers intertwining, their shared past binding them together even now. "Nell, you did what you thought was right, and I've carried no hate for you. Only sorrow. I lost the love of my life, and I lost my son. But I've forgiven you, Nell. I forgave you a long time ago."

She let out a shuddering breath, relief and sorrow mingling as she looked up at him, their eyes meeting. "Can you ever really forgive me, Tom? For leavin' you to raise Jimmy alone? For abandonin' our life?"

Tom nodded, his voice gentle. "You had your reasons, reasons I didn't understand then, but I understand more now. And besides, Jimmy's grown into a good man—a better man than I ever could've hoped for. He's strong, just like you, and he's found someone to share his life with. We've both made mistakes, Nell, but we still have this moment, and we still have our son."

A soft smile broke over her face, and she squeezed his hand. "You're right, Tom. We do have this moment, and for that, I'm grateful. I'm sorry for everything. I loved you then, and I love you still. Maybe in another time, in another life, we could've done things differently. But I'm thankful we can share this now, even if it's just for a little while."

Tom smiled, a flicker of the man he used to be shining through. "I'll take that, Nell. I'll take whatever time I can get."

They sat in silence, their hands entwined, the years of separation and pain finally finding a place to rest. And in that quiet moment, they both found a small measure of peace, their hearts finding a way to heal, even as the sun began to set outside.

When Jimmy and Fayteen returned to Golden Valley, a lightness filled them. They'd helped two people find a sliver of forgiveness and, in doing so, had brought a measure of healing to their own hearts. But now, something exciting awaited them.

As they neared their new home, Jimmy could see smoke curling from the chimney, a sign that the final touches had been made. The windows were clear and polished, the fresh wood gleaming in the afternoon sun, and there was a wreath hanging on the front door—a welcoming gesture that made Jimmy's heart swell.

Fayteen let out a delighted gasp, her eyes shining. "Jimmy! Look at it! It's beautiful!"

They stepped inside, the familiar scent of cedar filling the air, mingling with the faint aroma of lavender that Fayteen had insisted on using to freshen the rooms. The interior was warm and inviting, with rich wooden floors, wide windows that let in the light, and soft furnishings in shades of blue and cream.

They wandered through the rooms, their footsteps echoing slightly as they took in the details. The parlor was furnished with comfortable armchairs, a large hearth crackling with fire, and shelves lined with books and trinkets they'd collected. In the kitchen, copper pots gleamed on the walls, and a sturdy wooden table sat in the center, perfect for the meals they would share.

Fayteen laughed as she twirled around the kitchen, her joy infectious. "Oh, Jimmy, it's everything I ever dreamed of!"

Jimmy pulled her into his arms, his grin wide. "And it's all ours. We can fill it with memories, with laughter, with love. This is just the start, darlin'."

They made their way upstairs to the bedroom, where a large four-poster bed with a quilted coverlet awaited them. The room was cozy, with a window that looked out over the valley, the view stretching for miles. A copper tub sat in the corner, ready for long, luxurious baths after a day's work.

Fayteen's eyes sparkled as she ran her hand over the bed's smooth wood. "And you even got the copper tub," she said, a playful glint in her eyes.

Jimmy chuckled, leaning in close. "Only the best for my bride. And I've got a few more surprises up my sleeve, too."

He led her downstairs to a smaller room, where a beautifully crafted piano sat in the corner, a gift he'd acquired from a trader passing through town. Fayteen's mouth fell open, and she looked up at him, her eyes brimming with tears.

"Jimmy... a piano? For me?" she whispered, her hand covering her heart.

He nodded, his grin softening. "I know how much singin' means to you, Fayteen. Figured you could use this for rehearsals, for writin' new songs, for whatever your heart desires. Thought you could make this place your own, too."

She threw her arms around his neck, pulling him close, and he laughed, the sound filling the room as they held each other, swaying in the quiet. "Thank you, Jimmy. I don't know what I did to deserve you, but I'm thankful every day."

They spent the afternoon exploring every nook and cranny of their new home, each discovery bringing fresh laughter and playful moments. They found a small basket of preserves left by Ada from the mercantile, a note tucked inside wishing them happiness in their new home. In the pantry, they found a batch of cookies baked by Lou, and Fayteen laughed as she snuck one before dinner.

Later, as the sun dipped below the horizon, they settled by the fire in the parlor, sharing stories, their hands entwined as they spoke of dreams and the life they were building together. Jimmy pulled her close, his voice soft as he traced patterns along her hand. "I still can't believe this is real. I never thought I'd have this—a home, a wife, a family. Feels like a dream."

Fayteen nestled against him, her voice warm. "It's not a dream, Jimmy. It's our life, and we'll make it something to be proud of."

They shared a quiet moment, content in each other's arms, when Jimmy chuckled, a mischievous glint in his eye. "You know, I think we might need a few more chairs in the parlor. For when our family starts growin'."

Fayteen laughed, her cheeks flushing. "A family, huh? I think I'd like that, Jimmy Hawthorne."

The room fell into a comfortable silence, the crackle of the fire the only sound. Jimmy reached up, gently brushing a strand of hair away from her face, his eyes holding hers with a warmth that made her heart flutter. Slowly, he leaned in, pressing his lips to hers. Their kiss deepened, slow and tender, speaking the words they couldn't express, a reflection of the love they had nurtured through hardship and joy.

As they pulled each other closer, Jimmy's fingers moved to the laces of her dress, and Fayteen's hands found their way to the buttons of his shirt. Bit by bit, their clothes fell softly to the floor, forgotten in the warmth of the firelight. The room grew warmer, the flickering shadows casting a golden glow across their intertwined forms.

They lay together on the soft rug before the fire, wrapped in each other's arms, the quiet intimacy of their first night in their new home filling the space with a sense of peace and belonging. Their laughter was soft, mingling with whispered promises and gentle touches, each moment a step deeper into the life they were building together.

In that moment, they were more than just husband and wife—they were two souls bound by love, resilience, and the strength to face whatever lay ahead. Together, they found a world all their own, the warmth of the fire mirrored by the warmth of their embrace, a love that had been tested and had grown stronger with each challenge.

As they lay in each other's arms, drifting into the quiet of the night, they knew their journey was just beginning. The future stretched before them, vast and filled with possibilities, as boundless as the stars above.

34

Uncharted Paths

The morning sun rose over Golden Valley, bathing the newly-built Hawthorne home in a warm glow. The two-story house stood proudly at the edge of the valley, its exterior clad in rich cedar and framed by wide windows that welcomed the light. Jimmy had spent weeks collaborating with Andrew and Eli on the house, using the best materials Golden Valley could offer, and now, it was finally ready.

Wagons began arriving at dawn, each loaded with boxes, furniture, and a few surprises for the newlyweds. The dance troupe was the first to arrive, Lily Mae leading the group with her curly blonde hair bouncing as she directed the other girls. Ruby, with her striking red hair, trailed close behind, grinning as she hoisted a small chest from the back of the wagon.

"Alright, ladies!" Lily Mae called, flashing a mischievous smile at Fayteen. "We've got work to do! This ain't no time to stand around gawkin'!"

Fayteen laughed, playfully swatting at her. "Look at you, takin' charge! I knew I could count on my girls to keep things runnin' smoothly!"

Jimmy and Ahanu stood nearby, watching the bustling scene with smiles on their faces. Ahanu clapped Jimmy on the back. "Your wife has brought the whole town out to lend a hand. She has a way of rallying folks, doesn't she?"

Jimmy chuckled, crossing his arms as he took in the sight. "She sure does. I reckon Golden Valley wouldn't be the same without her."

As the townsfolk arrived, they brought gifts and supplies for the new home. Gideon and Martha Grady came with a beautifully carved rocking chair for the front porch, while Lou and Hattie from the café unloaded baskets filled with more preserves and homemade bread.

"We figured y'all could use a good supply," Lou said, setting the baskets down with a smile. "And don't worry, it's enough to last you a while!"

As the day wore on, the group carried in boxes and furniture, filling the house with memories and laughter. Fayteen guided them from room to room, marveling at how the sunlight danced across the polished wood floors and the high, open beams above.

The last item brought in was a large dining table, a gift from Reverend Thornton and the local parish. "A home needs a place to gather, a spot for sharing meals and stories," he said, his voice filled with warmth. "May this table see many happy days."

Once the moving was complete, they gathered outside at long tables set up for a community meal. Lou and Hattie had prepared a feast: roasted meats, fresh vegetables, and steaming biscuits, topped off with several pies. The townsfolk shared stories and laughter, the sounds of their voices filling the open air.

Fayteen stood, raising her glass. "To each of you, thank you for everything. Jimmy and I couldn't have done this without ya. We came to Golden Valley lookin' for a fresh start, and because of you all, we've found family and friends who mean the world to us."

Jimmy lifted his glass, echoing her sentiment. "This town's somethin' special, and y'all make it that way. Here's to Golden Valley and everyone who makes this place a home worth buildin'."

As the meal wound down, the dance troupe took to the center of the gathering, performing an impromptu routine that had everyone clapping along. Fayteen led them through lively steps, her face glowing with joy. Even a few of the townsfolk joined in, laughing as they tried to keep up with the girls' spirited moves.

Later, as the sun began to set, Fayteen took a moment to catch her breath under a large oak tree by the house. She was lost in thought when she noticed Josie standing nearby, her expression tense.

"Josie, are you alright?" Fayteen asked, concern filling her voice.

Josie shifted, wringing her hands. "Miss Fayteen... can I talk to ya? It's important."

Fayteen guided her to a bench under the tree, giving her a reassuring smile. "Of course. You know you can talk to me about anything."

Josie took a shaky breath, her voice barely above a whisper. "I went to see Dr. Harper a few days ago. I've been feelin'... different. Sick in the mornin', tired all the time. He said I'm expectin'."

Fayteen's heart went out to her, and she reached over, holding Josie's hand. "Oh, Josie. That must have come as quite a shock. But you're not alone. Dr. Harper and Eliza will help you, and I'm here for you too."

Josie's eyes filled with tears, and she nodded, her voice trembling. "I... I don't know who the father is. I've been tryin' to figure it out. I don't... entertain often, and when I do, I'm careful. I just don't understand how this happened. And I'm worried what Jimmy'll think. I know he's helped all of us girls, but..."

Fayteen gave her a gentle squeeze. "Josie, you don't need to worry about Jimmy. He's a good man, and he'll stand by you."

Together, they walked over to where Jimmy stood talking with Ahanu. He noticed Fayteen's expression and turned, his gaze shifting to Josie.

"Somethin' goin' on?" he asked, sensing the seriousness of the moment.

Fayteen nodded. "Josie has somethin' she needs to tell you."

Josie looked down, her voice barely a whisper. "I'm expectin', Jimmy. Dr. Harper confirmed it. I know this is a shock, and I'm sorry if it's disappointin' to ya..."

Jimmy's expression tightened, a flicker of frustration crossing his face. He turned away for a moment, collecting himself before speaking. "Josie, don't you go thinkin' this is on you. If anything, that fella who put you in this position should be the one answerin' for it. You don't have to carry the blame alone."

He softened, placing a hand on her shoulder. "You're part of this town, Josie, and you're part of our family. Dr. Harper and Eliza will make sure you're well cared for, and so will Fayteen and I. You focus on takin' care of yourself and that little one."

A tear slipped down Josie's cheek, and she managed a small smile. "Thank you, Jimmy. I didn't know what to expect, but I'm glad I have y'all."

Jimmy nodded, then glanced at Fayteen. "We've been blessed with a community that takes care of its own. I reckon that's what makes Golden Valley different."

As the evening settled in, Jimmy and Fayteen found themselves standing on the porch, watching the last of the day's light fade. The stars began to twinkle, casting a gentle glow over their new home.

Jimmy wrapped an arm around her waist, his voice soft. "We've built somethin' here, Fayteen. A place where folks know they're safe, where they can find support. This is exactly what we set out to do."

She leaned her head on his shoulder. "We're right where we're meant to be. But tell me, what'll happen to the third floor of the saloon now that we've moved out?"

Jimmy considered this, a thoughtful look in his eyes. "I think we'll need someone to manage things while we're here at the house. Maybe I'll find a reliable man to take over the daily runnin', someone I can trust with the girls and the business."

Fayteen nodded, intrigued. "Who do you have in mind? You'd need someone who's not only capable but respectful. The girls deserve that."

He smiled. "I'll be keepin' an eye out. Actually, come to think of it, the third-floor space can be for the new manager if they're keen. What'd ya think, darlin'?"

She laughed softly. "It's a great idea, Jimmy. You always thinkin' of ways to help. That's why I married you."

Jimmy pulled her close, brushing a kiss across her lips. "And that's why I'll keep doin' my best for you, for the girls, and for this town. Together, we'll make sure Golden Valley stays a place folks are proud to call home."

They stood there in the quiet of the evening, the warmth of their new home behind them, and the promise of the future stretching out before them. As the stars began to twinkle above, Jimmy and Fayteen turned to go inside. A cozy warmth settled over them, one that spoke of the life they were building together—a life of stability, responsibility, and care for those they had brought into their fold.

The next morning, Jimmy felt the familiar tug of duty as he headed into town to check on The Golden Nugget. Fayteen was staying back at the house to finish what Jimmy jokingly called "the last of the women's stuff"—setting up linens, choosing where the dishes would go, and arranging their pantry.

"Don't you go worryin', Jimmy Hawthorne," Fayteen had teased with a grin. "I'll make sure the house is ready by the time you're back, and I won't rearrange your whiskey collection without askin'."

He winked at her. "That's a relief. Don't want you gettin' too wild with the order of things."

As he rode into town, the saloon was bustling, and he could hear the clinking of glasses and the chatter of patrons long before he reached the doors. Inside, the girls were already busy with the morning crowd, and Ruby was wiping down tables, her red hair catching the light.

Jimmy moved through the saloon, pausing to take in the lively scene. Now that he and Fayteen had moved out, he knew it was time to bring someone else into the fold, someone who could handle the daily operations and look after the girls.

He approached the bar, where Antonio, their pianist, was enjoying a quiet moment. "Antonio, you know a lotta folks. You happen to know anyone who'd be a good fit for runnin' the saloon?"

Antonio raised an eyebrow, scratching his chin thoughtfully. "Funny you mention that, Jimmy. I know a fella by the name of Will Jeffries. Came into some hard times recently, but he's an honest man. Used to manage a stagecoach station, so he knows how to handle a rough crowd."

Jimmy nodded. "Bring him around, would ya? I'd like to meet him. Got to be someone I can trust with the girls and the business."

Just then, Josie entered, looking lighter, as if a weight had been lifted. Her brunette hair shone with the sun's reflection, and her warm brown eyes had a hint of confidence about them. She walked over to Jimmy, her eyes reflecting a newfound resolve.

"Jimmy, I've been thinkin'," she began, glancing around the saloon. "I love this place, but I don't know if it's the best place for me now, given... well, my situation."

Jimmy crossed his arms, leaning back against the bar. "You don't have to rush into anything, Josie. You've got time to figure things out. I'm not pushin' you out, if that's what you're worried about."

She smiled softly. "Thank you, Jimmy. But I reckon I need to start thinkin' about what's best for the little one. And the truth is, I don't want them growin' up around all this. I need to be thinkin' of other options, maybe a place of my own one day. For now, I'll keep dancin', but I wanted you to know where my mind's at."

Jimmy nodded, his gaze warm with understanding. "You do what's best for you and the child, Josie. And if you decide to move on, just say the word. You'll always have a place here, no matter what."

Moments later, Antonio returned with a tall, broad-shouldered man who had dark hair and a quiet, determined look. "Jimmy, this here's Will Jeffries. Will, meet Jimmy Hawthorne, the owner of The Golden Nugget."

Will extended his hand, meeting Jimmy's gaze with an unwavering, steady look. "Pleasure to meet you, Mr. Hawthorne. Heard a lot about you and the work you're doin' here."

Jimmy shook his hand, noting the firmness of Will's grip. "Good to meet you too, Will. Antonio here tells me you're lookin' for work. Can you tell me a bit about yourself?"

Will nodded, his face lined with experience. "I used to run the stagecoach stop over in Boise before the operation shut down. Been workin' odd jobs here and there since, but I'm lookin' for something steady. I know how to handle a crowd, keep order, and take care of folks."

Jimmy regarded him for a moment, then nodded. "Well, I'm lookin' for someone to manage this place. You'd be responsible for keepin' things runnin' smooth, watchin' out for the girls, and keepin' the patrons in line. This ain't a rough establishment, and I intend to keep it that way. You think you're up to the task?"

Will met Jimmy's gaze squarely. "Absolutely. I understand the importance of respectin' the girls and keepin' things orderly. You have my word on that."

After a few more questions, Jimmy made up his mind. "Alright, Will. Welcome aboard. I'll have you take over the third-floor quarters, so you're close to everything. You'll start tomorrow."

Will nodded gratefully, a hint of relief in his expression. "Thank you, Jimmy. You won't regret it."

Later that afternoon, when Jimmy returned to the house, Fayteen was arranging some flowers in a vase, the house looking more like a home with every touch she added.

"I found us a manager," Jimmy said, leaning in to kiss her cheek. "Good man, from what I can tell. Name's Will Jeffries."

Fayteen raised an eyebrow, intrigued. "Sounds like things are comin' together, then."

Jimmy took a deep breath, considering his words. "Which brings me to something else I wanted to ask ya. Now that we're married and moved out, do you still want to work at the saloon?"

Fayteen looked at him, surprised but thoughtful. "It's funny you ask, 'cause I've been thinkin' about that. I love dancin', Jimmy. I love bein' part of the show, the energy of it. But I reckon... well, I reckon I'd like to do it on my own terms. Maybe not every night, but I'd still like to be involved."

Jimmy smiled, wrapping an arm around her waist. "You're free to do just that. Whatever you want, darlin'. I just wanted to make sure you weren't feelin' obligated to stay on if you'd rather do somethin' else."

Fayteen rested her head on his shoulder, smiling. "No, I'm exactly where I want to be, Jimmy Hawthorne. Right here with you, buildin' this life together. And if that means a few nights dancin' and singin' at the saloon, well, that's just a bonus." Suddenly, she remembered their conversation from Paris and an earlier time, reminding Jimmy about hiring a chef to do meals. "What if I go about organizing that aspect of the business now? Is there any reason why we can't start that up? It would be a great addition to what we're already doing, and give our girls a new set of skills too."

Jimmy stood, thinking. "Darlin', it's a great time to get that that ball rollin'. Do you want to see about hiring a chef, or would you like me to?"

Fayteen looked at Jimmy with a slight smile and a twinkle in her eye, "I know just who to talk to!" With that, there was much more to think about and plan, but they would take it all in their stride.

They stood there, looking out at the open land that would soon be filled with memories. Together, they'd face the changes, challenges, and joys ahead with a love that had become the heart of Golden Valley itself.

35

The Golden Plate

The sun had just dipped below the horizon, casting a golden glow over Golden Valley as Fayteen sat at one of the tables in The Golden Nugget, sketching ideas onto a piece of paper. Jimmy stood nearby, polishing glasses behind the bar, his brow furrowed as he glanced over at his wife.

"I can see the wheels turnin'," he remarked with a soft smile. "What's got you thinkin' so hard?"

Fayteen tapped her pencil against her paper. "I've been goin' over this idea we had about servin' dinners here at the saloon. If we're gonna do it, we need to do it right. A proper kitchen, a chef who knows their way around good meals. Maybe even have the girls waitressing if they want?"

Jimmy leaned his elbows on the bar, nodding. "Who've you got mind, darlin'?"

"Well, Hattie and Lou have done wonders over at the café. Maybe they'd be interested in takin' on a new challenge? Or they might know someone who can handle the kitchen."

Fayteen smiled thoughtfully, sketching a little more. "It would only be a couple of nights a week at first. Just enough to see if it catches on with folks. The dance troupe girls could waitress if they want—a real step up for some of them who are ready to leave entertainin' behind."

Jimmy raised an eyebrow, his interest piqued. "You think the girls would want that?"

"I think some of them are lookin' for a change," Fayteen said softly. "Maggie, Anna, Sadie, Belle and Josie... they've all been talkin' about wanting somethin' different. And I reckon this could be a real opportunity for them. A fresh start, a way out if they want it."

Jimmy nodded, his gaze softening. "Then I say let's give them the chance."

Later that afternoon, Fayteen made her way down to the café, where Hattie and Lou were busy serving the last of the lunch crowd. Lou, with her bright smile and constant energy, greeted Fayteen warmly as soon as she stepped through the door.

"Well, look who it is! What brings you by, Fayteen?"

Fayteen took a seat at the counter, glancing around at the familiar, cozy atmosphere of the café. "I've got somethin' to ask you both. Jimmy and I have been talkin' about servin' dinners at The Golden Nugget a couple of nights a week, and I was wonderin' if you might be interested in helpin' us get it goin'."

Hattie, always the quieter of the two sisters, raised an eyebrow as she wiped her hands on her apron. "You're thinkin' of startin' a restaurant at the saloon?"

Fayteen nodded. "Not quite a restaurant, but more like a dinner service. We'd install a kitchen, bring in all the proper equipment, and serve up meals a few nights a week. It'd be a step up from just drinks and entertainment, and I think it'd bring in a new crowd."

Lou placed her hands on her hips, her eyes twinkling with curiosity. "And you're askin' us to cook for it?"

"Well," Fayteen smiled, "I thought I'd see if you were interested first. You're already runnin' a busy café, so I don't know if you'd have the time, but if you're not able, maybe you know someone who'd be up for the challenge?"

Lou exchanged a glance with Hattie before speaking up. "We could help get it goin', for sure. Might not be able to commit to it long-term, what with the café bein' our main focus, but we could help you find someone who can take it over once it's set up."

Fayteen's face lit up. "That's all I need to hear. I'm glad you're both on board. And the girls from the dance troupe—some of them are lookin' to leave the other line of work behind. They'd be interested in waitressing, I'm sure."

Hattie's eyes softened. "Those girls could use somethin' like that. It'd be a way for them to earn a livin' without feelin' like they've got no other options."

After finalizing the details with Hattie and Lou, Fayteen returned to The Golden Nugget, where the girls from the dance troupe were gathered backstage. Ruby, Maggie, Anna, Sadie, Belle, and Josie were lounging in their dressing room, laughing about something Maggie had said.

"Ladies," Fayteen greeted them with a warm smile. "I've got a proposition for you."

The girls turned their attention to her, curious looks on their faces.

"What kind of proposition?" Maggie asked, her eyes twinkling with mischief.

"Well," Fayteen began, "Jimmy and I are plannin' to start servin' dinners here at The Golden Nugget. We'll be open a couple of nights a week, and I was wonderin' if any of you might be interested in waitressing."

The room fell silent for a moment as the girls exchanged glances. Sadie was the first to speak up, her voice thoughtful. "You mean we wouldn't have to... entertain anymore?"

Fayteen nodded. "Not if you don't want to. This would be a real opportunity to do somethin' different. You'd be servin' meals, takin' care of customers in a way that's respectable, and it'd be a step up from what some of you have been doin'."

Maggie's eyes lit up. "I've been thinkin' about leavin' the entertainin' behind for a while now. This could be just what I need."

Anna nodded in agreement, her expression serious. "Me too. I've had enough of the men who think they can take liberties just because they paid for a drink. I want somethin' better."

Sadie, who had always been more reserved, spoke up next. "It sounds like a good idea, Fayteen. I'd like to try it."

Even Belle, who was often the most skeptical, seemed intrigued. "I'll give it a shot. Can't hurt to try somethin' new."

Fayteen smiled, feeling a sense of pride in the girls. They had come a long way since she first met them, and now they were ready to take control of their own futures. "That's settled then. We'll start gettin' the kitchen ready, and I'll let you all know when we're ready to start servin'."

Over the next few weeks, The Golden Nugget began its transformation. Jimmy oversaw the installation of a kitchen in the back of the saloon, bringing in a stove, ovens, and all the equipment needed to serve hearty meals. Hattie and Lou helped out where they could, guiding the process and offering advice on the menu.

On the first night of the new dinner service, the girls from the dance troupe stood nervously at the entrance, dressed in simple yet elegant uniforms. Maggie, Anna, Sadie, and Belle exchanged excited glances as the first customers began to arrive.

Maggie smiled as she greeted a couple at the door. "Good evenin'. Table for two?"

The couple nodded, and Maggie led them to their seats, her heart pounding with excitement. This was a new beginning, not just for her but for all of them.

As the evening wore on, the kitchen bustled with activity, the smell of roasted meats and freshly baked bread filling the air. Fayteen moved between the tables, checking on the customers and making sure everything was running smoothly. Jimmy stood at the bar, watching with pride as the saloon came alive in a new way.

"I think this is gonna be somethin' special," Fayteen said, stopping by Jimmy's side.

He smiled, sliding an arm around her waist. "It already is, Fayteen. You've done somethin' real good here. And I reckon the girls will feel the same."

As the night came to an end, the girls gathered together, their faces flushed with excitement and pride. They had taken the first step toward a new life, and as they looked around The Golden Nugget, they knew they were on the path to something better.

***

Later that evening, as Fayteen and Jimmy sat together on the patio outside their home, watching the stars begin to appear in the darkening sky, Jimmy glanced over at her. "Remember that proposal from Samuel Latham and Edwin Carver a few weeks back?"

Fayteen nodded. "The one where they wanted to invest in Golden Valley?"

"Yeah," Jimmy said, rubbing his chin thoughtfully. "They're talkin' about buildin' up the town, puttin' in shops, maybe even a theater. Sounds mighty temptin', but there's somethin' that doesn't sit right with me. They want a percentage of the profits, which means they'd have some say in how things run. I don't know if I'm ready for that."

Fayteen's brow furrowed. "I agree with you. This town is growin', sure, but I'd rather see it grow naturally, with more families and businesses comin' in on their own. If we let outsiders control too much, we might lose what makes Golden Valley special."

Jimmy nodded. "Exactly. I've been thinkin' we should talk to the founders—Henry, Gideon, Reverend Thornton, and Calvin, along with the womenfolk. See what they think. After all, this is their town too."

Fayteen smiled, resting her head on his shoulder. "I think that's a good idea. We'll figure it out together, just like we always do."

The next morning, Jimmy and Fayteen gathered the founders of Golden Valley at The Golden Nugget for a private meeting. Henry Wickham, with his ever-present warm demeanor, took a seat alongside his wife, Ada, while Gideon and Martha Grady, Reverend Thornton, and Calvin Dodd joined them at the table.

Jimmy laid out the proposal from Samuel Latham and Edwin Carver, explaining their offer to invest in the town and build up its infrastructure, but also sharing his concerns about the percentage they wanted in return.

"I'm just not sure if we're ready to hand over that kind of control," Jimmy said, glancing around at the gathered group. "What do y'all think?"

Henry was the first to speak. "You've got a point, Jimmy. This town's built on hard work, community, and the sweat of the folks who live here. Letting outsiders come in and start callin' the shots might be more trouble than it's worth."

Gideon nodded in agreement. "I've seen it happen before in other places. They come in with promises of growth and progress, but before you know it, the town don't feel like home no more. It's just another place where folks pass through, leavin' behind the people who built it."

Reverend Thornton leaned forward, his expression thoughtful. "I believe in progress, but I also believe in keeping the heart of this town intact. If we allow too much outside influence, we risk losin' the very thing that makes Golden Valley a place where people feel like they belong."

Calvin Dodd, always a man of few words, simply nodded. "Best we grow slow, but strong."

Jimmy glanced over at Fayteen, who gave him a reassuring smile. He turned back to the group. "I reckon we're all in agreement then. We'll tell Samuel and Edwin we appreciate their offer, but we're not ready for that kind of deal."

The decision made, Jimmy and Fayteen felt a sense of relief. Golden Valley would continue to grow on its own terms, with its heart and soul intact.

As they walked back upstairs, Jimmy turned to Fayteen with a grin. "Guess we'll keep buildin' this town our way."

Fayteen smiled, slipping her arm through his. "And I wouldn't have it any other way."

36

New Beginnings, Old Secrets

The next day dawned with the sound of laughter and chatter spilling from The Golden Nugget as patrons settled into the familiar rhythm of the saloon. Will Jeffries had taken to his new role like a fish to water, overseeing the morning's preparations and making sure everything ran as smoothly as Jimmy expected.

As he moved through the room, checking that the tables were set, Will caught sight of Josie carrying a tray of glasses. Their eyes met, and for a moment, the bustling noise of the saloon seemed to fade. Josie offered a tentative smile, which Will returned with a slight, respectful nod.

"Can I give ya a hand?" he asked, stepping over to relieve her of the heavy tray.

Josie blushed, a rare thing for her. "Thank you, Mr. Jeffries. Guess I'm a bit clumsy today."

"Call me Will," he replied, setting the tray down on the bar. "No need to fret about bein' clumsy," Will said with a warm smile. "You've got charm enough to make anyone forget a little stumble. Besides, this place is built to handle a bit of liveliness... and clumsiness!"

She laughed, surprised by his easy charm. "Well, you're in the right place, then."

The light moment was interrupted by the arrival of Calvin Dodd, the town's undertaker. A quiet man with neatly combed white hair, Calvin wasn't known for frequenting The Golden Nugget. His visits usually heralded a somber event, so his presence caused a ripple of curiosity.

Jimmy noticed him first and approached. "Calvin," he greeted, his brow furrowed. "Didn't expect to see you here. Everything alright?"

Calvin nodded, though a shadow of worry darkened his gaze. "Jimmy, I hate to be the bearer of strange news, but... well, I had an unusual visitor last night. Someone left a note pinned to my door. Didn't sign it, just left a message about 'unfinished business' in Golden Valley."

Jimmy felt a twinge of apprehension, his mind racing through the possibilities. "Do you have the note with you?"

Calvin reached into his coat pocket, pulling out a crumpled piece of paper. Jimmy unfolded it, reading the brief message:

The past isn't buried, not even in Golden Valley. Be prepared for what comes next.

Jimmy frowned, handing the note back. "Did you see who left it?"

Calvin shook his head. "Didn't hear a thing. Just found it there this morning."

Josie, who had lingered nearby, looked over at Will, her face clouded with worry. Will placed a reassuring hand on her shoulder. "Seems like this town's got a few ghosts," he muttered.

As the news spread through the saloon, the townsfolk began exchanging uneasy glances. Fayteen entered, catching sight of Jimmy's troubled expression as he filled her in on the note.

"Looks like Golden Valley's past might not be as settled as we thought," Jimmy said. He tried to keep his tone light, but there was a tension in his voice that Fayteen couldn't ignore.

They decided to continue with the day's business, putting the mysterious note on the back burner, at least for now. That evening, as dusk settled over the valley, Ahanu and Sahale Whispering Wind arrived at the saloon, having returned from visiting their family in the nearby Shoshone village. Their presence added a sense of comfort and calm that seemed to ease the tension hanging in the air.

"Ahanu!" Jimmy called, clapping him on the shoulder. "Just the man I was hopin' to see."

Ahanu's face split into a broad grin. "Jimmy Hawthorne, always a pleasure. Looks like you have a bit of a crowd here tonight."

Jimmy explained the situation with the note, showing it to Ahanu and Sahale. Ahanu read it, his face growing serious. "Jimmy, there are things—things that are hard to explain. But sometimes, the past doesn't stay buried, no matter how deep you think you have put it."

Sahale nodded, her expression thoughtful. "In our traditions, spirits have ways of leaving messages. If there is unrest in the land, you will know soon enough."

Josie, who had been listening from nearby, spoke up, a hint of fear in her voice. "Do you think it could be someone who holds a grudge against Golden Valley? Maybe someone from... before?"

Fayteen put an arm around her, offering a comforting smile. "We've faced plenty together. Whatever comes, we'll handle it."

Jimmy's mind drifted back to the fire that had been set before their wedding. At the time, he'd assumed it was Bear Langston's men trying to get back at him for not selling The Golden Nugget. But now, he wasn't so sure. The note and Calvin's encounter raised questions about the land itself, questions he'd never considered before.

"I'll admit," he said quietly to Fayteen, "I never knew much about this land when I bought it. There wasn't nothin' here but a couple of old shacks and an abandoned outhouse when I first laid eyes on it. Figured it was prime for buildin'. Never thought it might have a story of its own."

Ahanu placed a steady hand on his shoulder. "If there are spirits here, Jimmy, they will not rest until they are heard. In our ways, we honor the land and those who came before. Perhaps it is time to listen."

As the evening wore on, the tension seemed to ease, and the crowd relaxed into the usual festivities. Fayteen led the girls in a lively dance, their dresses twirling as they moved with joyful abandon. The music picked up, and patrons filled the floor, joining in the spirited dance.

Will, watching from the bar, found his gaze drawn to Josie. She seemed lighter, her smile brighter, despite the earlier tension. As the song ended, she joined him at the bar, her cheeks flushed from the dancing.

"Look at you, Will," she teased, her tone playful. "Standin' there like a watchdog. You ever dance?"

He grinned, shaking his head. "I'll leave that to the pros. My feet were made for walkin', not dancin'."

Josie raised an eyebrow, leaning in. "Everyone can dance, you know. Just takes a little trust."

Before he could reply, they were interrupted by a shout from outside. Jimmy and Fayteen exchanged a look, heading for the doors as a young boy burst in, out of breath.

"Mr. Hawthorne! Miss Fayteen!" the boy panted. "There's a fire over by the old stables. It's spreadin' fast!"

Everyone sprang into action, grabbing buckets and following Jimmy and Ahanu toward the stables. The fire, though fierce, was isolated, and they worked together to extinguish the flames. As the last embers died out, Jimmy noticed something peculiar in the ashes—a small, charred piece of paper, the edges curling with the faint remains of writing.

He picked it up, squinting to make out the words: *This isn't over.*

Jimmy's grip tightened on the paper, a sense of foreboding settling over him. He shared a look with Ahanu, who placed a hand on his shoulder. "We will find out who is behind this, Jimmy. Whoever they are, they have made their intentions clear."

Returning to the saloon, Jimmy called an impromptu meeting with the townsfolk, sharing the latest discovery. Calvin, the undertaker, spoke up, his voice steady. "Seems like we're facing more than just idle threats. We need to be prepared for whatever's coming."

Fayteen stood beside Jimmy, her face determined. "Golden Valley's stood strong through plenty of trials. Whoever this is, they won't tear us down."

Sahale stepped forward, her expression serene. "In times like these, we must look to our ancestors and the wisdom they have left behind. I will perform a cleansing ritual at dawn. It may help bring peace to this place and guide us in the days ahead."

As the crowd dispersed, Jimmy, Fayteen, Ahanu, and Sahale stayed behind, discussing what measures could be taken to protect Golden Valley. Ahanu suggested bringing in additional help from the Shoshone village, warriors who could stand guard at night.

Fayteen squeezed Jimmy's hand, sensing his tension. "We'll get through this. Whatever it is, we're ready."

But even as she spoke, an uneasy feeling settled in the pit of her stomach. She glanced back toward the saloon, where Will and Josie stood talking quietly, their faces etched with concern.

As the moonlight spread over Golden Valley, a sense of calm seemed to return—at least for the moment. They knew, however, that this peace was temporary, a brief respite before the next storm.

And as they made their way back inside, Jimmy's mind turned to the future, knowing that the path ahead would require strength, unity, and a willingness to face whatever shadows the past might bring.

Unseen in the distance, a lone figure watched from the hills, their gaze fixed on Golden Valley. The note, the fire—these were only the beginning. Soon enough, they'd make their presence known, and Golden Valley would be forced to confront the ghosts that refused to stay buried.